Mistakes Can Kill You

Mistakes Can Kill You

A Collection of Western Stories

By

Louis L'Amour

Skyhorse Publishing

Skyhorse Publishing books may be purchased in bulk at special discounts for sales promotion, corporate gifts, fund-raising, or educational purposes. Special editions can also be created to specifications. For details, contact the Special Sales Department, Skyhorse Publishing, 307 West 36th Street, 11th Floor, New York, NY 10018 or info@skyhorsepublishing.com.

www.skyhorsepublishing.com

10 9

Library of Congress Cataloging-in-Publication Data is available on file.

ISBN: 978-1-62636-542-1

Printed in China

TABLE OF CONTENTS

THE BLACK ROCK COFFIN-MAKERS

CHAPTER ONE:
Five Thousand Dollar Fake

Jim Gatlin had been up the creek and over the mountains, and more than once had been on both ends of a six-shooter. Lean and tall, with shoulders wide for his height and a face like saddle leather, he was, at the moment, doing a workmanlike job of demolishing the last of a thick steak and picking off isolated beans that had escaped his initial attack. He was a thousand miles from home and knew nobody in the town of Tucker.

He glanced up as the door opened and saw a short, thick-bodied man. The man gave one startled look at Jim and ducked back out of sight. Gatlin blinked in surprise, then shrugged and filled his coffee cup from the pot standing on the restaurant table.

Puzzled, he listened to the rapidly receding pound of a horse's hoofs, then rolled a smoke, sitting back with a contented sigh. Two hundred and fifty odd miles to the north was the herd he had drifted northwest from Texas. The money the critters had brought was in the belt around his waist, and his pants' pockets. Nothing remained now but to return to Texas, bank the profit, and pick up a new herd.

The outer door opened again and a tall girl entered the restaurant. Turning right, she started for the door leading to the hotel. She stopped abruptly as though his presence had only then registered. She turned, and her eyes widened in alarm. Swiftly she crossed the room to him. "Are you insane?" she whispered. "Sitting here like that when the town is full of Wing Cary's hands? They know you're coming and have been watching for you for days!"

Gatlin looked up, smiling. "Ma'am, you've sure got the wrong man, although if a girl as purty as you is worried about him, he sure is a lucky fellow. I'm a stranger here. I never saw the place until an hour ago!"

She stepped back, puzzled, and then the door slammed open once more and a man stepped into the room. He was as tall as Jim, but thinner, and his dark eyes were angry. "Get away from him, Lisa! I'm killin' him—right now!"

The man's hand flashed for a gun, and Gatlin dove sidewise to the floor, drawing as he fell. A gun roared in the room, then Gatlin fired twice.

The tall man caught himself, jerking his left arm against his ribs, his face twisted as he gasped for breath. Then he wilted slowly to the floor, his gun sliding from his fingers.

Gatlin got to his feet, staring at the stranger. He swung his eyes to the girl staring at him. "Who is that hombre?" he snapped. "What's this all about? Who did he think I was?"

"You—you're not—you aren't Jim Walker?" Her voice was high, amazed.

"Walker?" He shook his head. "I'm sure as hell not. The name is Gatlin. I'm just driftin' through."

There was a rush of feet in the street outside. She caught his hand. "Come! Come quickly! They won't listen to you! They'll kill you! All the Gary outfit are in town!"

She ran beside him, dodging into the hotel, and then swiftly down a hall. As the front door burst open, they plunged out the back and into the alley behind the building. Unerringly, she led him to the left, and then opened the back door of another building and drew him inside. Silently she closed the door and stood close beside him, panting in the darkness.

Shouts and curses rang from the building next door. A door banged, and men charged up and down outside. Jim was still holding his gun, but now he withdrew the empty shells and fed two into the cylinder to replace those fired. He slipped a sixth into the usually empty chamber. "What is this place?" he whispered. "Will they come here?"

"It's a law office," she whispered. "I work here part time, and I left the door open myself. They'll not think of this place." Stealthily, she lifted the bar and dropped it into place. "Better sit down. They'll be searching the streets for some time."

He found the desk and seated himself on the corner, well out of line with the windows. He could see only the vaguest outline of her face. She was, he remembered, pretty. The gray eyes were wide and clear, her figure rounded yet slim. "What is this?" he repeated. "What was he gunnin' for me for?"

"It wasn't you. He thought you were Jim Walker, of the XY. If you aren't actually him you look enough like him to be a brother, a twin brother."

"Where is he? What goes on here? Who was that hombre who tried to gun me?"

She paused, and seemed to be thinking, and he had the idea she was still uncertain whether to believe him or not. "The man you killed was Bill Trout. He was the bad man of Paradise country and segundo on Wing Cary's Flying C spread. Walker called him a thief and a murderer in talking to Cary, and Trout threatened to shoot him on sight. Walker hasn't been seen since, and that was four days ago, so everybody believed Walker had skipped the country. Nobody blamed him much."

"What's it all about?" Gatlin inquired.

"North of here, up beyond Black Rock, is Alder Creek country, with some rich bottom hayland lying in several corners of the mountains. This is dry country, but that Alder Creek area has springs and some small streams flowing down out of the hills. The streams flow into the desert and die there, so the water is good only for the man who controls the range."

"And that was Walker?"

"No, up until three weeks ago it was old Dave Butler. Then Dave was thrown from his horse and killed, and when they read his will, he had left the property to be sold at auction and the money paid to his nephew and niece back in New York. However, the joker was, he stipulated that Jim Walker was to get the ranch if he would bid ten thousand cash and forty thousand on his note, payable in six years."

"In other words, he wanted Walker to have the property?" Jim asked. "He got first chance at it?"

"That's right. And I was to get second chance. If Jim didn't want to make the bid, I could have it for the same price. If neither of us wanted it, the ranch was to go on public auction, and that means that Cary and Horwick would get it. They have the money, and nobody around here could outbid them."

The street outside was growing quieter as the excitement of the chase died down. "I think," Lisa continued, "that Uncle Dave wanted Jim to have the property because Jim did so much to develop it. Jim was foreman of the XY acting for Dave. Then, Uncle Dave knew my father and liked me, and he knew I loved the ranch, so he wanted me to have second chance, but I don't have the money, and they all know it. Jim had some of it, and he could get the rest. I think that was the real trouble behind his trouble with Trout. I believe Wing deliberately set Trout to kill him, and Jim's statements about Bill were a result of the pushing around Bill Trout had given him."

The pattern was not unfamiliar, and Gatlin could easily appreciate the situation. Water was gold in this country of sparse grass. To a cattleman, such a ranch as Lisa described could be second to none, with plenty of water and grass and good hay meadows. Suddenly she caught his arm. Men were talking outside the door.

"Looks like he got plumb away, Wing. Old Ben swears there was nobody in the room with him but that Lisa Cochrane, an' she never threw that gun, but how Jim Walker ever beat Trout is more'n I can see. Why, Bill was the fastest man around here unless it's you or me."

"That wasn't Walker, Pete. It couldn't have been!"

"Ben swears it was, an' Woody Hammer busted right through the door in front of him. Said it was Jim, all right."

Wing Cary's voice was irritable. "I tell you, it couldn't have been!" he flared. "Jim Walker never saw the day he dared face Trout with a gun," he added. "I've seen Walker draw an' he never was fast."

"Maybe he wasn't," Pete Chasin agreed dryly, "but Trout's dead, ain't he?"

"Three days left," Cary mused. "Lisa Cochrane hasn't the money, and it doesn't look like Walker will even be bidding. Let it ride, Pete, I don't think we need to worry about anything. Even if that was Walker, an' I'd take an oath it wasn't, he's gone for good now. All we have to do is sit tight."

The two moved off, and Jim Gatlin, staring at the girl in the semi-darkness, saw her lips were pressed tight. His eyes had grown accustomed to the dim light, and he could see around the small office. It was a simple room with a desk, chair, and filing cabinets. Well-filled bookcases lined the walls.

He got to his feet. "I've got to get my gear out of that hotel," he said, "and my horse."

"You're leaving?" she asked.

Jim glanced at her in surprise. "Why, sure! Why stay here in a fight that's not my own? I've already killed one man, and if I stay I'll have to kill more or be killed myself. There's nothing here for me."

"Did you notice something?" she asked suddenly. "Wing Cary seemed very sure that Jim Walker wasn't coming back, that you weren't he."

Gatlin frowned. He had noticed it, and it had him wondering. "He did sound mighty sure. Like he might know he wasn't coming back."

They were silent in the dark office, yet each knew what the other was thinking. Jim Walker was dead. Pete Chasin had not known it. Neither, obviously, had Bill Trout.

"What happens to you then?" Gatlin asked suddenly. "You lose the ranch?"

She shrugged. "I never had it, and never really thought I would have it, only . . . well, if Jim had lived . . . I mean, if Jim got the ranch we'd have made out. We were very close, like brother and sister. Now, I don't know what I can do."

"You haven't any people?"

"None that I know of." Her head came up suddenly. "Oh, it isn't myself I'm thinking of, it's all the old hands, the ranch itself. Uncle Dave hated Cary, and so do his men. Now he'll get the ranch and they'll all be fired, and he'll ruin the place! That what he's wanted all along."

Gatlin shifted his feet. "Tough," he said, "mighty tough."

He opened the door slightly. "Thanks," he said, "for getting me out of there." She didn't reply, so after a moment he stepped out of the door and drew it gently to behind him.

There was no time to lose. He must be out of town by daylight and with miles behind him. There was no sense getting mixed up in somebody else's fight, for all he'd get out of it would be a bellyful of lead. There was nothing he could do to help. He moved swiftly, and within a matter of minutes was in his hotel room. Apparently, searching for Jim Walker, they hadn't considered his room in the hotel, so Gatlin got his duffle together, stuffed it into his saddlebags, and picked up his rifle. With utmost care he eased down the back stairs and into the alley.

The streets were once more dark and still. What had become of the Flying C hands, he didn't know, but none were visible. Staying on back streets, he made his way carefully to the livery barn, but here his chance of cover grew less, for he must enter the wide door with a light glowing over it.

After listening, he stepped out and, head down, walked through the door. Turning, he hurried to the stall where his powerful black waited. It was the work of only a few minutes to saddle up. He led the horse out of the stall and caught up the bridle. With a hand on the pommel a voice stopped him.

"Lightin' out?"

It was Pete Chasin's voice. Slowly he released his grip on the pommel and turned slightly. The man was hidden in a stall. "Why not?" Gatlin asked. "I'm not goin' to be a shootin' gallery for nobody. This ain't my range, an' I'm slopin' out of here for Texas. I'm no trouble hunter."

He heard Chasin's chuckle. "Don't reckon you are. But it seems a shame not to make the most of your chance. What if I offered you five thousand to stay? Five thousand, in cash?"

"Five thousand?" Gatlin blinked. That was half as much as he had in his belt, and the ten thousand he carried had taken much hard work and bargaining to get. Buying a herd, chancing the long drive.

"What would I have to do?" he demanded.

Chasin came out of the stall. "Be yourself," he said, "just be yourself—but let folks think you're Jim Walker. Then you buy a ranch here . . . I'll give yuh the money, an' then yuh hit the trail."

Chasin was trying to double-cross Cary! To get the ranch for himself!

Gatlin hesitated, "That's a lot of money, but these boys toss a lot of lead. I might not live to spend the dough."

"I'll hide yuh out," Chasin argued. "I've got a cabin in the hills. I'd hide yuh out with four, five of my boys to stand guard. Yuh'd be safe enough. Then yuh could come down, put your money on the line an' sign the papers."

"Suppose they want Walker's signature checked?"

"Jim Walker never signed more'n three, four papers in his life. He left no signatures hereabouts. I've took pains to be sure."

Five thousand because he looked like a man. It was easy money, and he'd be throwing a monkey wrench into Wing Cary's plans. Cary, a man he'd decided he disliked. "Sounds like a deal," he said. "Let's go!"

The cabin on the north slope of Bartlett Peak was well hidden, and there was plenty of grub. Pete Chasin left him there with two men to guard him, and two more standing by on the trail toward town. All through the following day, Jim Gatlin loafed, smoking cigarettes and talking idly with the two men. Hab Johnson was a big, unshaven hombre with a sullen face and a surly manner. He talked little, and then only to growl. Pink Stabineau was a wide-chested, flat-faced jasper with an agreeable grin.

Gatlin had a clear idea of his own situation. He could use five thousand, but he knew Chasin never intended him to leave the country with it, and doubted if he would last an hour after the ranch was transferred to Chasin himself. Yet Gatlin had been around the rough country and he knew a trick or two of his own. Several times he thought of Lisa Cochrane, but avoided that angle as much as he could.

After all, she had no chance to get the ranch, and Walker was probably dead. That left it between Cary and Chasin. The unknown Horwick of whom he had heard mention was around, too, but he seemed to stand with Cary in everything. Yet he was restless and irritable, and he kept remembering the girl beside him in the darkness, and her regrets at breaking up the old outfit. Jim Gatlin had been a hand who rode for the brand; he knew what it meant to have a ranch sold out from under a bunch of old hands. The home that had been theirs gone, the friends drifting apart never to meet again, everything changed.

He finished breakfast on the morning of the second day, then walked out of the cabin with his saddle, Hab Johnson looked up sharply. "Where yuh goin'?" he demanded.

"Ridin'," Gatlin said briefly, "an' don't worry. I'll be back."

Johnson chewed a stem of grass, his hard eyes on Jim's. "Yuh ain't goin' nowheres. The boss said to watch yuh an' keep yuh here. Here yuh stay."

Gatlin dropped his saddle. "You aren't keepin' me nowheres, Hab," he said flatly. "I've had enough sittin' around. I aim to see a little of this country."

"I reckon not." Hab got to his feet. "Yuh may be a fast hand with a gun, but yuh ain't gittin' both of us, nor yuh ain't so foolish as to try." He waved a big hand. "Now yuh go back an' set down."

"I started for a ride," Jim said quietly, "an' a ride I'm takin'." He stooped to pick up the saddle and saw Hab's boots as the big man started for him. Jim had lifted the saddle clear of the ground, and now he hurled it, suddenly, in Hab's path. The big man stumbled and hit the ground on his hands and knees, then started up.

As he came up half way, Jim slugged him. Hab tottered, fighting for balance, and Gatlin moved in, striking swiftly with a volley of lefts and rights to the head. Hab went down and hit hard, then came up with a lunge, but Gatlin dropped him again. Blood dripped from smashed lips and a cut on his cheekbone.

Gatlin stepped back, working his fingers. His hard eyes flicked to Pink Stabineau, who was smoking quietly, resting on one elbow, looking faintly amused. "You stoppin' me?" Gatlin demanded.

Pink grinned. "Me? Now where did yuh get an idea like that? Take your ride. Hab's just too pernickety about things. Anyway, he's always wantin' to slug somebody. Now maybe he'll be quiet for a spell."

There was a dim trail running northwest from the cabin and Gatlin took it, letting his horse choose his own gait. The black was a powerful animal, not only good on a trail but an excellent roping horse and he moved out eagerly, liking the new country. When he had gone scarcely more than two miles, he skirted the edge of a high meadow with plenty of grass, then left the trail and turned off along a bench of the mountain, riding due north.

Suddenly the mountain fell away before him, and below in a long finger of grass he saw the silver line of a creek, and nestled against a shoulder of the mountain he discerned roofs among the trees. Pausing, Jim rolled a smoke and studied the lie of the land. Northward, for all of ten miles, there was good range. Dry, but not so bad as over the mountain, and in the spring and early summer it would be good grazing land. He had looked at too much range not to detect, from the colors of the valley before him, some of the varieties of grass and brush. Northwest the range stretched away through a wide gap in the mountains, and he seemed to distinguish a deeper green in the distance.

Old Dave Butler had chosen well, and his XY had, Gatlin could see as he rode nearer, been well handled. Tanks had been built to catch some of the overflow from the mountains and to prevent the washing of valuable range. The old man, and evidently Jim Walker, had worked hard to build this ranch into something. Even while wanting money for his relatives in the east, Butler had tried to insure that the work would be continued after his death. Walker would continue it, and so would Lisa Cochrane.

CHAPTER TWO:
Kill-Branded Pardner

All morning he rode, and well into the afternoon, studying the range but avoiding the buildings. Once, glancing back, he saw a group of horsemen riding swiftly out of the mountains from which he had come and heading for the XY. Reining in, he watched from a vantage point among some huge boulders. Men wouldn't ride that fast without adequate reason . . .

Morosely, he turned and started back along the way he had come, thinking more and more of Lisa. Five thousand was a lot of money, but what he was doing was not dishonest and so far he had played the game straight. Still why think of that? In a few days he'd have the money in his pocket and be headed for Texas. He turned on the brow of the hill and glanced back, carried away despite himself by the beauty of the wide sweep of range.

Pushing on, he skirted around and came toward the cabin from the town trail. He was riding with his mind far away when the black snorted violently and shied. Jim drew up, staring at the man who lay sprawled in the trail. It was the cowhand Pete Chasin had left on guard there. He'd been shot through the stomach and a horse had been ridden over him.

Swinging down, a quick check showed the man was dead. Jim grabbed up the reins and sprang into the saddle. Sliding a sixgun from its holster, he pushed forward, riding cautiously. The tracks told him that a party of twelve horsemen had come this way.

He heard the wind in the trees, the distant cry of an eagle, but nothing more. He rode out into the clearing before the cabin and drew up. Another man had died here. It wasn't Stabineau nor Hab Johnson, but the other guard, who must have retreated to this point for aid.

Gun in hand, Gatlin pushed the door open and looked into the cabin. Everything was smashed, yet when he swung down and went in, he found his own gear intact, under the overturned bed. He threw his bed roll on his horse and loaded up his saddle-bags. He jacked a shell into the chamber of the Winchester and was about to mount up when he heard a muffled cry.

Turning, he stared around, then detected a faint stir among the leaves of a mountain mahogany. Warily he walked over and stepped around the bush.

Pink Stabineau, his face pale, and his shirt dark with blood, lay sprawled on the ground. Curiously there was still a faint touch of humor in his eyes when he looked up at Gatlin. "Got me," he said finally. "It was that damned Hab. He sold us out . . . to Wing Cary. The damn' dirty son!"

Jim dropped to his knees and gently unbuttoned the man's shirt. The wound was low down on the left side and although he seemed to have lost much blood, there was a chance. Working swiftly, he built a fire, heated water and bathed and then dressed the wound. From time to time Pink talked, telling him much of what he suspected, that Cary would hunt Chasin down now, and kill him.

"If they fight," Jim asked, "who'll win?"

Stabineau grinned wryly. "Cary . . . he's tough, an' cold as ice. Pete's too jumpy. He's fast, but mark my words, if they face each other he'll shoot too fast and miss his first shot. Wing won't miss!

"But it won't come to that. Wing's a cinch player. He'll chase him down an' the bunch will gun him to death. Wing's blood-thirsty."

Leaving food and a canteen of water beside the wounded man, and giving him two blankets, Jim Gatlin mounted. His deal was off then. The thought left him with a distinct feeling of relief. He had never liked any part of it, and he found himself without sympathy for Pete Chasin. The man had attempted a double-cross and failed.

Well, the road was open again now, and there was nothing between him and Texas but the miles. Yet he hesitated, and then turned his horse toward the XY. He rode swiftly, and at sundown was at the ranch. He watched it for a time, and saw several hands working around, yet there seemed little activity. No doubt they were waiting to see what was to happen.

Suddenly, a sorrel horse started out from the ranch and swung into the trail toward town. Jim Gatlin squinted his eyes against the fading glare of the sun and saw the rider was a woman. That would be Lisa Cochrane. Suddenly he swung the black and, touching spurs to the horse, raced down the mountains to intercept her.

Until that moment he had been uncertain as to the proper course, but now he knew, yet for all his speed, his eyes were alert and watchful for he realized the risk he ran. Wing Cary would be quick to discover that as long as he was around and alive that there was danger, and even now the rancher might have his men out, scouring the country for him. Certainly, there were plausible reasons enough, for it could be claimed that he had joined with Chasin in a plot to get the ranch by appearing as Jim Walker.

Lisa's eyes widened when she saw him. "I thought you'd be gone by now. There's a posse after you!"

"You mean some of Cary's men?" he corrected.

"I mean a posse. Wing has men on your trail, too, but they lost you somehow. He claims that you were tied up in a plan with Pete Chasin to get the ranch, and that you killed Jim Walker!"

"That I did?" his eyes searched her face. "You mean that? He actually claims that?"

She nodded, watching him. "He says that story about your being here was all nonsense, that you actually came on purpose, that you an' Chasin rigged it that way! You'll have to admit it looks funny, you arriving right at this time and looking just like Jim."

"What if it does?" he demanded impatiently. "I never heard of Jim Walker until you mentioned him to me, and I never heard of the town of Tucker until a few hours before I met you."

"You'd best go, then," she warned, "they're all over the country. Sheriff Eaton would take you in, but Wing wouldn't, nor any of his boys. They'll kill you on sight."

"Yeah," he agreed, "I can see that." Nevertheless, he didn't stir, but continued to roll a cigarette. She sat still, watching him curiously. Finally he looked up. "I'm in a fight," he admitted, "and not one I asked for. Cary is making this a mighty personal thing, ma'am, an' I reckon I ain't even figurin' on leavin'." He struck a match. "You got any chance of gettin' the ranch?"

"How could I? I have no money!"

"Supposin'," he suggested, squinting an eye against the smoke, "you had a pardner—with ten thousand dollars?"

Lisa shook her head. "Things like that don't happen," she said. "They just don't."

"I've got ten thousand dollars on me," Gatlin volunteered, "an' I've been pushed into this whether I like it or not. I say we ride into Tucker now, an' we see this boss of yours, the lawyer. I figure he could get the deal all set up for us tomorrow. Are you game?"

"You—you really have that much?" She looked doubtfully at his shabby range clothes. "It's honest money?"

"I drove cattle to Montana," he said. "That was my piece of it. Let's go."

"Not so fast!" The words rapped out sharply. "I'll take that money, an' take it now! Woody, get that girl!"

For reply Jim slapped the spurs to the black and at the same instant, slapped the sorrel a ringing blow. The horses sprang off together in a dead run! Behind them a rifle shot rang out and Jim felt the bullet clip past his skull. "Keep goin'!" he yelled. "Ride!"

At a dead run they swung down the trail, and then Jim saw a side trail he had noticed on his left. He jerked his head at the girl and grabbed at her bridle. It was too dark to see the gesture, but she felt the tug and turned the sorrel after him, mounting swiftly up the steep side hill under the trees. Here the soft needles made it impossible for their horses' hoofs to be heard, and Jim led the way, pushing on under the pines.

That it would be only a minute or so before Cary discovered his error was certain, but each minute counted. A wall lifted on their right and they rode on, keeping in the intense darkness close under it, but then another wall appeared on their left and they were boxed in. Behind them they heard a yell, distant now, but indication enough their trail had been found. Boulders and slabs of rock loomed before them, but the black horse turned down a slight incline and worked his way around the rocks. From time to time they spoke to each other to keep together, but he kept moving, knowing that Wing Cary would be close behind.

The canyon walls seemed to be drawing closer and the boulders grew larger and larger. Somewhere Jim heard water running, and the night air was cool and slightly damp on his face. He could smell pines, so knew there were trees about and they had not ridden completely out of them. Yet Jim was becoming worried, for the canyon walls towered above them and obviously there was no break. If this turned out to be a box canyon, they were bottled up. One man could hold this canyon corked with no trouble at all.

The black began to climb and in a few minutes walked out on a flat of grassy land. The moon was rising but as yet there was no light in this deep canyon.

Lisa rode up beside him. "Jim," it was the first time she had ever called him by name, "I'm afraid we're in for it now. Unless I'm mistaken this is a box canyon. I've never been up here, but I've heard of it, and there's no way out."

"I was afraid of that." The black horse stopped as he spoke and he heard water falling ahead. He urged the horse forward but he refused to obey. Jim swung down into the darkness. "Pool," he said. "We'll find some place to hole up and wait for daylight."

They found a group of boulders and seated themselves among them, stripping the saddles from their horses and picketing them on a small patch of grass behind the boulders. Then for a long time they talked, the casual talk of two people finding out about each other. Jim talked of his early life on the Neuces, of his first trip into Mexico after horses when he was fourteen, and how they were attacked by Apaches. There had been three Indian fights that trip, two south of the border and one north of it.

He had no idea when sleep took him, but he awakened with a start to find the sky growing gray, and to see Lisa Cochrane sleeping on the grass six feet away. She looked strangely young with her face relaxed and her lips slightly parted. A dark tendril of hair had blown across her cheek. He turned away and walked out to the horses. The grass was thick and rich here.

He studied their position with care, and found they were on a terrace separated from the end wall of the canyon only by the pool, at least an acre of clear, cold water into which a small fall fell from the cliff above. There were a few trees, and some of the scattered boulders they had encountered the previous night. The canyon on which they had come was a wild jumble of boulders and brush surmounted on either side by cliffs that lifted nearly three hundred feet. While escape might be impossible if Wing Cary attempted, as he surely would, to guard the opening, yet their own position was secure, too, for one man with a rifle might stand off an army from the terrace.

After he had watered the horses, he built a fire and put water on for coffee. Seeing some trout in the pool, he tried his luck, and from the enthusiasm with which they went for his bait the pool could never have been fished before, or not in a long time. Lisa came from behind the boulders just as the coffee came to a boil. "What is this, a picnic?" she asked brightly.

He grinned, touching his unshaven jaw. "With this beard?" He studied her a minute. "You'd never guess you'd spent the night on horseback or sleeping at the end of a canyon," he said. Then his eyes sobered. "Can you handle a rifle? I mean, well enough to stand off Cary's boys if they tried to come up here?"

She turned quickly and glanced down the canyon. The nearest boulders to the terrace edge were sixty yards away, and the approach even that close would not be easy. "I think so," she said. "What are you thinking of?"

He gestured at the cliff. "I've been studyin' that. With a mite of luck a man might make it up there."

Her face paled. "It isn't worth it. We're whipped, and we might as well admit it. All we can do now is sit still and wait until the ranch is sold."

"No," he said positively. "I'm goin' out of here if I have to blast my way out. They've made a personal matter out of this, now," he glanced at her, "I sort of have a feeling you should have that ranch. Lookin' at it yesterday I just couldn't imagine it without you. You lived there, didn't you?"

"Most of my life. My folks were friends of Uncle Dave's, and after they were killed I stayed on with him."

"Did he leave you anything?" he asked.

She shook her head. "I . . . I think he expected me to marry Jim . . . he always wanted it that way, but we never felt like that about each other, and yet Jim told me after Uncle Dave died that I was to consider the place my home, if he got it."

As they ate, he listened to her talk while he studied the cliff. It wasn't going to be easy, and yet it could be done.

A shout rang out from the rocks behind them, and they both moved to the boulders, but there was nobody in sight. A voice yelled again that Jim spotted as that of Wing Cary. He shouted a reply, and Wing yelled back, "We'll let Lisa come out if she wants, an' you, too, if you come with your hands up!"

Lisa shook her head, so Gatlin shouted back, "We like it here! Plenty of water, plenty of grub! If you want us you'll have to come an' get us!"

In the silence that followed, Lisa said, "He can't stay, not if he attends the auction."

Jim turned swiftly. "Take the rifle. If they start to come, shoot an' shoot to kill! I'm going to take a chance!"

Keeping out of sight behind the worn gray boulders, Gatlin worked his way swiftly along the edge of the pool toward the cliff face. As he felt his way along the rocky edge, he stared down into the water. That pool was deep, from the looks of it. And that was something to remember.

At the cliff face he stared up. It looked even easier than he thought, and at one time and another he had climbed worse faces. However, once he was well up the face he would be within sight of the watchers below . . . or would he?

CHAPTER THREE:
Hell's Chimney

He put a hand up and started, working his way to a four-inch ledge that projected from the face of the rock and slanted sharply upward. There were occasional clumps of brush growing from the rock, and they would offer some security. A rifle shot rang out behind him, then a half dozen more, farther off. Lisa had fired at something and had been answered from down the canyon.

The ledge was steep, but there were good handholds and he worked his way along it more swiftly than he would have believed possible. His clothing blended well with the rock, and by refraining from any sudden movements there was a chance that he could make it.

When almost two hundred feet up the face, he paused, resting on a narrow ledge, partly concealed by an outcropping. He looked up, but the wall was sheer. Beyond there was a chimney, but almost too wide for climbing and the walls looked slick as a blue clay sidehill. Yet study the cliff as he would, he could see no other point where he might climb farther. Worse, part of that chimney was exposed to fire from below.

If they saw him he was through. He'd be stuck, with no chance of evading the fire. Yet he knew he'd take the chance. Squatting on the ledge, he pulled off his boots, and running a loop of piggin' string through their loops, he slung them from his neck. Slipping thongs over his guns, he got into the chimney and braced his back against one side, then lifted his feet, first his left, then his right, against the opposite wall.

Whether Lisa was watching or not, he didn't know, but almost at that instant she began firing. The chimney was, at this point, all of six feet deep, and wide enough to allow for climbing, but very risky climbing. His palms flat against the slippery wall, he began to inch himself upward, working his stocking feet up the opposite wall. Slowly, every movement a danger, his breath coming slow, his eyes riveted on his feet, he began to work his way higher.

Sweat poured down his face and smarted in his eyes, and he could feel it trickling down his stomach under his wool shirt. Before he was halfway up his breath was coming in great gasps and his muscles were weary with the strain of opposing their strength against the walls to keep from falling. Then, miraculously, the chimney narrowed a little, and climbing was easier.

He glanced up. Not over twenty feet to go! His heart bounded and he renewed his effort. A foot slipped, and he felt an agonizing moment when fear throttled him and he seemed about to fall. To fall meant to bound from that ledge and go down, down into that deep green pool at the foot of the cliff, a fall of nearly three hundred feet!

Something smacked against the wall near him and from below there was a shout. Then Lisa opened fire, desperately, he knew, to give him covering fire. Another shot splashed splinters in his face and he struggled wildly, sweat poured from him, to get up those last few feet. Suddenly the rattle of fire ceased, and then opened up again. He risked a quick glance and saw Lisa Cochrane running out in the open, and as she ran, she halted and fired!

She was risking her life, making her death or capture inevitable, to save him!

Suddenly a breath of air was against his cheek and he hunched himself higher, his head reaching the top of the cliff. Another shot rang out and howled off the edge of the rock beside him. Then his hands were on the edge, and he rolled over on solid ground, trembling in every limb.

A moment only, for there was no time to waste. He got to his feet, staggering, and stared around. He was on the very top of the mountain and Tucker lay far away to the south. He seated himself and got his boots on, then slipped the thongs from his guns. Walking swiftly as his still trembling muscles would allow, he started south.

There was a creek, he remembered, that flowed down into the flatlands from somewhere near here, an intermittent stream, but with a canyon that offered an easy outlet to the plain below. Studying the terrain, he saw a break in the rocky plateau that might be it, and started down the steep mountainside through the cedar, toward that break.

A horse was what he needed most. With a good horse under him he might make it. He had a good lead, for they must come around the mountain, a good ten miles by the quickest trail. That ten miles might get him to town before they could catch him, to town and to the lawyer who would make the bid for them, even if Eaton had him in jail by that time. Suddenly, remembering how Lisa had run out into the open, risking her life to protect him, he realized he would willingly give his own to save her.

He stopped, mopping his face with a handkerchief. The canyon broke away before him and he dropped into it, sliding and climbing to the bottom. When he reached the bottom he started off toward the flat country at a swinging stride. A half hour later, his shirt dark with sweat, the canyon suddenly spread wide into the flat country. Dust hung in the air, and he slowed down, hearing voices.

"Give 'em a blow." It was a man's voice speaking. "Hear any more shootin'?"

"Not me." The second voice was thin and nasal. "Reckon it was my ears mistakin' themselves."

"Let's go, Eaton." another voice said. "It's too hot here. I'm pinin' for some o' that good XY well water!"

Gatlin pushed his way forward. "Hold it, Sheriff! You huntin' me?"

Sheriff Eaton was a tall, gray-haired man with a handlebar mustache and keen blue eyes. "If you're Gatlin, an' from the looks of yuh, yuh must be, I sure am! How come you're so all fired anxious to get caught?"

Gatlin explained swiftly. "That girl's back there, an' they got her!" he finished. "Sheriff, I'd be mighty pleased if yuh'd send a few men after her, or go yourself an' let the rest of them go to Tucker with me."

Eaton studied him. "What you want in Tucker?"

"To bid that ranch in for Lisa Cochrane!" he said flatly. "Sheriff, that girl saved my bacon back there, an' I'm a grateful man! You get me to town to get that money in Lawyer Ashton's hands, an' I'll go to jail!"

Eaten rolled his chaw in his lean jaws. "Dave Butler come over the Cut-Off with me, seen this ranch, then, an' nothin' would have it but that he come back here to settle. I reckon I know what he wanted." He turned. "Doc, you'll git none of that XY water today! Take this man to Ashton, then put him in jail! An' make her fast!"

Doc was a lean, saturnine man with a lantern jaw and cold eyes. He glanced at Gatlin, then nodded, "If yuh say so, Sheriff. I sure was hopin' for some o' that good XY water, though. Come on, podner."

They wheeled their horses and started for Tucker, Doc turning from the trail to cross the desert through a thick tangle of cedar and sage brush. "Mite quicker this-away. Ain't nobody ever rides it, an' she's some rough."

It was high noon and the sun was blazing. Doc led off, casting only an occasional glance back at Gatlin. Jim was puzzled, for the man made no show of guarding him. Was he deliberately offering him the chance to make a break? It looked it, but Jim wasn't having any. His one idea was to get to Tucker, see Ashton, and get his money down. They rode on, pushing through the dancing heat waves, no breeze stirring the air, and the sun turning the bowl into a baking oven.

Doc slowed the place a little. "Hosses won't stand it," he commented, then glanced at Gatlin. "I reckon you're honest. Yuh had a chance for a break an' didn't take it." He grinned wryly. "Not that yuh'd have got fur. This here ol' rifle o' mine sure shoots where I aim it at."

"I've nothin' to run from," Gatlin replied. "What I've said was true. My bein' in Tucker was strictly accidental."

The next half mile they rode side by side, entering now into a devil's playground of boulders and arroyos. Doc's hand went out and Jim drew up. Buzzards roosted in a tree not far off the trail, a half dozen of the great birds. "Somethin' dead," Doc said. "Let's have a look."

Two hundred yards farther and they drew up. What had been a dappled gray horse lay in a saucerlike depression among the cedars. Buzzards lifted from it, flapping their great wings. Doc's eyes glinted and he spat. "Jim Walker's mare," he said, "an' his saddle."

They pushed on, circling the dead horse. Gatlin pointed. "Look," he said, "he wasn't killed. He was crawlin' away."

"Yeah," Doc was grim, "but not fur. Look at the blood he was losin'."

They got down from their horses, their faces grave. Both men knew what they'd find, and neither man was happy. Doc slid his rifle from the scabbard. "Jim Walker was by way o' bein' a friend o' mine," he said. "I take his goin' right hard."

The trail was easy. Twice the wounded man had obviously lain still for a long time. They found torn cloth where he had ripped up his shirt to bandage a wound. They walked on until they saw the gray rocks and the foot of the low bluff. It was a cul-de-sac.

"Wait a minute," Gatlin said. "Look at this." He indicated the tracks of a man who had walked up the trail. He had stopped here, and there was blood on the sage, spattered blood. The faces of the men hardened, for the deeper impression of one foot, the way the step was taken and the spattered blood told but one thing. The killer had walked up and kicked the wounded man!

They had little farther to go. The wounded man had nerve, and nothing had stopped him. He was backed up under a clump of brush that grew from the side of the bluff, and he lay on his face. That was an indication to these men that Walker had been conscious for some time, that he had sought a place where the buzzards couldn't get at him.

Doc turned, and his gray white eyes were icy. "Step your boot beside that track," he said, his rifle partly lifted.

Jim Gatlin stared back at the man and felt something cold and empty inside him. At that moment, familiar with danger as he was, he was glad he wasn't the killer. He stepped over to the tracks and made a print beside them. His boot was almost an inch shorter and of a different type.

"Didn't figger so," Doc said. "But I aimed to make sure."

"On the wall there," Gatlin said. "He scratched somethin'."

Both men bent over. It was plain, scratched with an edge of whitish rock on the slate of a small slab, Cary done . . . and no more.

Doc straightened. "He kin wait a few hours more. Let's git to town."

Tucker's street was more crowded than usual when they rode up to Ashton's office and swung down. Jim Gatlin pulled open the door and stepped in. The tall, gray-haired man behind the desk looked up. "You're Ashton?" Gatlin demanded.

At the answering nod, he opened his shirt and unbuckled his money belt. "There's ten thousand there. Bid in the XY for Cochrane an' Gatlin."

Ashton's eyes sparkled with sudden satisfaction. "You're her partner?" he asked. "You're putting up the money? It's a fine thing you're doing, man."

"I'm a partner only in name. My gun backs the brand, that's all. She may need a gun behind her for a little while, an' I've got it."

He turned to Doc, but the man was gone. Briefly, Gatlin explained what they had found, and added, "Wing Cary's headed for town now."

"Headed for town?" Ashton's head jerked around. "He's here. Came in about twenty minutes ago!"

Jim Gatlin spun on his heel and strode from the office. On the street, pulling his hat brim low against the glare, he stared left, then right. There were men on the street, but they were drifting inside now. There was no sign of the man called Doc or of Cary.

Gatlin's heels were sharp and hard on the boardwalk. He moved swiftly, his hands swinging alongside his guns. His hard brown face was cool and his lips were tight. At the Barrelhouse, he paused, put up his left hand and stepped in. All faces turned toward him, but none was that of Cary. "Seen Wing Cary?" he demanded. "He murdered Jim Walker."

Nobody replied, and then an oldish man turned his head and jerked it down the street. "He's gettin' his hair cut, right next to the livery barn. Waitin' fur the auction to start up."

Gatlin stepped back through the door. A dark figure, hunched near the blacksmith shop, jerked back from sight. Jim hesitated, alert to danger, then quickly pushed on.

The red-and-white barber pole marked the frame building. Jim opened the door and stepped in. A sleeping man snored with his mouth open, his back to the street wall. The bald barber looked up, swallowed and stepped back.

Wing Cary sat in the chair, his hair half trimmed, the white cloth draped around him. The opening door and sudden silence made him look up. "You, is it?" he said.

"It's me. We found Jim Walker. He marked your name, Cary, as his killer."

Cary's lips tightened and suddenly a gun bellowed and something slammed Jim Gatlin in the shoulder and spun him like a top, smashing him sidewise into the door. That first shot saved him from the second. Wing Cary had held a gun in his lap and fired through the white cloth. There was sneering triumph in his eyes, and as though time stood still Jim Gatlin saw the smoldering of the black-rimmed circles of the holes in the cloth.

He never remembered firing, but suddenly Cary's body jerked sharply, and Jim felt the gun buck in his hand. He fired again then, and Wing's face twisted and his gun went into the floor, narrowly missing his own foot.

Wing started to get up, and Gatlin fired the third time, the shot nicking Wing's ear and smashing a shaving cup, spattering lather. The barber was on his knees in one corner, holding a chair in front of him. The sleeping man had dived through the window, glass and all.

Men came running, and Jim leaned back against the door. One of the men was Doc, and he saw Sheriff Eaton, and then Lisa tore them aside and ran to him. "Oh, you're hurt! You've been shot! You've . . . !"

His feet gave away slowly and he slid down the door to the floor. Wing Cary still sat in the barber shop, his hair half clipped.

Doc stepped in and glanced at him, then at the barber. "Yuh can't charge him fur it, Tony. Yuh never finished!"

THE NESTER AND THE PIUTE

He was ridin' loose in the saddle when we first saw him, and he was wearing a gun, which was some unusual for the Springs, these days. Out on the range where a man might have a run-in with a locoed steer or maybe a rattler, most of the boys carried guns, but around town Sheriff Todd had sort of set up a rulin' against it.

It was the second time I'd seen him, but he looked some different this mornin', and it took me a minute or two to decide what it was made the difference, and then I decided it was partly the gun and partly that look in his eyes.

He reined in that yellow horse in front of Green's and hooked one long leg around the saddle-horn.

"Howdy."

"Howdy." Hatcher was the only one who answered, only the rest of us sort of looked up at him. He dug in his shirt pocket for the makin's and started to build a smoke.

Nobody said anything, just sort of waitin' to see what was on his mind. He had an old carbine in a saddle scabbard, and the scabbard wasn't under his leg, but with the muzzle pointed down and the stock close to his hand. A man ridin' thataway ain't rightly figurin' on usin' a rope on no stock. That rifle would be in the way, but if he was figurin' on needin' a rifle right quick, it would be a plumb handy way to carry it.

When he had his smoke built he lit it with his left hand, and I got a good glimpse of his eyes, kind of cold and gray, and them lookin' us over.

Nobody here was friendly to him, yet nobody was unfriendly, neither. All of us had been around the Springs for years, all but him. He was the nester from Squaw Rock, an' nesters aren't right popular around cow range. However, the times was a changin' an' we all knowed it, so it wasn't like it might have been a few years before, when the country was new.

"Seen a tall-like hombre on a black horse?"

He asked the question like maybe it was a formality that he wanted to get over with, and not like he expected an answer.

"What sort of man?"

It was Hatcher who had started the talkin', as if he was ridin' point for the rest of us.

"Maybe two hundred pounds, sort of limp in his right leg, maybe. Rides him a black horse, long-gaited crittur, and he wears two guns, hangin' low."

"Where'd you see him?"

"Ain't never seed him. I seen his sign."

Yanell, who lived over nigh to Squaw Rock himself looked up from under his hat brim, and spat into the dust. What he was thinkin' we was all thinkin'. If this nester read sign that well, and trailed the Piute clean from Squaw Rock, he was no pilgrim.

That description fitted the Piute like a glove, and nobody amongst us had any love for the Piute. He'd been livin' in the hills over toward White Hills for the last six years, ever since he come back to the country after his trouble. The Piute had done a bit of horse stealin' and rustlin' from time to time and we all knowed it, but none of us were right anxious to trail him down.

Not that we were afraid. Only, none of us had ever caught him in the act, so we just left it up to Sheriff Todd, who wanted it that way. This here nester seemed to have some ideas of his own.

"No," Hatcher said, "I ain't seen nobody like that. Not lately."

The nester—his name was Bin Morley—nodded like he'd expected nothin' else. "Reckon I'll ride along," he said. "Be seein' you!"

He swung his leg back over the saddle and kicked his toe into a stirrup. The yellow horse started to walk like it was a signal for something, and we sat there watchin' him fade out down toward the cottonwoods at the end of town.

Hatcher bit off a hunk of chewing and rolled it in his jaws. "If he meets up with the Piute," he said, "he's askin' for trouble."

Yanell spit into the dust. "Reckon he'll handle it," he said drily. "Somethin' tells me the Piute rustled cows off the wrong hombre."

"Wonder what Sheriff Todd'll say?" Hatcher wanted to know.

"This here Morley, now," Yanell said, "he sort of looks like a man who could do his own lawin'. He's one of them hombres what ain't felt the civilizin' influences of Sheriff Todd's star, nor he ain't likely to!"

The nester's yellow horse ambled casually out over the trail toward White Hills. From time to time Bin Morley paused to study the trail, but from here it was much easier. He knew the look of the big black's track now, and from what was said later, I reckon the Piute wasn't really expectin' no trouble. Me, I was plumb curious. My Pappy always did tell me my bump of curiosity was too big for my britches, but after a few minutes I got up off the porch and walked around to where my steeldust was standin' three-legged in the dust. I throwed a leg over him and trailed out after the nester.

Maybe I'd been listenin' too much to the old-timers around tellin' of cattle drives and Injun fightin'. You listen to the stories a mite and you get to honin' to see some of them fracases yourself.

Now I knowed the Piute. Actually, he was only part Piute, and the rest was some brand of white, but whatever it was, the combination had resulted in pure D poison. That was one reason everybody was plenty willin' to accept Sheriff Todd's orders to leave law enforcement to him. I will say, he done a good job. He done a good job until it come to the Piute.

It was understandable about the Piute. That Injun left no more trail than a snake goin' over a flat rock, and no matter how much we suspected, nobody could ever get any evidence on him. Sheriff Todd had been on his trail a dozen times, but each time he lost it. I knew what Yanell was thinkin' just as well as if it was me. Anybody who could trail the Piute plumb from Squaw Creek wasn't likely to holler calf rope for any Injun rustler without smokin' things up a mite.

Me, I was just curious enough and ornery enough to want to see what would happen when this nester cornered the Piute.

He was a big, sullen brute, the Piute was. Rumor had it he'd killed a half dozen men, and certainly there was several that started out huntin' him that never showed up until somebody found 'em dead, but there'd never been evidence to prove a thing. He could sling a gun, and when we had the turkey shoot around about Thanksgiving, he used to fetch his guns down, and nine times out of ten, he got himself a turkey—and he used a six-gun. You take a man that moves around over the hills like a ghost, Injun footin' it over the rocks an' through the brush, and who shoots like that, and you get an idea why nobody was just too worried about gettin' him in a corner.

Six miles out I got a glimpse of the nester. The yellow horse was amblin' along, takin' it easy in a sort of loose-jointed trot that didn't look like much but seemed to eat up the country right fast.

The day wore on and I kept to the brush, not knowing how Morley would take it if he knew I was trailin' him. Then all of a sudden I saw him swing the yellow horse off the trail and drop to the ground. He was there for a minute, and ridin' closer, I could see he was bendin' over the body of a man. Then he swung back into the saddle and moseyed off down the trail.

When he went over the next rise I turned my horse down the hill. Even before I rode up, I knew who the dead man was. I could see his horse lying in the cactus off to one side, and only one man in that country rode a bay with a white splash on the shoulder. It was Sheriff Todd.

There was a sign around, but I didn't need more than a glance at it to tell me what had happened. Sheriff Todd had run into the Piute unexpectedlike, and caught him flat-footed with stolen stock, the first time he had ever had that chance. Only from the look of it, Todd had been caught flat-footed himself. His gun was out, but unfired, and he had been shot twice in the stomach.

Lookin' down at that body, I felt something change inside me. I knowed right then, no matter how the nester come out, I was goin' to foiler on my own hook. For Sheriff Todd was still alive when he hit the ground, and that Piute had bent over him, put a pistol to the side of his head, and blowed half his head off! There were powder burns around that hole in his temple where the bullet went in. It had been cold-blooded murder.

Swinging a leg over that gelding, I was startin' off when I happened to think of a gun, and turned back and recovered the one Sheriff Todd had worn. I also got his saddle-gun out of the scabbard and started off, trailin' the nester.

From now on the sign was bad. The Piute knowed he was up against it now. He was takin' time to blot his tracks, and if it hadn't been for Morley, I'd never have trailed him half as far as I did.

We hadn't gone more than a few miles further before I saw something that turned me plumb cold inside. The Piute had turned off at the Big Joshua and was headin' down the trail toward Rice Flats!

That scared me, because Rice Flats was where my girl lived down there in a cabin with her kid brother and her ma, and they had lived there alone ever since her dad fell asleep and tumbled off his spring wagon into the canyon. The Piute had been nosin' around the Flats long enough to scare Julie some, but I reckon it was the sheriff who had kept him away.

Now that Sheriff Todd was gone, and the Piute knowed he was on the dodge from here on. He would know that killin' Sheriff Todd was the last straw, and he'd have to get clean out of the country. Knowin' that, he'd know he might's well get hung for one thing as another.

As my gelding was a right fast horse, I started him movin' then. I jacked a shell into the chamber of the sheriff's carbine and I wasn't thinkin' much about the nester. Yet by the time I got to the cabin on the Flats, I knowed I was too late.

My steeldust came into the yard at a dead run and I hit the dust and went for that house like a saddle tramp for a chuck wagon. I busted inside and took a quick look around. Ma Frank was lyin' on the bed with a big gash in her scalp, but she was conscious.

"Don't mind me!" she said. "Go after that Injun! He has taken out with Julie on her black!"

"What about you?" I asked, although goodness knows I was wantin' nothin' more than to be out and after Julie.

"'Brose'll be back right soon. He rid over to Elmer's after some side meat."

'Brose was short for Ambrose, her fourteen-year-old boy, so knowin' he'd be back, I swung a leg over that saddle and headed out for the hills. My steeldust knowed somethin' was in the wind and he hustled his hocks for those hills like he was headin' home from a trail drive.

The Piute had Julie and he was a killin' man, a killin' man who knowed he was up the crick without a paddle now, and if he was got alive he'd rope meat shore. No man ever bothered a woman or killed a man as well liked in that country as Sheriff Todd without ridin' under a cottonwood limb. Me, I'm a plumb peaceable sort of hand, but when I seen the sheriff back there I got my dander up. Now that Piute had stole my girl, I was a wild man.

Ever see that country out toward White Hills? God must have been cleanin' up the last details of the job when He made that country, and just dumped a lot of the slag and wastin's down in a lot of careless heaps. Ninety per cent of that country stands on end, and what doesn't stand on end is dryer than a salt desert, and hotter than a bronc on a hot rock.

The Piute knowed every inch of it, and he was showin' us all he knowed. We went down across a sunbaked flat where weird dust devils danced like crazy in a world where there was nothin' but heat and dust and misery for man and beast. No cactus there, not even salt grass or yeso, nothin' growed there, and the little winds that stirred along the dusty levels made you think of snakes glidin' along the ground.

My gelding slowed to a walk an' we plodded on and somewhere miles ahead beyond the wall of sun dancin' heat waves, there was a column of dust, a thin, smoky trail where the nester rode ahead of me. Right then, I began to have a sight of respect for that long-legged yellow horse he was ridin' because he kept on goin' an' even gained ground on my steeldust.

Finally we got out of that hell's valley and took a trail along the rusty edge of some broken rock, windin' higher toward some sawtooth ridges that gnawed at the sky like starvin' coyotes in a dry season. That trail hung like an eyebrow to the face of the cliff we skirted, an' twice, away up ahead, I heard shots. I knowed they was shots from the Piute, because I'd seen that carbine the nester carried. It was a Spencer .56.

Never seen one? Mister, all they lack is wheels! A caliber .56, with a bore like a cannon, and them shootin' soft-nosed lead bullets. What they do to a man ain't pretty, like you'll know. I knowed well enough it wasn't the nester shootin' because when you unlimber a Spencer .56 she had a bellow like a mad bull in a rock canyon.

Sundown came and then the night, an' little breezes picked up and blew cool and pleasant down from the hills. Stop? There was no time for stoppin'. I knew my gelding would stand anything the Piute's horse would, and I knowed by the shootin' that the Piute knowed the nester was on his trail. He wasn't goin' to get nary a chance to cool his heels with that nester tailin' him down them draws and across the bunch grass levels.

The Piute? I wasn't worried so much about Julie now. He might kill her, but that I doubted as long as he had a prayer of gettin' away with her. He was goin' to have to keep movin' or shoot it out.

The longer I rode, the more respect I got for Bin Morley. He stuck to that Piute's trail like a cockle burr to a sheep, and that yellow horse of his just kept his head down and kept moseyin' along those trails like he was born to 'em, and he probably was.

The stars come out and then the moon lifted, and they kept on goin'. My steeldust was beginnin' to drag his heels, and so I knowed the end was comin'. At that, it was most mornin' before it did come.

How far we'd come or where we were I had no idea. All I know was that up ahead of me was the Piute with my girl, and I wanted a shot at him. Nobody needed to tell me I was no hand to tie in a gun battle with the Piute with him holdin' a six-gun. He was too slick a hand for me.

Then all of a sudden as the sky was turnin' gray and the hills were losin' their shadows, I rounded a clump of cotton woods and there was that yellow horse, standin' three-footed, croppin' absently at the first green grass in miles.

The nester was nowhere in sight, but I swung down and with the carbine in hand, started down through the trees, catfootin' in along with no idea what I might see or where they could have gone. Then all of a sudden I come out on the edge of a cliff and looked down at a cabin in a grassy basin, maybe a hundred feet below, and a good four hundred yards away.

Standin' in front of that cabin were two horses. My face was pretty pale, an' my stomach felt sick, but I headed for the trail down, when I heard a scream. It was Julie!

Then, in front of the cabin, I heard a yell, and that durned nester stepped right out in plain sight and started walking up to the cabin, and he wasn't more than thirty yards away from it.

That fool nester knowed he was askin' for it. The Piute might have shot from behind the door jamb, or from a window, but the nester figured I was behind him and he might draw him out for my fire. Or maybe he figured his comin' out in the open would make him leave the girl alone. Whatever his reason, it worked. The Piute stepped outside the door.

Me? I was standin' up there like a fool, just a-gawkin', while there, right in front of my eyes, the Piute was goin' to kill a man. Or was he?

He was playin' big Injun right then. Maybe he figured Julie was watchin', or maybe he thought the nester would scare. Mister, that nester wouldn't scare a copper cent.

The Piute swaggered about a dozen steps out from the cabin and stood there, his thumbs in his belt, sneerin'. The nester, he just moseyed along kind of lazylike, carryin' his old Spencer in his right hand like he'd plumb forgot about his hand gun.

Then, like it was on a stage, I seen it happen. That Piute went for his guns and the nester swung up his Spencer. There was two shots—then a third.

It's a wonder I didn't break my neck gettin' down that trail, but when I run up, the Piute was lyin' there on his back with his eyes blazin' over. I took one look, an' then turned away and you can call me a pie eatin' tenderfoot, but I was sick as I could be. Mister, did you ever see a man who'd been hit by two soft-nosed .56 caliber bullets? In the stummick?

Bin Morley come out with Julie, and I straightened up and she run over to me and began askin' how Ma was. She wasn't hurt none, as the nester got there just in time.

We took the horses back, and then I fell behind with the nester. I jerked my head toward the Piute's body.

"You goin' to bury him?" I asked.

He looked at me like he thought I was soft in the head.

"What fur? He picked the place hisself, didn't he?"

We mounted up.

"Besides," he said, "I've done lost two whole days as it is, and gettin' behind on my work ain't goin' to help none." He was stuffin' something in his slicker on the back of his horse.

"What's that?" I asked.

"A ham," he said grimly, "a whole ham. I brung it clean from Tucson an' that durned Piute stole it off me. Right out of my cabin. Ma, she was out pickin' berries when it happened."

"You mean," I said, "you trailed the Piute clean over here just for a ham?"

"Mister," the nester spat, "you durned right I did! Why Ma and me ain't et no hawg meat since we left Missoury, comin' three year ago!"

The steeldust started to catch up with Julie's pony, but I heard the nester sayin', "Never was no hand to eat beef, nohow. Too durned stringy. Gets in my teeth!"

MISTAKES CAN KILL YOU

Ma Redlin looked up from the stove. "Where's Sam? He still out yonder?"

Johnny rubbed his palms on his chaps. "He ain't comin' to supper, Ma. He done rode off."

Pa and Else were watching him and Johnny saw the hard lines of temper around Pa's mouth and eyes. Ma glanced at him apprehensively, but when Pa did not speak, she looked to her cooking. Johnny walked around the table and sat down across from Else.

When Pa reached for the coffee pot he looked over at Johnny. "Was he alone, boy? Or did he ride off with that no account Albie Bower?"

It was in Johnny neither to lie nor to carry tales. Reluctantly, he replied. "He was with somebody. I reckon I couldn't be sure who it was."

Redlin snorted and put down his cup. It was a sore point with Joe Redlin that his son and only child should take up with the likes of Albie Bower. Back in Pennsylvania and Ohio the Redlins had been good God-fearing folk, while Bower was no good, and came from a no-good outfit. Lately, he had been flashing money around, but he claimed to have won it gambling at Degner's Four Star Saloon.

"Once more I'll tell him," Redlin said harshly. "I'll have no son of mine traipsin' with that Four Star outfit. Pack of thieves, that's what they are."

Ma looked up worriedly. She was a buxom woman with a round apple-cheeked face. Good humor was her normal manner. "Don't you be sayin' that away from home, Joe Redlin. That Loss Degner is a gun-slinger, and he'd like nothin' so much as to shoot you after you takin' Else from him."

"I ain't afeerd of him." Redlin's voice was flat. Johnny knew that what he said was true. Joe Redlin was not afraid of Degner but he avoided him, for Redlin was a small rancher, a one-time farmer, and not a fighting man. Loss Degner was bad all through and made no secret of it. His Four Star was the hangout for all the tough element and Degner had killed two men since Johnny had been in the country, as well as pistol whipping a half dozen more.

It was not Johnny's place to comment, but secretly he knew the older Redlin was right. Once he had even gone so far as to warn Sam, but it only made the older boy angry.

Sam was almost twenty-one, and Johnny but seventeen, but Sam's family had protected him and he had lived always close to the competence of Pa Redlin. Johnny had been doing a man's work since he was thirteen, fighting a man's battles, and making his own way in a hard world.

Johnny also new what only Else seemed to guess, that it was Hazel, Degner's red-haired singer, who drew Sam Redlin to the Four Star. It was rumored that she was Degner's woman, and Johnny had said as much to Sam. The younger Redlin had flown into a rage and whirling on Johnny had drawn back his fist. Something in Johnny's eyes stopped him and although Sam would never have admitted it, he was suddenly afraid.

Like Else, Johnny had been adrift when he came to the R Bar. Half dead with pneumonia he had come up to the door on his black gelding, and the Redlin's hospitality had given him a bed, the best care the frontier could provide, and when Johnny was well, he went to work to repay them. Then he stayed on for the spring roundup as a forty-a-month hand.

He volunteered no information and they asked him no questions. He was slightly built and below medium height, but broad shouldered and wiry. His shock of chestnut hair always needed cutting, and his green eyes held a lurking humor. He moved with deceptive slowness, for he was quick at work, and skillful with his hands. Nor did he wait to be told about things, but even before he began riding he had mended the buckboard, cleaned out and shored up the spring, repaired the door hinges, and cleaned all the guns.

"We collect from Walters tomorrow," Redlin said suddenly. "Then I'm goin' to make a payment on that Sprague place and put Sam on it. With his own place he'll straighten up and go to work."

Johnny stared at his plate, his appetite gone. He knew what that meant, for it had been in Joe Redlin's mind that Sam should marry Else and settle on that place. Johnny looked up suddenly, and his throat tightened as he looked at her. The gray eyes caught his, searched them for an instant, then moved away, and Johnny watched the lamplight in her ash blonde hair, turning it to old gold.

He pushed back from the table and excused himself, going out into the moonlit yard. He lived in a room he had built into a corner of the barn. They had objected at first, wanting him to stay at the house, but he could not bear being close to Else, and then he had the lonely man's feeling for seclusion. Actually, it had other advantages, for it kept him near his horse, and he never knew when he might want to ride on.

That black gelding and his new .44 Winchester had been the only incongruous notes in his getup when he arrived at the R Bar, but he had hidden his guns and his best clothes in a cave up the mountain, riding down to the ranch in shabby range clothes with only the .44 Winchester for safety.

He had watched the ranch for several hours despite his illness before venturing down to the door. It paid to be careful, and there were men about who might know him.

Later, when securely in his own room, he had returned to his cache and dug out the guns and brought his outfit down to the ranch. Yet nobody had ever seen him with guns on, nor would they, if he was lucky.

The gelding turned its head and nickered at him, rolling its eyes at him. Johnny walked into the stall and stood there, one hand on the horse's neck. "Little bit longer, boy, then we'll go. You sit tight now."

There was another reason why he should leave now, for he had learned from Sam that Flitch was in town. Flitch had been on the Gila during the fight, and he had been a friend of Card Wells, whom Johnny had killed at Pichacho. Moreover, Flitch had been in Cimarron a year before that when Johnny, only fifteen then, had evened the score with the men who killed his father and stole their outfit. Johnny had gunned two of them down and put the third into the hospital.

Johnny was already on the range when Sam Redlin rode away the next morning to make his collection. Pa Redlin rode out with Else and found Johnny branding a yearling. Pa waved and rode on, but Else sat on her horse and watched him. "You're a good hand, Johnny," she said when he released the calf. "You should have your own outfit."

"That's what I want most," he admitted, "But I reckon I'll never have it."

"You can if you want it enough. Is it because of what's behind you?"

He looked up quickly then. "What do you know of me?"

"Nothing, Johnny, but what you've told us. But once, when I started into the barn for eggs, you had your shirt off and I saw those bullet scars. I know bullet scars because my own father had them. And you've never told us anything, which usually means there's something you aren't anxious to tell."

"I guess you're right." He tightened the girth on his saddle. "There ain't much to tell, though. I come west with my Pa, and he was a lunger. I drove the wagon myself after we left Independence. Clean to Caldwell, then on to Santa Fe. We got us a little outfit with what Pa had left, and some mean fellers stole it off us, and they killed Pa."

Joe Redlin rode back to join them as Johnny was swinging into the saddle. He turned and glanced down at the valley. "Reckon that range won't get much use, Johnny," he said, anxiously, "and the stock sure need it. Fair to middlin' grass, but too far to water."

"That draw, now," Johnny suggested, "I been thinkin' about that draw. It would take a sight of work, but a couple of good men with teams and some elbow grease could build them a dam across that draw. There's a sight of water comes down when it rains, and enough to last most of the summer if it was damned. Maybe even the whole year."

The three horses started walking toward the draw, and Johnny pointed out what he meant. "A feller' over to Mobeetie did that one time," he said, "and it washed his dam out twice, but the third time she held, and he had him a little lake, all the year around."

"That's a good idea, Johnny." Redlin studied the setup, then nodded. "A right good idea."

"Sam and me could do it," Johnny suggested, avoiding Pa Redlin's eyes.

Pa Redlin said nothing, but both Johnny and Else knew that Sam was not exactly ambitious about extra work. He was a good hand, Sam was, strong and capable, but he was big-headed about things and was little inclined to sticking with a job.

"Reminds me," Pa said, glancing at the sun, "Sam should be back soon."

"He might stop in town," Else suggested, and was immediately sorry she had said it for she could see the instant worry on Redlin's face. The idea of Sam Redlin stopping at the Four Star with seven thousand dollars on him was scarcely a pleasant one. Murder had been done there for much, much less. And then Sam was overconfident. He was even cocky.

"I reckon I'd better ride in and meet him," Redlin said, genuinely worried now. "Sam's a good boy, but he sets too much store by himself. He figures he can take care of himself anywhere, but that pack of wolves . . ." His voice trailed off to silence.

Johnny turned in his saddle. "Why, I could just as well ride in, Pa," he said casually, "I ain't been to town for a spell, and if anything happened, I could lend a hand."

Pa Redlin was about to refuse, but Else spoke up quickly. "Let him go, Pa. He could do some things for me, too, and Johnny's got a way with folks. Chances are he could get Sam back without trouble."

That's right! Johnny's thoughts were grim. Send me along to save your boy. You don't care if I get shot, just so's he's been saved. Well, all right, I'll go. When I come back I'll climb my gelding and light out. Up to Oregon. I never been to Oregon.

Flitch was in town. His mouth tightened a little, but at that, it would be better than Pa going. Pa always said the wrong thing, being outspokenlike. He was a man who spoke his mind, and to speak one's mind to Flitch or Loss Degner would mean a shooting. It might be he could get Sam out of town all right. If he was drinking it would be hard. Especially if that redhead had her hands on him.

"You reckon you could handle it?" Pa asked doubtfully.

"Sure," Johnny said, his voice a shade hard, "I can handle it. I doubt if Sam's in any trouble. Later, maybe. All he'd need is somebody to side him."

"Well," Pa was reluctant, "better take your Winchester. My six-gun, too."

"You hang onto it. I'll make out."

Johnny turned the gelding and started back toward the ranch, his eyes cold. Seventeen he might be, but four years on the frontier on your own make pretty much of a man out of you. He didn't want any more shooting, but he had six men dead on his back trail now, not counting Comanches and Kiowas. Six, and he was seventeen. Next thing they would be comparing him to the Kid and to Wes Hardin.

He wanted no gunfighter's name, only a little spread of his own where he could run a few cows and raise horses, good stock, like some he had seen in East Texas. No range ponies for him, but good blood. That Sprague place now . . . but that was Sam's place, or as good as his. Well, why not? Sam was getting Else, and it was little enough he could do for Pa and Ma, to bring Sam home safe.

He left the gelding at the water trough and walked into the barn. In his room he dug some saddle gear away from a corner and out of a hiding place in the corner he took his guns. After a moment's thought, he took but one of them, leaving the .44 Russian behind. He didn't want to go parading into town with two guns on him, looking like a sure enough shooter. Besides, with only one gun and the change in him, Flitch might not spot him at all.

Johnny was at the gate riding out when Else and Pa rode up. Else looked at him, her eyes falling to the gun on his hip. Her face was pale and her eyes large. "Be careful, Johnny. I had to say that because you know how hot-headed Pa is. He'd get killed, and he might get Sam killed."

That was true enough, but Johnny was aggrieved. He looked her in the eyes. "Sure, that's true, but you didn't think of Sam, now, did you? You were just thinking of Pa."

Her lips parted to protest, then her face seemed to stiffen. "No, Johnny, it wasn't only Pa I thought of. I did think of Sam. Why shouldn't I?"

That was plain enough. Why shouldn't she? Wasn't she going to marry him? Wasn't Sam getting the Sprague place when they got that money back safe?

He touched his horse lightly with a spur and moved on past her. All right, he would send Sam back to her, if he could. It was time he was moving on, anyway.

The gelding liked the feel of the trail and moved out fast. Ten miles was all, and he could do that easy enough, and so he did it, and Johnny turned the black horse into the street and stopped before the livery stable, swinging down. Sam's horse was tied at the Four Star's hitchrail. The saddle-bags were gone.

Johnny studied the street, then crossed it and walked down along the buildings on the same side as the Four Star. He turned quickly into the door.

Sam Redlin was sitting at a table with the redhead, the saddle-bags on the table before him, and he was drunk. He was very drunk. Johnny's eyes swept the room. The bartender and Loss Degner standing together, talking. Neither of them paid any attention to Johnny, for neither knew him. But Flitch did.

Flitch was standing down the bar with Albie Bower, but none of the old Gila River outfit. Both of them looked up, and Flitch kept looking, never taking his eyes from Johnny. Something bothered him, and maybe it was the one gun.

Johnny moved over to Sam's table. They had to get out of here fast, before Flitch remembered. "Hi, Sam," he said, "just happened to be in town, and Pa said if I saw you, to side you on the way home."

Sam stared at his sullenly. "Side me? You?" He snorted his contempt. "I need no man to side me. You can tell Pa I'll be home later tonight." He glanced at the redhead. "Much later."

"Want I should carry this stuff home for you?" Johnny put his hand on the saddle-bags.

"Leave him be!" Hazel protested angrily. "Can't you see he don't want to be bothered? He's capable of takin' care of himself, an' he don't need no kid for gardeen!"

"Beat it," Sam said. "You go on home. I'll come along later."

"Better come now, Sam." Johnny was getting worried, for Loss Degner had started for the table.

"Here, you!" Degner was sharp. "Leave that man alone! He's a friend of mine, and I'll have no saddle tramp annoying my customers!"

Johnny turned on him. "I'm no saddle tramp. I ride for his Pa. He asked me to ride home with him—now. That's what I aim to do."

As he spoke he was not thinking of Degner, but of Flitch. The gunman was behind him now, and neither Flitch, fast as he was, nor Albie Bower were above shooting a man in the back.

"I said to beat it." Sam stared at him drunkenly. "Saddle tramp's what you are. Folks never should have took you in."

"That's it," Degner said. "Now get out! He don't want you nor your company."

There was a movement behind him, and he heard Flitch say, "Loss, let me have him. I know this hombre. This is that kid gunfighter, Johnny O'Day, from the Gila."

Johnny turned slowly, his green eyes flat and cold. "Hello, Flitch. I heard you were around." Carefully, he moved away from the table, aware of the startled look on Hazel's face, the suddenly tight awareness on the face of Loss Degner. "You lookin' for me, Flitch?" It was a chance he had to take. His best chance now. If shooting started, he might grab the saddle-bags and break for the door, and then the ranch. They would be through with Sam Redlin once the money was gone.

"Yeah," Flitch stared at him, his unshaven face hard with the lines of evil, and shadowed by the intent that rode him hard, "I'm lookin' for you. Always figured you got off easy, made you a fast rep gunnin' down your betters."

Bower had moved up beside him, but Loss Degner had drawn back to one side. Johnny's eyes never left Flitch. "You in this, Loss?"

Degner shrugged. "Why should I be? I was no Gila River gunman. This is your quarrel, finish it between you."

"All right, Flitch," Johnny said, "you want it. I'm givin' you your chance to start the play."

The stillness of a hot midafternoon lay on the Four Star. A fly buzzed against the dusty, cobwebbed back window. Somewhere in the street a horse stamped restlessly, and a distant pump creaked. Flitch stared at him, his little eyes hard and bright. His sweat-stained shirt was torn at the shoulder, and there was dust ingrained in the pores of his face.

His hands dropped in a flashing draw, but he had only cleared leather when Johnny's first bullet hit him, puncturing the Bull Durham tag that hung from his shirt pocket. The second shot cut the edge of it, and the third, fourth and fifth slammed Albie Bower back, knocking him back step by step, but Albie's gun was hammering, and it took the sixth shot to put him down.

Johnny stood over them, staring down at their bodies, and then he turned to face Loss Degner.

Degner was smiling, and he held a gun in his hand from which a thin tendril of smoke lifted. Startled, Johnny's eyes flickered to Sam Redlin.

Sam lay across the saddle-bags, blood trickling from the temples. He had been shot through the head by Degner under cover of the gun battle, murdered without a chance!

Johnny O'Day's eyes lifted to Loss Degner's. The saloon keeper was still smiling. "Yes, he's dead, and I've killed him. He had it coming, the fool! Thinking we cared to listen to his bragging! All we wanted was that money, and now we've got it. Me, Hazel and I! We've got it."

"Not yet," Johnny's lips were stiff and his heart was cold. He was thinking of Pa, Ma, and Else. "I'm still here."

"You?" Degner laughed. "With an empty gun? I counted your shots, boy. Even Johnny O'Day is cold turkey with an empty gun. Six shots, two for Flitch, and beautiful shooting, too, but for four shots for Albie who was moving and shooting, not so easy a target. But now I've got you. With you dead, I'll just say Sam came here without any money, that he got shot during the fight. Sound good to you?"

Johnny still faced him, his gun in his hand. "Not bad," he said, "but you still have me here, Loss. And this gun ain't empty!"

Degner's face tightened, then relaxed. "Not empty? I counted the shots, kid, so don't try bluffing me, Now, I'm killing you." He tilted his gun toward Johnny O'Day, and Johnny fired, once, twice . . . a third time. As each bullet hit him, Loss Degner jerked and twisted, but the shock of the wounds, and death wounds they were, was nothing to the shock of bullets from that empty gun.

He sagged against the bar, then slipped floorward. Johnny moved in on him. "You can hear me, Loss?" The killer's eyes lifted to his. "This ain't a six shooter. It's a Walch twelve-shot Navy gun, thirty-six caliber. She's right handy, Loss, and it only goes to show you shouldn't jump to conclusions."

Hazel sat at the table, staring at the dying Degner. "You better go to him, Red," Johnny said quietly. "He's only got a minute."

She stared at him as he picked up the saddle-bags and backed to the door.

Russell, the storekeeper, was on the steps with a half dozen others, none of whom he knew. "Degner killed Sam Redlin," he said. "Take care of Sam, will you?"

At Russell's nod, Johnny swung to the saddle and turned the gelding toward home.

He wouldn't leave now. He couldn't leave now. They would be all alone there, without Sam. Besides, Pa was going to need help on that dam. "Boy," he touched the gelding's neck, "I reckon we got to stick around for awhile."

FOUR CARD DRAW

When a man drew four cards he could expect something like this to happen. Ben Taylor had probably been right when he told him his luck had run out. Despite that, he had a place of his own, and come what may, he was going to keep it.

Nor was there any fault to find with the place. From the moment Allen Ring rode his claybank into the valley he knew he was coming home. This was it, this was the place. Here he would stop. He'd been tumbleweeding all over the West now for ten years, and it was time he stopped if he ever did, and this looked like his fence corner.

Even the cabin looked good, although Taylor told him the place had been empty for three years. It looked solid and fit, and while the grass was waist high all over the valley, and up around the house, he could see trails through it, some of them made by unshod ponies, which mean wild horses, and some by deer. Then there were the tracks of a single shod horse, always the same one.

Those tracks always led right up to the door, and they stopped there, yet he could see that somebody with mighty small feet had been walking up to peer into the windows. Why would a person want to look into a window more than once? The window of an empty cabin? He had gone up and looked in himself, and all he saw was a dusty, dark interior with a ray of light from the opposite window, a table, a couple of chairs, and a fine old fireplace that had been built by skilled hands.

"You never built that fireplace, Ben Taylor," Ring had muttered, "you who never could handle anything but a running iron or a deck of cards. You never built anything in your life as fine and useful as that."

The cabin sat on a low ledge of grass backed up against the towering cliff of red rock, and the spring was not more than fifty feet away, a stream that came out of the rock and trickled pleasantly into a small basin before spilling out and winding throughtfully down the valley to join a larger stream, a quarter of a mile away.

There were some tall spruces around the cabin, a couple of sycamores and a cottonwood near the spring. Some gooseberry bushes, too, and a couple of apple trees. The trees had been pruned.

"And you never did that, either, Ben Taylor!" Allen Ring said soberly. "I wish I knew more about this place."

Time had fled like a scared antelope, and with the scythe he found in the pole barn, he cut off the tall grass around the house, patched up the holes in the cabin where the pack rats had got in, and even thinned out the bushes—it had been several years since they had been touched—and repaired the pole barn.

The day he picked to clean out the spring was the day Gail Truman rode up to the house. He had been putting the finishing touches on a chair bottom he was making when he heard a horse's hoof strike stone, and he straightened up to see the girl sitting on the red pony. She was staring open mouthed at the stacked hay from the grass he had cut, and the washed windows of the house. He saw her swing down and run up to the window, and dropping his tools he strolled up.

"Huntin' somebody, Ma'am?"

She wheeled and stared at him, her wide blue eyes accusing. "What are you doing here?" she demanded. "What do you mean by moving in like this?"

He smiled, but he was puzzled, too. Ben Taylor had said nothing about a girl, especially a girl like this. "Why, I own the place!" he said. "I'm fixin' it up so's I can live here."

"You own it?" Her voice was incredulous, agonized. "You couldn't own it! You couldn't. The man who owns this place is gone, and he would never sell it! Never!"

"He didn't exactly sell it, Ma'am," Ring said gently, "he lost it to me in a poker game. That was down Texas way."

She was horrified. "In a poker game? Whit Bayly in a poker game? I don't believe it!"

"The man I won it from was called Ben Taylor, Ma'am." Ring took the deed from his pocket and opened it. "Come to think of it, Ben did say that if anybody asked about Whit Bayly to say that he died down in the Guadaloupes—of lead poisoning."

"Whit Bayly is dead?" The girl looked stunned. "You're sure? Oh!"

Her face went white and still and something in it seemed to die. She turned with a little gesture of despair and stared out across the valley, and his eyes followed hers. It was strange, Allen Ring told himself, that it was the first time he had looked just that way, and he stood there, caught up by something nameless, some haunting sense of the familiar.

Before him lay the tall grass of the valley, turning slightly now with the brown of autumn, and to his right a dark stand of spruce, standing stiffly, like soldiers on parade, and beyond them the swell of the hill, and further to the right the hill rolled up and stopped, and beyond lay a wider valley fading away into the vast purple and mauve of distance, and here and there spotted with the golden candles of cottonwoods, their leaves bright yellow with nearing cold.

There was no word for this, it was a picture, yet a picture of which a man could only dream and never reproduce.

"It—it's beautiful, isn't it?" he said.

She turned on him, and for the first time she seemed really to look at him, a tall young man with a shock of rust brown hair and sombre gray eyes, having about him the look of a rider and a look of a lonely man.

"Yes, it is beautiful. Oh, I've come here so many times to see it, the cabin, too. I think this is the most lovely place I have ever seen. I used to dream about—" She stopped, suddenly confused. "Oh, I'm sorry. I shouldn't talk so."

She looked at him soberly. "I'd better go. I guess this is yours now."

He hesitated. "Ma'am," he said sincerely, "the place is mine, and sure enough, I love it. I wouldn't swap this place for anything. But that view, that belongs to no man. It belongs to whoever looks at it with eyes to see it, so you come any time you like, and look all you please."

Ring grinned. "Fact is," he said, "I'm aimin' to fix the place up inside, an' I'm sure no hand at such things. Maybe you could sort of help me. I'd like it kind of homey like." He flushed. "You see, I sort of lived in bunkhouses all my life, an' never had no such place."

She smiled with a quick understanding and sympathy. "Of course! I'd love to, only—" her face sobered, "you won't be able to stay here. You haven't seen Ross Bilton yet, have you?"

"Who's he?" Ring asked, curiously. He nodded toward the horsemen he saw approaching. "Is this the one?"

She turned quickly, and nodded. "Be careful! He's the town marshal. The men with him are Ben Hagen and Stan Brule."

Brule he remembered—but would Brule remember him?

"By the way, my name is Allen Ring," he said, low voiced.

"I'm Gail Truman. My father owns the Tall T brand."

Bilton was a big man with a white hat. Ring decided he didn't like him and that the feeling was going to be mutual. Brule he knew, so the stocky man was Ben Hagen. Brule had changed but little, some thinner, maybe, but his hatchet face as lean and poisonous as always.

"How are you, Gail?" Bilton said briefly. "Is this a friend of yours?"

Allen Ring liked to get his cards on the table. "Yes, a friend of hers, but also the owner of the place."

"You own Red Rock?" Bilton was incredulous. "That will be very hard to prove, my friend. Also, this place is under the custody of the law."

"Whose law?" Ring wanted to know. He was aware that Brule was watching him, wary but uncertain as yet.

"Mine. I'm the town marshal. There was a murder committed here, and until that murder is solved and the killer brought to justice this place will not be touched. You have already seen fit to make changes, but perhaps the court will be lenient."

"You're the town marshal?" Allen Ring shoved his hat back on his head and reached for his tobacco. "That's mighty interestin'. Howsoever, let me remind you that you're out of town right now."

"That makes no difference!" Bilton's voice was sharp. Ring could see that he was not accustomed to being told off. That his orders were usually obeyed. "You will get off this place before nightfall!"

"It makes a sight of difference to me," Allen replied calmly. "I bought this place by stakin' everything I had against it in a poker game. I drew four cards to win, a nine to match one I had, and three aces. It was a fool play that paid off. I registered the deed. She's mine legal. I know of no law that allows a place to be kept idle because there was a murder committed on it. If after three years it hasn't been solved, I suggest the town get a new marshal."

Ross Bilton was angry, but he kept himself under control. "I've warned you, and you've been told to leave. If you do not leave, I'll use my authority to move you."

Ring smiled. "Now listen, Bilton! You might pull that stuff on some folks that don't like trouble! You might bluff somebody into believin' you had the authority to do this. You don't bluff me, an' I simply don't scare—do I, Brule?"

He turned on Brule so sharply that the man stiffened in his saddle, his hand poised as though to grab for a gun. The breed's face stiffened with irritation, and then recognition came to him. "Allen Ring!" he said. "You again!"

"That's right, Brule. Only this time I'm not takin' cattle through the Indian Nation. Not pushin' them by that ratty bunch of rustlers an' highbinders you rode with." Ring turned his eyes toward Bilton. "You're the law? An' you ride with him? Why, the man's wanted in ever' county in Texas for everythin' from murder to horse thievin'."

Ross Bilton stared at Ring for a long minute. "You've been warned," he said.

"An' I'm stayin'," Ring replied sharply. "And keep your coyotes away, if you come again. I don't like 'em!"

Brule's fingers spread and his lips stiffened with cold fury. Ring watched him calmly. "You know better than that, Brule. Wait until my back is turned. If you reach for a gun I'll blow you out of your saddle."

Stan Brule slowly relaxed his hand, and then wordless, he turned to follow Bilton and Hagen, who had watched with hard eyes.

Gail Truman was looking at him curiously. "Why, Brule was afraid of you!" she exclaimed. "Who are you, anyway?"'

"Nobody, Ma'am," he said simply. "I'm no gunfighter, just an hombre who ain't got brains enough to scare proper. Brule knows it. He knows he might beat me, but he knows I'd kill him. He was there when I killed a friend of his, Blaze Garden."

"But—but then you must be a gunman. Blaze Garden was a killer! I've heard Dad and the boys talk about him!"

"No, I'm no gunman. Blaze beat me to the draw. In fact, he got off his first shot before my gun cleared the holster, only he shot too quick and missed. His second and third shots hit me while I was walkin' to him. The third shot wasn't so bad because I was holdin' my fire and gettin' close. He got scared an' stepped back and the third shot was too high. Then I shot and I was close up to him then. One was enough. One is always enough if you place it right."

He gestured at the place. "What's this all about? Mind tellin' me?"

"It's very simple, really. Nothing out here is very involved when you come to that. It seems that there's something out here that brings men to using guns much faster than in other places, and one thing stems from another.

"Whit Bayly owned this place. He was a fixing man, always tinkering and fixing things up. He was a tall, handsome man whom all the girls loved—"

"You, too?" he asked quizzically.

She flushed. "Yes, I guess so, only I'm only eighteen now, and that was three, almost four years ago. I wasn't very pretty, or very noticeable, and much too young.

"Sam Hazlitt was one of the richest men in the country around here, and Whit had a run-in with him over a horse. There had been a lot of stealing going on around, and Hazlitt traced some stock of his to this ranch, or so he claimed. Anyway, he accused Bayly of it, and Whit told him not to talk foolish. Furthermore, he told Hazlitt to stay off of his ranch. Well, folks were divided over who was in the right, but Whit had a lot of friends and Hazlitt had four brothers and clannish as all get out.

"Not long after some riders from Buck Hazlitt's ranch came by that way and saw a body lying in the yard, right over near the spring. When they came down to have a look, thinking Whit was hurt, they found Sam Hazlitt, and he'd been shot dead—in the back.

"They headed right for town, hunting Whit, and they found him. He denied it, and they were goin' to hang him, had a rope around his neck, and then I—I—well, I swore he wasn't anywhere near his ranch all day."

"It wasn't true?" Ring asked keenly, his eyes searching the girl's face. She avoided his eyes, flushing even more.

"Not—not exactly. But I knew he wasn't guilty! I just knew he wouldn't shoot a man in the back! I told them he was over to our place, talking with me, and he hadn't time to get back there and kill Sam.

"Folks didn't like it much. Some of them still believed he killed Sam, and some didn't like it because despite the way I said it, they figured he was sparking a girl too young for him. I always said it wasn't that. As a matter of fact, I did see Whit over our way, but the rest of it was lies. Anyway, after a few weeks Whit up and left the country."

"I see—and nobody knows yet who killed Sam Hazlitt?"

"Nobody. One thing that was never understood was what became of Sam's account book—sort of a tally book, but more than that. It was a sort of record he kept of a lot of things, and it was gone out of his pocket. Nobody ever found it, but they did find the pencil Sam used on the sand nearby. Dad always figured Sam lived long enough to write something, but that the killer stole the book and destroyed it."

"How about the hands? Could they have picked it up? Did Bilton question them about that?"

"Oh, Bilton wasn't marshal then! In fact, he was riding for Buck Hazlitt then! He was one of the hands who found Sam's body!"

After the girl had gone Allen Ring walked back to the house and thought the matter over. He had no intention of leaving. This was just the ranch he wanted, and he intended to live right here, yet the problem fascinated him.

Living in the house and looking around the place had taught him a good deal about Whit Bayly. He was, as Gail had said, "a fixin' man," for there were many marks of his handiwork aside from the beautifully made fireplace and the pruned apple trees. He was, Ring was willing to gamble, no murderer.

Taylor had said he died of lead poisoning. Who had killed Bayly? Why? Was it a casual shooting over some rangeland argument, or had he been followed from here by someone on vengeance bent? Or someone who thought he might know too much?

"You'll like the place." Taylor had said—that was an angle he hadn't considered before. Ben Taylor had actually seen this place himself! The more sign he read, the more tricky the trail became, and Allen walked outside and sat down against the cabin wall when his supper was finished, and lighted a smoke.

Stock had been followed to the ranch by Sam Hazlitt. If Whit was not the thief, then who was? Where had the stock been driven? He turned his eyes almost automatically toward the Mogollons, the logical place. His eyes narrowed, and he recalled that one night while playing cards they had been talking of springs and waterholes, and Ben Taylor had talked about Fossil Springs, a huge spring that roared thousands of gallons of water out of the earth.

"Place a man could run plenty of stock," he had said and winked, "and nobody the wiser!"

Those words had been spoken far away and long ago, and the Red Rock ranch had not yet been put on the table; that was months later. There was, he recalled, a Fossil Creek somewhere north of here. And Fossil Creek might flow from Fossil Spring—perhaps Ben Taylor had talked more to effect than he knew. That had been Texas, and this was Arizona, and a casual bunkhouse conversation probably seemed harmless enough.

"We'll see, Ben!" Ring muttered grimly. "We'll see!"

Ross Bilton had been one of the Hazlitt hands at the time of the killing, one of the first on the scene. Now he was town marshal but interested in keeping the ranch unoccupied—why?

None of it made sense, yet actually it was no business of his. Allen Ring thought that over, and decided it was his business in a sense. He now owned the place, and lived on it. If an old murder was to interfere with his living there, it behooved him to know the facts. It was a slight excuse for his curiosity.

Morning came and the day drew on toward noon, and there was no sign of Bilton or Brule. Ring had loaded his rifle and kept it close to hand, and he was wearing two guns, thinking he might need a loaded spare, although he rarely wore more than one. Also, inside the cabin door he had his double-barreled shotgun.

The spring drew his attention. At the moment he did not wish to leave the vicinity of the cabin, and that meant a good time to clean out the spring. Not that it needed it, but there loose stones in the bottom of the basin, and some moss. With this removed he would have more water and clearer water. With a wary eye toward the canyon mouth, he began his work.

The sound of an approaching horse drew him erect. His rifle stood against the rocks at hand, and his guns were ready, yet as the rider came into sight, he saw there was only one man, and a stranger.

He rode a fine bay gelding and he was not a young man, but thick and heavy with drooping mustache and kind blue eyes. He drew up.

"Howdy!" he asid affably, yet taking a quick glance around before looking again at Ring. "I'm Rolly Truman, Gail's father."

"It's a pleasure," Ring said, wiping his wet hands on a red bandana. "Nice to know the neighbors." He nodded at the spring. "I picked me a job. That hole's deeper than it looks!"

"Good flow of water," Truman agreed. He chewed his mustache thoughtfully. "I like to see a young man with get up about him, startin' his own spread, willin' to work."

Allen Ring waited. The man was building up to something; what, he knew not. It came then, carefully at first, yet shaping a loop as it drew near.

"Not much range here, of course," Truman added, "you should have more graze. Ever been over in Cedar Basin? Or up along the East Verde bottom? Wonderful land up there, still come wild, but a country where a man could do something with a few white-face cattle."

"No, I haven't seen it," Ring replied, "but I'm satisfied. I'm not land hungry. All I want is a small place, an' this suits me fine."

Truman shifted in his saddle and looked uncomfortable. "Fact is, Son, you're upsettin' a lot of folks by bein' here. What you should do is to move."

"I'm sorry," Ring said flatly, "I don't want to make enemies, but I won this place on a four card draw. Maybe I'm a fatalist, but somehow or other, I think I should stick here. No man's got a right to think he can draw four cards and win anythin', but I did, an' in a plenty rough game. I had everythin' I owned in that pot. Now I got the place."

The rancher sat his horse uneasily, then he shook his head. "Son, you've sure got to move! There's no trouble here now, and if you stay she's liable to open old sores, start more trouble than any of us can stop. Besides, how did Ben Taylor get title to this place? Bayly had no love for him. I doubt if your title will stand up in court."

"As to that I don't know." Ring persisted stubbornly, "I have a deed that's legal enough, and I've registered that deed, an' my brand along with it. I did find out that Bayly had no heirs. So I reckon I'll sit tight until somebody comes along with a better legal claim than mine."

Truman ran his hand over his brow. "Well, I guess I don't blame you much, Son. Maybe I shouldn't have come over, but I know Ross Bilton and his crowd, and I reckon I wanted to save myself some trouble as well as you. Gail, she thinks you're a fine young man. In fact, you're the first man she's ever showed interest in since Whit left, and she was a youngster then. It was a sort of hero worship she had for him. I don't want trouble."

Allen Ring leaned on the shovel and looked up at the older man. "Truman," he said, "are you sure you aren't buyin' trouble by tryin' to avoid it? Just what's your stake in this?"

The rancher sat very still, his face drawn and pale. Then he got down from his horse and sat on a rock. Removing his hat, he mopped his brow.

"Son," he said slowly, "I reckon I got to trust you. You've heard of the Hazlitts. They are a hard, clannish bunch, men who lived by the gun most of their lives. Sam was murdered. Folks all know that when they find out who murdered him and why, there's goin' to be plenty of trouble around here. Plenty."

"Did you kill him?"

Truman jerked his head up. "No! No, you mustn't get that idea, but—well, you know how small ranchers are. There was a sight of rustlin' them days, and the Hazlitts were the big outfit. They lost cows."

"And some of them got your brand?" Ring asked shrewdly.

Truman nodded. "I reckon. Not so many, though. And not only me. Don't get me wrong, I'm not beggin' off the blame. Part of it is mine, all right, but I didn't get many. Eight or ten of us hereabouts slapped brands on Hazlitt stock—and at least five of us have the biggest brands around here now, some as big almost as the Hazlitts."

Allen Ring studied the skyline thoughtfully. It was an old story and one often repeated in the west. When the War between the States ended, men came home to Texas and the southwest to find cattle running in thousands, unbranded and unowned. The first man to slap on a brand was the owner, and no way he could be contested.

Many men grew rich with nothing more than a wide loop and a running iron. Then the unbranded cattle were gone, the ranches had settled into going concerns, and the great days of casual branding had ended, yet there was still free range, and a man with that same loop and a running iron could still build a herd fast.

More than one of the biggest ranchers had begun that way, and many of them continued to brand loose stock wherever found. No doubt that had been true here, and these men like Rolly Truman, good, able men who had fought Indians and built their homes to last, had begun just that way. Now the range was mostly fenced, ranches had narrowed somewhat, but Ring could see what it might mean to open an old sore now.

Sam Hazlitt had been trailing rustlers—he had found out who they were, and where the herds were taken, and he had been shot down from behind. The catch was that the tally book, with his records, was still missing. That tally book might contain evidence as to the rustling done by men who were now pillars of the community, and open them to the vengeance of the Hazlitt outfit.

Often western men threw a blanket over a situation. If a rustler had killed Sam, then all the rustlers involved would be equally guilty. Anyone who lived on this ranch might stumble on that tally book and throw the range into a bloody gun war in which many men now beyond the errors of their youth, with homes, families, and different customs, would die.

It could serve no purpose to blow the lid off the trouble now, yet Allen Ring had a hunch. In their fear of trouble for themselves they might be concealing an even greater crime, aiding a murderer in his escape. There were lines in the face of Rolly Truman that a settled, established rancher should not have.

"Sorry," Ring said, "I'm stayin'. I like this place."

All through the noon hour the tension was building. The air was warm and sultry, and there was a thickening haze over the mountains. There was that hot thickness in the air that presaged a storm. Yet when he left his coffee to return to work, Ring saw three horsemen coming into the canyon mouth at a running walk. He stopped in the door and touched his lips with his tongue.

They reined up at the door, three hard-bitten, hard-eyed men with rifles across their saddle bows. Men with guns in their holsters and men of a kind that would never turn from trouble. These were men with the bark on, lean fanatics with lips thinned with old bitterness.

The older man spoke first. "Ring, I've heard about you. I'm Buck Hazlitt. These are my brothers, Joe and Dolph. There's talk around that you aim to stay on this place. There's been talk for years that Sam hid his tally book here. We figure the killer got that book and burned it. Maybe he did, and again, maybe not. We want that book. If you want to stay on this place, you stay. But if you find that book, you bring it to us."

Ring looked from one to the other, and he could see the picture clearly. With men like these, hard and unforgiving, it was no wonder Rolly Truman and the other ranchers were worried. The years and prosperity had eased Rolly and his like into comfort and softness, but not there. The Hazlitts were of feudal blood and background.

"Hazlitt," Ring said, "I know how you feel. You lost a brother, and that means somethin', but if that book is still around, which I doubt, and I find it, I'll decide what to do with it all by myself. I don't aim to start a range war. Maybe there's some things best forgotten. The man who murdered Sam Hazlitt ought to pay."

"We'll handle that," Dolph put in grimly. "You find that book, you bring it to us. If you don't—" His eyes hardened. "Well, we'd have to class you with the crooks."

Ring's eyes shifted to Dolph. "Class, if you want," he flared. "I'll do what seems best to me with that book. But all of you folks are plumb proddy over that tally book. Chances are nine out of ten the killer found it and destroyed it."

"I don't reckon he did," Buck said coldly, "because we know he's been back here, a-huntin' it. Him an' his girl."

Ring stiffened. "You mean—?"

"What we mean is our figger, not yours." Buck Hazlitt reined his horse around. "You been told. You bring that book to us. You try to buck the Hazlitts and you won't stay in this country."

Ring had his back up. Despite himself he felt cold anger mounting within him. "Put this in your pipe, friend." he said harshly, "I came here to stay. No Hazlitt will change that. I ain't huntin' trouble but if you bring trouble to me, I'll handle it. I can bury a Hazlitt as easy as any other man!"

Not one of them condescended to notice the remark. Turning their horses they walked them down the canyon and out of it into the sultry afternoon. Allen Ring mopped the sweat from his face, and listened to the deep rumbling of far-off thunder, growling among the canyons like a grizzly with a toothache. It was going to rain. Sure as shootin', it was going to rain—a regular gully washer.

There was yet time to finish the job on the spring, so he picked up his shovel and started back for the job. The rock basin was nearly cleaned and he finished removing the few rocks and the moss that had gathered. Then he opened the escape channel a little more to insure a more rapid emptying and filling process in the basin into which the trickle of water fell.

The water emerged from a crack in the rocks and trickled into the basin, and finishing his job, Ring glanced thoughtfully to see if anything remained undone. There was still some moss on the rocks from which the water flowed, and kneeling down, he leaned over to scrape it away and pulling away the last shreds, he noticed a space from which a rock had recently fallen. Pulling more moss away, he dislodged another rock, and there, pushed into a niche, was a small black book!

Sam Hazlitt, dying, had evidently managed to shove it back in this crack in the rocks, hoping it would be found by someone not the killer.

Sitting back on his haunches, Ring opened the faded, canvas bound book. A flap crossed over the page ends and the book had been closed by a small tongue that slid into a loop of the canvas cover. Opening the book, he saw the pages were stained, but still legible.

The next instant he was struck by lightning. At least, that was what seemed to happen. Thunder crashed, and something struck him on the skull and he tried to rise and something struck again. He felt a drop of rain on his face and his eyes opened wide and then another blow caught him and he faded out into darkness, his fingers clawing at the grass to keep from slipping down into that velvety, smothering blackness.

He was wet. He turned a little, lying there, thinking he must have left a window open and the rain was—his eyes opened and he felt rain pounding on his face and he stared, not at a boot with a California spur, but at dead brown grass, soaked with rain now, and the glistening smoothness of water-worn stones. He was soaked to the hide.

Struggling to his knees, he looked around, his head heavy, his lips and tongue thick. He blinked at a gray, rain-slanted world and at low gray clouds and a distant rumble of thunder following a streak of lightning along the mountain tops.

Lurching to his feet, he stumbled toward the cabin and pitched over the door sill to the floor. Struggling again to his feet he got the door closed and in a vague, misty half world of consciousness he struggled out of his clothes and got his hands on a rough towel and fumblingly dried himself.

He did not think. He was acting purely from vague instinctive realization of what he must do. He dressed again, in dry clothes and dropped at the table. After awhile he sat up and it was dark and he knew he had blacked out again. He lighted a light and nearly dropped it to the floor, then stumbled to the wash basin and splashed his face with cold water. Then he bathed his scalp, feeling tenderly of the lacerations there.

A boot with a California spur.

That was all he had seen. The tally book was gone, and a man wearing a new boot with a California type spur, a large rowel, had taken it. He got coffee on, and while he waited for it he took his guns out and dried them painstakingly, wiping off each shell, then replacing them in his belt with other shells from a box on a shelf.

He reloaded the guns, then slipping into his slicker he went outside for his rifle. Between sips of coffee, he worked over his rifle until he was satisfied, then threw a small pack together, and stuffed his slicker pockets with shotgun shells.

The shotgun was an express gun and short barreled. He slung it from a loop under the slicker. Then he took a lantern and went to the stable and saddled the claybank. Leading the horse outside into the driving rain, he swung into the saddle and turned along the road toward Basin.

There was no letup in the rain. It fell steadily and heavily, yet the claybank slogged along, alternating between a shambling trot and a fast walk. Allen Ring, his chin sunk in the upturned collar of his slicker watched the drops fall from the brim of his Stetson and felt the bump of the shotgun under his coat.

He had seen little of the tally book, but sufficient to know that it would blow the lid off the very range war they were fearing. Knowing the Hazlitts, he knew they would bring fire and gunplay to every home even remotely connected with the death of their brother.

The horse slid down a steep bank and shambled across the wide wash. Suddenly, the distant roar that had been in his ears for some time sprang into consciousness and he jerked his head up. His horse snorted in alarm, and Ring stared, open mouthed at the wall of water towering all of ten feet high, that was rolling down the wash toward him.

With a shrill rebel yell he slapped the spurs to the claybank and the startled horse turned loose with an astounded leap and hit the ground in a dead run. There was no time to slow for the bank of the wash and the horse went up, slipped at the very brink and started to fall back.

Ring hit the ground with both boots, scrambled over the brink, and even as the flood roared down upon them, he heaved on the bridle and the horse cleared the edge and stood trembling. Swearing softly, Ring kicked the mud from his boots and mounted again. Leaving the raging torrent behind him he rode on.

Thick blackness of night and heavy clouds lay upon the town when he sloped down the main street and headed the horse toward the barn. He swung down, handed the bridle to the handy man.

"Rub him down," he said. "I'll be back."

He started for the doors, then stopped, staring at the three horses in neighboring stalls. The liveryman noticed his glance, and looked at him.

"The Hazlitts. They come in about an hour ago, ugly as sin."

Allen Ring stood wide legged, staring grimly out the door. There was a coolness inside him now that he recognized. He dried his hands carefully.

"Bilton in town?" he asked.

"Sure is. Playin' cards over to the Mazatzal Salloon."

"He wear Mex spurs? Big rowels?"

The man rubbed his jaw. "I don't remember. I don't know at all. You watch out," he warned, "folks are on the prod."

Ring stepped out into the street and slogged through the mud to the edge of the boardwalk before the darkened general store. He kicked the mud from his boots and dried his hands again, after carefully unbuttoning his slicker.

Nobody would have a second chance after this. He knew well enough that his walking into the Mazatzal would precipitate an explosion. Only, he wanted to light the fuse himself, in his own way.

He stood there in the darkness alone, thinking it over. They would all be there. It would be like tossing a match into a lot of fused dynamite. He wished then that he was a better man with a gun than he was, or that he had someone to side him in this, but he had always acted alone and would scarcely know how to act with anyone else.

He walked along the boardwalk with long strides, his boots making hard sounds under the steady roar of the rain. He couldn't lace that spur, that boot. Yet he had to. He had to get his hands on that boot.

Four horses stood, heads down in the rain, saddles covered with slickers. He looked at them, and saw they were of three different brands. The window of the Mazatzal was rain wet, yet standing at one side he glanced within.

The long room was crowded and smoky. Men lined the bar, feet on the brass rail. A dozen tables were crowded with card players. Everyone seemed to have taken refuge here from the rain. Picking out the Hazlitt boys, Allen saw them gathered together at the back end of the room. Then he got Ross Bilton pegged. He was at a table playing cards, facing the door. Stan Brule was at this end of the bar, and Hagen was at a table against the wall, the three of them making three points of a flat triangle whose base was the door.

It was no accident. Bilton then, expected trouble, and he was not looking toward the Hazlitts. Yet, on reflection, Ring could see the triangle could center fire from three directions on the Hazlitts as well. There was a man with his back to the door who sat in the game with Bilton. And not far from Hagen, Rolly Truman was at the bar.

Truman was toying with his drink, just killing time. Everybody seemed to be waiting for something.

Could it be he they waited upon? No, that was scarcely to be considered. They could not know he had found the book, although it was certain at least one man in the room knew, and possibly others. Maybe it was just the tension, the building up of feeling over his taking over of the place at Red Rock. Allen Ring carefully turned down the collar of his slicker and wiped his hands dry again.

He felt jumpy, and could feel that dryness in his mouth that always came on him at times like this. He touched his gun butts, then stepped over and opened the door.

Every one looked up or around at once. Ross Bilton held a card aloft and his hand froze in the act of dealing, holding still for a full ten seconds while Ring closed the door. He surveyed the room again, saw Ross play the card and say something in an undertone to the man opposite him. The man turned his head slightly and it was Ben Taylor!

The gambler looked around, his face coldly curious, and for an instant their eyes met across the room, and then Allen Ring started toward him.

There was no other sound in the room, although they could all hear the unceasing roar of the rain of the roof. Ring saw something leap up in Taylor's eyes and his own took on a sardonic glint.

"That was a good hand you dealt me down Texas way," Ring said. "A good hand!"

"You'd better draw more cards," Taylor said, "you're holdin' a small pair!"

Ring's eyes shifted as the man turned slightly. It was the jingle of his spurs that drew his eyes, and there they were, the large rowelled California style spurs, not common here. He stopped beside Taylor so the man had to tilt his head back to look up. Ring was acutely conscious that he was not centered between the fire and Brule and Hagen. The Hazlitts looked on curiously, uncertain as to what was happening.

"Give it to me, Taylor," Ring said quietly, "give it to me now."

There was ice in his voice, and Taylor, aware of the awkwardness of his position, got to his feet, inches away from Ring.

"I don't know what you're talking about," he flared.

"No?"

Ring was standing with his feet apart a little, and his hands were breast high, one of them clutching the edge of his raincoat. He hooked with his left from that position, and the blow was too short, too sudden, and too fast for Ben Taylor.

The crack of it on the angle of his jaw was audible, and then Ring's right came up in the gambler's solar plexus and the man's knees sagged. Spinning him around, Ring ripped open his coat with a jerk that scattered buttons across the room, then from an inside pocket he jerked the tally book.

He saw the Hazlitts start at the same instant that Bilton sprang back from the chair, upsetting it.

"Get him!" Bilton roared. "Get him!"

Ring shoved Taylor hard into the table, upsetting it and causing Bilton to spring back to keep his balance, and at the same instant, Ring dropped to a half crouch and turning left he drew with a flash of speed, saw Brule's gun come up at almost the same instant, and then he fired!

Stan Brule was caught with his gun just level and the bullet smashed him on the jaw. The tall man staggered, his face a mask of hatred and astonishment mingled, and then Ring fired again, did a quick spring around with his knees bent, turning completely around in one leap, and firing as his feet hit the floor. He felt Hagen's bullet smash into him, and he tottered, then fired coolly, and swinging as he fired, he caught Bilton right over the belt buckle.

It was fast action, snapping, quick, yet deliberate. The four fired shots had taken less than three seconds.

Stepping back, he scooped the tally book from the floor where it had dropped, then pocketed it. Bilton was on the floor, coughing blood. Hagen had a broken right arm and was swearing in a thick, stunned voice.

Stan Brule had drawn his last gun. He had been dead before he hit the floor. The Hazlitts started forward with a lunge, and Allen Ring took another step backward, dropping his pistol and swinging the shotgun, still hanging from his shoulder, into firing position.

"Get back!" he said thickly. "Get back or I'll kill the three of you! Back—back to where you stood!"

Their faces wolfish, the three stood lean and dangerous, yet the shotgun brooked no refusal and slowly, bitterly, and reluctantly, the three moved back, step by step.

Ring motioned with the shotgun. "All of you—along the wall!"

The men rose and moved back, their eyes on him, uncertain, wary, some of them frightened.

Allen Ring watched them go, feeling curiously lightheaded and uncertain. He tried to frown away the pain from his throbbing skull, yet there was a pervading weakness from somewhere else.

"My gosh!" Rolly Truman said. "The man's been shot! He's bleeding!"

"Get back!" Ring said thickly.

His eyes shifted to the glowing pot-bellied stove, and he moved forward, the shotgun waist high, his eyes on the men who stared at him, awed.

The sling held the gun level, his hand partly supporting it, a finger in the trigger. With his left hand he opened the stove, then fumbled in his pocket.

Buck Hazlitt's eyes bulged. "No!" he roared "No, you don't!"

He lunged forward, and Ring tipped the shotgun and fired a blast into the floor, inches ahead of Hazlitt's feet. The rancher stopped so suddenly he almost fell, the shotgun tipped to cover him.

"Back!" Ring said. He swayed on his feet. "Back!" He fished out the tally book and threw it into the flames.

Something like a sigh went through the crowd. They stared, awed as the flames seized hungrily at the opened book, curling around the leaves with hot fingers, turning them brown, then black and to ashes.

Half hypnotized the crowd watched, then Ring's eyes swung to Hazlitt. "It was Ben Taylor killed him," he muttered. "Taylor, an' Bilton was with him. He—he seen it."

"We take your word for it?" Buck Hazlitt demanded furiously.

Allen Ring's eyes widened and he seemed to gather himself. "You want to question it? You want to call me a liar?"

Hazlitt looked at him, touching his tongue to his lips. "No," he said, "I figured it was them."

"I told you true," Ring said, and then his legs seemed to fold up under him and he went to the floor.

The crowd surged forward and Rolly Truman stared at Buck as Hazlitt neared the stove. The big man stared into the flames for a minute, then he closed the door.

"Good!" he said. "Good thing! It's been a torment, that book, like a cloud hangin' over us all!"

The sun was shining through the window when Gail Truman came to see him. He was sitting up in bed, and feeling better. It would be good to be back on the place again, for there was much to do. She came in, slapping her boots with her quirt and smiling.

"Feel better?" she asked brightly. "You certainly look better. You've shaved."

He grinned and rubbed his jaw. "I needed it. Almost two weeks in this bed. I must have been hit bad."

"You lost a lot of blood. It's lucky you've a strong heart."

"It ain't—isn't so strong any more," he said, "I think it's grown mighty shaky here lately."

Gail blushed. "Oh? It has? Your nurse, I suppose?"

"She is pretty, isn't she?"

Gail looked up, alarmed. "You mean, you—"

"No, honey," he said, "you!"

"Oh." She looked at him, then looked down. "Well, I guess—"

"All right?"

She smiled then, suddenly and warmly. "All right."

"I had to ask you," he said. "We had to marry."

"Had to? Why?"

"People would talk, a young, lovely girl like you over at my place all the time—would they think you were looking at the view?"

"If they did," she replied quickly, "they'd be wrong!"

"You're telling me?" he asked.

LAW OF THE DESERT BORN

Shad Marone crawled out of the water swearing, and slid into the mesquite. Suddenly, for the first time since the chase began, he was mad. He was mad clear through. "The hell with it!" He got to his feet, his eyes blazing. "I've run far enough! If they cross Black River, they're askin' for it!"

For three days he had been on the dodge, using every stratagem known to men of the desert, but they clung to him like leeches. That was what came of killing a sheriff's brother, and the fact that he killed in self-defense wasn't going to help a bit. Especially when the killer was Shad Marone.

That was what you could expect when you were the last man of the losing side in a cattle war. All his friends were gone now but Madge.

The best people of Puerto de Luna hadn't been the toughest in this scrap, and they had lost. And Shad Marone, who had been one of the toughest, had lost with them. His guns hadn't been enough to outweigh those of the other faction.

Of course, he admitted to himself, those on his side hadn't been angels. He'd branded a few head of calves himself from time to time, and when cash was short he had often run a few steers over the border. But hadn't they all?

Truman and Dykes had been good men, but Dykes had been killed at the start, and Truman had fought like a gentleman, and that wasn't any way to win in the Black River country.

Since then, there had been few peaceful days for Shad Marone.

After they'd elected Clyde Bowman sheriff, he knew they were out to get him. Bowman hated him, and Bowman had been one of the worst of them in the cattle war.

The trouble was, Shad was a gun fighter and they all knew it. Bowman was fast with a gun, and in a fight could hold his own. Also, he was smart enough to leave Shad Marone strictly alone. So they just waited, watched, and planned.

Shad had taken their dislike as a matter of course. It took tough men to settle a tough country, and if they started shooting, somebody got hurt. Well, he wasn't getting hurt. There had been too much shooting to suit him.

He wanted to leave Puerto de Luna, but Madge was still living on the old place, and he didn't want to leave her there alone. So he stayed on, knowing it couldn't last.

Then Jud Bowman rode into town. Shad was thoughtful when he heard that. Jud was notoriously quarrelsome, and was said to have twelve notches on his gun. Shad had a feeling that Jud hadn't come to Puerto de Luna by accident.

Jud hadn't been in town two days before the grapevine had the story that if Clyde and Lopez were afraid to run Marone out of town, he wasn't.

Jud Bowman might have done it too, if it hadn't been for Tips. Tips Hogan had been tending bar in Puerto de Luna for a long time. He'd come over the trail as wagon boss for Shad's old man, something everyone had forgotten but Shad and Tips himself.

Tips saw the gun in Bowman's lap, and he gave Marone a warning. It was just a word, through unmoving lips, while he mopped the bar.

After a moment, Shad turned, his glass in his left hand, and he saw the way Bowman was sitting, and how the table top would conceal a gun in his lap. Even then, when he knew they had set things up to kill him, he hadn't wanted trouble. He decided to get out while the getting was good. Then he saw Slade near the door and Henderson across the room.

He was boxed. They weren't gambling this time. Tips Hogan knew what was coming, and he was working his way down the bar.

Marone took it easy. He knew it was coming, and it wasn't a new thing. That was his biggest advantage, he thought. He had been in more fights than any of them. He didn't want any more trouble, but if he got out of this it would be right behind a sixgun. The back door was barred and the window closed.

Jud Bowman looked up suddenly. He had a great shock of blonde, coarse hair, and under bushy brows his eyes glinted. "What's this about you threatenin' to kill me, Marone?"

So that was their excuse. He had not threatened Bowman, scarcely knew him, in fact, but this was the way to put him in wrong, to give them the plea of self-defense.

He let his eyes turn to Bowman, saw the tensity in the man's face. A denial, and there would be shooting. Jud's right-hand finger tips rested on the table's edge. He had only to drop a hand and fire.

"Huh?" Shad said stupidly, as though startled from a day dream. He took a step toward the table, his face puzzled. "Wha'd you say? I didn't get it."

They had planned it all very carefully. Marone would deny, Bowman would claim he'd been called a liar, there would be a killing. They were tense, all three of them set to draw.

"Huh?" Shad repeated, blankly.

They were caught flat-footed. After all, you couldn't shoot a man in cold blood. You couldn't shoot a man who was half asleep. Most of the men in the saloon were against Marone, but they would never stand for murder.

They were poised for action, and nothing happened. Shad blinked at them. "Sorry," he said, "I must've been dreamin'. I didn't hear you."

Bowman glanced around uncertainly, wetting his lips with his tongue. "I said I heard you threatened to kill me," he repeated. It sounded lame, and he knew it, but Shad's response had been unexpected. What happened then was even more unexpected.

Marone's left hand shot out and before anyone could move, the table was spun from in front of Bowman. Everyone saw the naked gun lying in his lap.

Every man in the saloon knew that Jud Bowman, for all his reputation, had been afraid to shoot it out with an even break. It would have been murder.

Taken by surprise, Bowman blinked foolishly. Then his wits came back. Blood rushed to his face. He grabbed the gun. "Why, you . . . !"

Then Shad Marone shot him. Shad shot him through the belly, and before the other two could act, he wheeled, not toward the door, but to the closed window. He battered it with his shoulder and went right on through. Outside, he hit the ground on his hands, but came up in a lunging run. Then he was in the saddle and on his way.

There were men in the saloon who would tell the truth—two at least, although neither had much use for him. But Marone knew that with Clyde Bowman as sheriff he would never be brought to trial. He would be killed "evading arrest."

For three days he fled, and during that time they were never more than an hour behind him. Then, at Forked Tree, they closed in. He got away, but they clipped his horse. The roan stayed on his feet, giving all he had, as horses always had given for Shad Marone, and then died on the river bank, still trying with his last breath.

Marone took time to cache his saddle and bridle, then started on afoot. He made the river, and they thought that would stop him, for he couldn't swim a stroke. But he found a drift log, and with his guns riding high, he shoved off. Using the current and his own kicking, he got to the other bank, considerably downstream.

The thing that bothered him was the way they clung to his trail. Bowman wasn't the man to follow as little trail as he left. Yet the man hung to him like an Apache.

Apache!

Why hadn't he thought of that? It would be Lopez, following that trail, not Bowman. Bowman was a bulldog, but Lopez was wily as a fox and bloodthirsty as a weasel.

Shad got to his feet and shook the water from him like a dog. He was a big, rawboned, sun-browned man. His shirt was half torn away, and a bandolier of cartridges was slung across his shoulder and chest. His sixgun was on his hip, his rifle in his hand.

He poured the water out of his boots. Well, he was through playing now. If they wanted a trail, he'd see that they got one.

Lopez was the one who worried him. He could shake the others, but Lopez was one of the men who had built this country. He was ugly, he killed freely and often, he was absolutely ruthless, but he had nerve. You had to hand it to him. The man wasn't honest, and he was too quick to kill, but it had taken men like him to tame this wild, lonely land. It was a land that didn't tame easy.

Well, what they'd get now would be death for them all. Even Lopez. This was something he'd been saving.

Grimly he turned up the steep, little-used path from the river. They thought they had him at the river. And they would think they had him again at the lava beds.

Waterless, treeless, and desolate, the lava beds were believed to harbor no life of any kind. Only sand, and great, jagged rocks—rocks shaped like flame—grotesque, barren, awful. More than seventy miles long, never less than thirty miles wide, and so rough a pair of shoes wouldn't last five miles and footing next to impossible for horses.

On the edge of the lava, Shad Marone sat down and pulled off his boots. Tying their strings, he hung them to his belt. Then he pulled out a pair of moccasins he always carried, and slipped them on. Pliable and easy on his feet, they would give to the rough rock, and would last many times as long in this terrain as boots. He got up and walked into the lava beds.

The bare lava caught the fierce heat and threw it back in his face. A trickle of sweat started down his cheek. He knew the desert, knew how to live in the heat, and he did not try to hurry. That would be fatal. Far ahead of him was a massive tower of rock, jutting up like a church steeple from a tiny village. He headed that way, walking steadily. He made no attempt to cover his trail, no attempt to lose his pursuers. He knew where he was going.

An hour passed, and then another. It was slow going. The rock tower had come abreast of him and then fallen behind. Once he saw the trail of some tiny creature, perhaps a horned frog.

Once, when he climbed a steep declivity, he glanced back. They were still coming. They hadn't quit.

Lopez: That was like Lopez. He wouldn't quit. Shad smiled then, but his eyes were without humor. All right, they wanted to kill him bad enough to try the lava beds. They would have to learn the hard way—learn when they could never profit from the lesson.

He kept working north, using the shade carefully. There was little of it, only here and there in the lee of a rock. But each time he stopped, he cooled off a little. So far he hadn't taken a drink.

After the third hour he washed his lips and rinsed his mouth. Twice, after that, he took only a spoonful of water and rinsed his mouth before swallowing.

Occasionally he stopped and looked around to get his bearings. He smiled grimly when he thought of Bowman. The sheriff was a heavy man. Davis would be there, too. Lopez was lean and wiry. He would last. He would be hard to kill.

By his last count there were eight left. Four had turned back at the lava beds. He gained a little.

At three in the afternoon he finally stopped. It was a nice piece of shade, and would grow better as the hours went on. The ground was low, and in one corner there was a pocket. He dug with his hands until the ground became damp. Then he lay back on the sand and went to sleep.

He wasn't worried. Too many years he had been awakening at the hour he wished, his senses alert to danger. He was an hour ahead of them, at least. He would need this rest he was going to get. What lay ahead would take everything he had. He knew that.

Their feet would be punishing them cruelly now. Three of them still had their horses, leading them.

He rested his full hour, then got up. He had cut it very thin. Through a space in the rocks he could see them, not three hundred yards away. Lopez, as he had suspected, was in the lead. How easy to pick them off now! But no, he would not kill again. Let their own anxiety to kill him kill them.

Within a hundred yards he had put two jumbled piles of boulders between himself and his pursuers. A little farther then, and he stopped.

Before him was a steep slide of shale, near the edge of a great basin. Standing where he did, he could see far away in the distance, a purple haze over the mountains. Between there was nothing but a great white expanse, shimmering with heat.

He slid down the shale and brought up at the bottom. He was now, he knew, seventy feet below sea level. He started away, and at every step dry, powdery dust lifted in clouds. It caked in his nostrils, filmed his eyelashes, and covered his clothes with whitish, alkaline dust. Far across the Sink, and scarcely discernible from the crest behind him, was the Window in the Rock. He headed for it, walking steadily. It was ten miles if you walked straight across.

"So far that Navajo was right," Shad told himself. "An' he said to make it before dark . . . or else!"

Shad Marone's lips were dry and cracked. After a mile he stopped, tilting his canteen until he could get his finger into the water, then carefully moistened his lips. Just a drop then, inside his mouth.

All these men were desertwise. None of them, excepting perhaps Lopez, would know about the Sink. They would need water. They would have to know where to find it. By day they could follow his trail, but after darkness fell . . . ?

And then, the Navajo had said, the wind would begin to blow. Shad looked at the dry, powdery stuff under him. He could imagine what a smothering, stifling horror this would be if the wind blew. Then, no man could live.

Heat waves danced a queer rigadoon across the lower sky, and heat lifted, beating against his face from the hot white dust beneath his feet. Always it was over a man's shoe tops, sometimes almost knee deep. Far away the mountains were a purple line that seemed to waver vaguely in the afternoon sun. He walked on, heading by instinct rather than sight for the Window.

Dust arose in a slow, choking cloud. It came up from his feet in little puffs, like white smoke. He stumbled, then got his feet right, and kept on. Walking in this was like dragging yourself through heavy mud. The dust pulled at his feet. His pace was slow.

Thirst gathered in his throat, and his mouth seemed filled with something thick and clotted. His tongue was swollen, his lips cracked and swollen. He could not seem to swallow.

He could not make three miles an hour. Darkness would reach him before he made the other side. But he would be close. Close enough. Luckily, at this season, the light stayed long in the sky.

After a long time, he stopped and looked back. Yes, they were coming. But there was not one dust cloud. There were several. Through red-rimmed, sun-squinted eyes, he watched. They were straggling. Every straggler would die. He knew that. Well, they had asked for it.

Dust covered his clothing, and only his gun he kept clean. Every half hour he stopped and wiped it as clean as he could. Twice he pulled a knotted string through the barrel.

Finally he used the last of his water. Every half hour he had been wetting his lips. He did not throw the canteen away, but slung it back upon his hip. He would need it, later, when he got to the Nest. His feet felt very heavy, his legs seemed to belong to an automaton. Head down, he slogged wearily on. In an hour he made two miles.

There is a time when human nature seems able to stand no more. There is a time when every iota of strength seems burned away. This was the fourth day of the chase. Four days without a hot meal, four days of riding, walking, running. Now this. He had only to stop, they would come up with him, and it would be over.

The thought of how easy it would be to quit came to him. He considered the thought. But he did not consider quitting. He could no more have stopped than a bee could stop making honey. Life was ahead, and he had to live. It was a matter only of survival now. The man with the greatest urge to live would be the one to survive.

Those men behind him were going to die. They were going to die for three reasons. First, he alone knew where there was water, and at the right time he would lose them.

Second, he was in the lead, and after dark they would have no trail, and if they lived through the night there would be no trail left in the morning.

Third, at night, at this season, the wind always blew, and their eyes and mouths and ears would fill with soft, white filmy dust, and if they lay down, they would be buried by the sifting, swirling dust.

They would die then, every man jack of them.

They had it coming. Bowman deserved it, so did Davis and Gardner. Lopez most of all. They were all there, he had seen them. Lopez was a killer. The man's father had been Spanish and Irish, his mother an Apache.

Without Lopez he would have shaken them off long ago. Shad Marone tried to laugh, but the sound was only a choking grunt. Well, they had followed Lopez to their death, all of them. Aside from Lopez, they were weak sisters.

He looked back again. He was gaining on them now. The first dust cloud was farther behind, and the distance between the others was growing wider. It was a shame Lopez had to die, at that. The man was tough and had plenty of trail savvy.

Shad Marone moved on. From somewhere within him he called forth a new burst of strength. His eyes watched the sun. While there was light, they had a chance. What would they think in Puerto de Luna when eight men did not come back?

Marone looked at the sun, and it was low, scarcely above the purple mountains. They seemed close now. He lengthened his stride again. The Navajo had told him how his people once had been pursued by Apaches, and had led the whole Apache war party into the Sink. There they had been caught by darkness, and none were ever seen again according to the Indian's story.

Shad stumbled then, and fell. Dust lifted thickly about him, clogging his nostrils. Slowly, like a groggy fighter, he got his knees under him and using his rifle for a staff, pushed himself to his feet.

He started on, driven by some blind, brute desire for life. When he fell again he could feel rocks under his hands. He pulled himself up.

He climbed the steep, winding path toward the Window in the Rock. Below the far corner of the Window was the Nest. And in the Nest there was water. Or so the Navajo had told him.

When he was halfway up the trail he turned and looked back over the Sink. Far away, he could see the dust clouds. Four of them. One larger than the others. Probably there were two men together.

"Still coming," he muttered grimly, "and Lopez leading them!"

Lopez, damn his soul!

The little devil had guts, though; you had to give him that. Suddenly, Marone found himself almost wishing Lopez would win through. The man was like a wolf. A killer wolf. But he had guts. And it wasn't just the honest men who had built up this country to what it was today.

Maybe, without the killers and rustlers and badmen, the West would never have been won so soon. Shad Marone remembered some of them: Wild, dangerous men, who went into country where nobody else dared venture. They killed and robbed to live, but they stayed there.

It took iron men for that: Men like Lopez, who was a mongrel of the Santa Fe Trail. Lopez had drunk water from a buffalo track many a time. Well, so have I, Shad told himself.

Shad Marone took out his six-shooter and wiped it free of dust. Only then did he start up the trail.

He found the Nest, a hollow among the rocks, sheltered from the wind. The Window loomed above him now, immense, gigantic. Shad stumbled, running, into the Nest. He dropped his rifle and lunged for the water hole, throwing himself on the ground to drink. Then he stared, unbelieving.

Empty!

The earth was dry and parched where the water had been, but only cracked earth remained.

He couldn't believe it. It couldn't be! It couldn't. . . ! Marone came to his feet, glaring wildly about. His eyes were red-rimmed, his face heat-flushed above the black whiskers now filmed with gray dust.

He tried to laugh. Lopez dying down below there, he dying up here! The hard men of the West, the tough men! He sneered at himself. Both of them now would die, he at the waterhole, Lopez down there in the cloying, clogging dust!

He shook his head. Through the flame-sheathed torment of his brain there came a cool ray of sanity.

There had been water here. The Indian had been right. The cracked earth showed that. But where?

Perhaps a dry season. . . . But no; it had not been a dry season. Certainly no dryer than any other year at this time.

He stared across the place where the pool had been. Rocks, and a few rock cedar, and some heaped up rocks from a small slide. He stumbled across and began clawing at the rocks, pulling, tearing. Suddenly a trickle of water burst through! He got hold of one big rock and in a mad frenzy, tore it from its place. The water shot through then, so suddenly he was knocked to his knees.

He scrambled out of the depression, splashing in the water. Then, lying on his face, he drank, long and greedily.

Finally he rolled away and lay still, panting. Dimly he was conscious of the wind blowing. He crawled to the water again and bathed his face, washing away the dirt and grime. Then, careful as always, he filled his canteen from the fresh water bubbling up from the spring.

If he only had some coffee. . . . But he'd left his food in his saddlebags.

Well, Madge would be all right now. He could go back to her. After this, they wouldn't bother him. He would take her away. They would go to the Blue Mountains in Oregon. He had always liked that country.

The wind was blowing more heavily now, and he could smell the dust. That Navajo hadn't lied. It would be hell down in the Sink. He was above it now, and almost a mile away.

He stared down into the darkness, wondering how far Lopez had been able to get. The others didn't matter; they were weak sisters, who lived on the strength of better men. If they didn't die there they would die elsewhere, and the West could spare them. He got to his feet.

Lopez would hate to die. The ranch he had built so carefully in a piece of the wildest, roughest country was going good. It took a man with guts to settle where he had and make it pay. Shad Marone rubbed the stubble on his jaw. "That last thirty head of his cows I rustled for him brought the best price I ever got!" he remembered thoughtfully. "Too bad there ain't more like him!"

Well, after this night there would be one less. There wouldn't be anything to guide Lopez down there now. A man caught in a thick whirlpool of dust would have no landmarks; there would be nothing to get him out except blind instinct. The Navajos had been clever, leading the Apaches into a trap like that. Odd, that Lopez's mother had been an Apache, too.

Just the same, Marone thought, he had nerve. He'd shot his way up from the bottom until he had one of the best ranches.

Shad Marone began to pick up some dead cedar. He gathered some needles for kindling, and in a few minutes had a fire going.

Marone took another drink. Somehow, he felt restless. He got up and walked to the edge of the Nest. How far had Lopez come? Suppose . . . Marone gripped his pistol.

Suddenly, he started down the mountain. "The hell with it!" he muttered.

A stone rattled.

Shad Marone froze, gun in hand.

Lopez, a gray shadow, weaving in the vague light from the cliff, had a gun in his hand. For a full minute they stared at each other.

Marone spoke first. "Looks like a dead heat," he said.

Lopez said, "How'd you know about that waterhole?"

"Navajo told me," Shad replied, watching Lopez like a cat. "You don't look so bad," he added. "Have a full canteen?"

"No. I'd have been a goner. But my mother was an Apache. A bunch of them got caught in the Sink once. That never happened twice to no Apache. They found this waterhole then, and one down below. I made the one below, an' then I was finished. She was a dry hole. But then water began to run in from a crack in the rock."

"Yeah?" Marone looked at him again. "You got any coffee?"

"Sure."

"Well," Shad holstered his gun, "I've got a fire."

THE TRAIL TO PEACH MEADOW CANYON

I

Winter snows were melting in the forests of the Kaibab, and the red-and-orange hue of the thousand-foot Vermilion Cliffs was streaked with the dampness of melting frost. Deer were feeding in the forest glades among the stands of ponderosa and fir, and the trout were leaping in the streams. Where sunlight trailed through the webbed overhang of the leaves, the water danced and sparkled.

Five deer were feeding on the grass along a mountain stream back of Finger Butte, their coats mottled by the light and shadow of the sun shining through the trees.

A vague something moved in the woods behind them and the five-pronged buck lifted his regal head and stared curiously about. He turned his nose into the wind, reading it cautiously.

But his trust was betrayal, for the movement was downwind of him.

The movement came again and a young man stepped from concealment behind a huge fir not twenty feet from the nearest deer. He was straight and tall in gray, fringed buckskins, and he wore no hat. His hair was thick, black, and wavy, growing full over the temples, and his face was lean and brown. Smiling, he walked toward the deer with quick, lithe strides, and had taken three full steps before some tiny sound betrayed him.

The buck's head came up and swung around, and then with a startled snort it sprang away, the others following.

Mike Bastian stood grinning, his hands on his hips.

"Well, what do you think now, Roundy?" he called. "Could your Apache beat that? I could have touched him if I had jumped after him!"

Rance Roundy came out of the trees—a lean, wiry old man with a gray mustache and blue eyes that were still bright with an alert awareness.

"No, I'll be darned if any Apache ever lived as could beat that!" he chortled. "Not a mite of it! An' I never seen the day I could beat it, either. You're a caution, Mike, you sure are. I'm glad you're not sneakin' up after my hair!" He drew his pipe from his pocket and started stoking it with tobacco. "We're goin' back to Toadstool Canyon, Mike. Your dad sent for us."

Bastian looked up quickly. "Is there trouble, is that it?"

"No, only he wants to talk with you. Maybe—" Roundy was cautious— "he figures it's time you went out on a job. On one of those rides."

"I think that's it," Mike nodded. "He said in the spring, and it's about time for the first ride. I wonder where they'll go, this time?"

"No tellin'. The deal will be well planned, though. That dad of yours would have made a fine general, Mike. He's got the head for it, he sure has. Never forgets a thing, that one."

"You've been with him a long time, haven't you?"

"Sure—since before he found you. I knowed him in Mexico in the war, and that was longer ago than I like to think. I was a boy then, my ownself.

"Son," Roundy said suddenly, "look!"

He tossed a huge pine cone into the air, a big one at least nine inches long.

With a flash of movement. Mike Bastian palmed his gun and almost as soon as it hit his hand it belched flame—and again. The second shot spattered the cone into a bunch a flying brown chips.

"Not bad!" Roundy nodded. "You still shoot too quick, though. You got to get over that, Mike. Sometimes one shot is all you'll ever get."

Side by side the two walked through the trees, the earth spongy with a thick blanket of pine needles. Roundy was not as tall as Mike, but he walked with the long, springy stride of the woodsman. He smoked in silence for some distance, and then he spoke up.

"Mike, if Ben's ready for you to go out, what will you do?"

For two steps, Bastian said nothing. Then he spoke slowly. "Why, go, I guess. What else?"

"You're sure? You're sure you want to be an outlaw?"

"That's what I was raised for, isn't it?" There was some bitterness in Mike's voice. "Somebody to take over what Ben Curry started?"

"Yeah, that's what you were raised for, all right. But this you want to remember, Mike: It's you life. Ben Curry, for all his power, can't live it for you. Moreover, times have changed since Ben and me rode into this country. It ain't free and wild like it was, because folks are comin' in, settlin' it up, makin' homes. Gettin' away won't be so easy, and your pards will change too. In fact, they have already changed.

"When Ben and me come into this country," Roundy continued, "it was every man for himself. More than one harum-scarum fella, who was otherwise all right, got himself the name of an outlaw. Nobody figured much about it them. We rustled cows, but so did half the big ranchers of the West. And if a cow-poke got hard up and stopped a stage, nobody made much fuss unless he killed somebody. They figured it was just high spirits. But the last few years, it ain't like that no more. And it ain't only that the country is growin' up—it's partly Ben Curry himself."

"You mean he's grown too big?" Mike put in.

"What else? Why, your dad controls more land than there is in New York State! Got it right under his thumb! And he's feared over half the West by those who know about him, although not many do.

"Outside of this country around us nobody ain't seen Ben Curry in years, not leastwise to know him. But they've heard his name, and they know that somewhere an outlaw lives who rules a gang of almost a thousand men. That he robs and rustles where he will, and nobody has nerve enough to chase him.

"He's been smart, just plenty smart," old Roundy went on. "Men ride out and they meet at a given point. The whole job is planned in every detail, it's rehearsed, and then they pull it and scatter and meet again here. For a long time folks laid it to driftin' cowpunchers or to gangs passin' through. The way he's set up, one of the gangs he sends out might pull somethin' anywhere from San Antone to Los Angeles, or from Canada to Mexico, although usually he handles it close around.

"He's been the brains, all right, but don't ever forget it was those guns of his that kept things in line. Lately, he hasn't used his guns. Kerb Perrin and Rigger Molina or some of their boys handle the discipline. He's become too big, Ben Curry has. He's like a king, and the king isn't getting any younger. How do you suppose Perrin will take it when he hears about you takin' over? You think he'll like it?"

"I don't imagine he will," Mike replied thoughtfully. "He's probably done some figuring of his own."

"You bet he has! So has Molina, and neither of them will stop short of murder to get what they want. Your dad still has them buffaloed, I think, but that isn't going to matter when the showdown comes. And I think it's here!"

"You do?" Mike said, surprise in his voice.

"Yeah, I sure do!" Roundy hesitated. "You know, Mike, I never told you this, but Ben Curry has a family."

"A family?" Despite himself, Mike Bastian was startled.

"Yes, he has a wife and two daughters, and they don't have any idea he's an outlaw. They live down near Tucson somewhere. Occasionally, they come to a ranch he owns in Red Wall Canyon, a ranch supposedly owned by Voyle Ragan. He visits them there."

"Does anybody else know this?"

"Not a soul. And don't you be tellin' anybody. You see, Ben always wanted a son, and he never had one. When your real dad was killed down in Mesilla, he took you along with him, and later he told me he was going to raise you to take over whatever he left. That was a long time ago, and since then he's spent a sight of time and money on you.

"You can track like an Apache," Roundy said looking at the tall lad beside him. "In the woods you're a ghost, and I doubt if old Ben Curry himself can throw a gun any faster than you. I'd say you could ride anything that wore hair, and what you don't know about cards, dice and roulette wheels ain't in it. You can handle a knife, fight with your fists, and you can open anything a man has ever made in the way of safes and locks. Along with that, you've had a good education, and you could take care of yourself in any company. I don't reckon there ever was a boy had the kind of education you got, and I think Ben's ready to retire."

"You mean, to join his wife and daughters?" Mike questioned.

"That's it. He's gettin' no younger, and he wants it easy-like for the last years. He was always scared of only one thing, and he had a lot of it as a youngster. That's poverty. Well, he's made his pile and now he wants to step out. Still and all, he knows he can't get out alive unless he leaves somebody behind him that's strong enough and smart enough to keep things under control. That's where you come in."

"Why don't he let Perrin have it?"

"Mike, you know Perrin. He's dangerous, that one. He's poison mean and power-crazy. He'd have gone off the deep end a long time ago if it wasn't for Ben Curry. And Rigger Molina is kill-crazy. He would have killed fifty men if it hadn't been that he knew Ben Curry would kill him when he got back. No, neither of them could handle this outfit. The whole shebang would go to pieces in ninety days if they had it."

Mike Bastian walked along in silence. There was little that was new in what Roundy was saying, but he was faintly curious as to the old man's purpose. The pair had been much together, and they knew each other as few men ever did. They had gone through the storm and hunger and thirst together, living in the desert, mountains and forest, only rarely returning to the rendezvous in Toadstool Canyon.

Roundy had a purpose in his talking and Bastian waited, listening. Yet even as he walked he was conscious of everything that went on around him. A quail had moved back into the tall grass near the stream, and there was a squirrel up ahead in the crotch of a tree. Not far back a gray wolf had crossed the path only minutes ahead of them.

It was as Roundy had said. Mike was a woodman, and the thought of taking over the outlaw band filled him with unease. Always, he had been aware this time would come, that he had been schooled for it. But before, it had seemed remote and far off. Now, suddenly, it was at hand, it was facing him.

"Mike," Roundy want on, "the country is growin' up. Last spring some of our raids raised merry hell, and some of the boys had a bad time gettin' away. When they start again, there will be trouble and lots of it. Another thing: folks don't look at an outlaw like they used to. He isn't just a wild young cowhand full of liquor, nor a fellow who needs a poke, nor somebody buildin' a spread of his own. Now, he'll be like a wolf, with every man huntin' him. Before you decide to go into this, you think it over, make up your own mind.

"You know Ben Curry, and I know you like him. Well, you should! Nevertheless, Ben had no right to raise you for an outlaw. He went his way of his own free will, and if he saw it that way, that was his own doin'. But no man has a right to say to another, 'This you must do; this you must be.' No man has a right to train another, startin' before he has a chance to make up his mind, and school him in any particular way."

The old man stopped to relight his pipe, and Mike kept silence, would let Roundy talk out what seemed to bother him.

"I think every man should have the right to decide his own destiny, in so far as he can, " Roundy said, continuing his trend of thought. "That goes for you, Mike, and you've got the decision ahead of you. I don't know which you'll do. But if you decide to step out of this gang, then I don't relish bein' arond when it happens, for old Ben will be fit to be tied.

"Right now, you're an honest man. You're clean as a whistle. Once you become an outlaw, a lot of things will change. You'll have to kill, too—don't forget that. It's one thing to kill in defense of your home, your family, or your country. It's another thing when you kill for money or for power."

"You think I'd have to kill Perrin and Molina?" Mike Bastian asked.

"If they didn't get you first!" Roundy spat. "Don't forget this, Mike: You're fast. You're one of the finest, and aside from Ben Curry probably the finest shot I ever saw. But that ain't shootin' at a man who's shootin at you. There's a powerful lot of difference, as you'll see!

"Take Billy the Kid, this Lincoln County gunman we hear about. Frank and George Coe, Dick Brewer, Jesse Evans—any one of them can shoot as good as him. The difference is that the part down inside of him where the nerves should be was left out. When he starts shootin' and when he's bein' shot at, he's like ice! Kerb Perrin's that way, too. Perrin's the cold type, steady as a rock. Rigger Molina's another kind of cat—he explodes all over the place. He's white-hot, but he's deadly as a rattler."

Mike was listening intently as Roundy continued his description:

"Five of them cornered him one time at a stage station out of Julesburg. When the shootin' was over, four of them were down and the fifth was holdin' a gun-shot arm. Molina, he rode off under his own power. He's a shaggy wolf, that one! Wild and uncurried and big as a bear!"

Far more than Roundy realized did Mike Bastian know the facts about Ben Curry's empire of crime. For three years now, Curry had been leading his foster son through all the intricate maze of his planning. There were spies and agents in nearly every town in the Southwest, and small groups of outlaws quartered here and there on ranches who could be called upon for help at a moment's notice.

Also, there were ranches where fresh horses could be had, and changes of clothing, and where the horses the band had ridden could be lost. At Toadstool Canyon were less than two hundred of the total number of outlaws, and many of those, while living under Curry's protection, were not of his band.

Also, the point Roundy raised had been in Mike's mind, festering there, an abcess of doubt and dismay. The Ben Curry he knew was a huge, kindly man, even if grim and forbidding at times. He had taken the homeless boy and given him kindness and care; had, indeed, trained him as a son. Today, however, was the first inkling Mike had of the existence of that other family. Ben Curry had planed and acted with shrewdness and care.

Mike Bastian had a decision to make, a decision that would change his entire life, whether for better or worse.

Here in the country around the Vermilion Cliffs was the only world he knew. Beyond it? Well, he supposed he could punch cows. He was trained to do many things, and probably there were jobs awaiting such a man as himself.

He could become a gambler, but he had seen and known a good many gamblers and did not relish the idea. Somewhere beyond this wilderness was a larger, newer, wealthier land—a land where honest men lived and reared their families.

II

In the massive stone house at the head of Toadstool Canyon, so called because of the gigantic toadstool-like stone near the entrance, Ben Curry leaned his great weight back in his chair and stared broodingly out the door over the valley below.

His big face was blunt and unlined as rock, but the shock of hair above his leonine face was turning to gray. He was growing old. Even spring did not bring the old fire to his veins again, and it had been long since he had ridden out on one of the jobs he planned so shrewdly. It was time he quit.

Yet, for a man who had made decisions sharply and quickly, he was, for the first time in his life, uncertain. For six years he had ruled supreme in this remote corner north of Colorado. For twenty years he had been an outlaw, and for fifteen of those twenty years he had ruled a gang that grew and extended its ramifications until it was an empire in itself.

Six years ago he had moved to this remote country and created the stronghold where he now lived. Across the southern limit rolled the Colorado River, with its long canyons and maze of rocky wilderness, a bar to any pursuit from the country south of the river where he operated.

Only at Lee's Ferry was there a crossing, and in a cabin nearby his men watched it, night and day. That is, it was the only crossing known to other men. There were two more crossings—one that the gang used in going to and from their raids, and the other known only to himself. It was his ace-in-the-hole, even if not his only one.

One law of the gang, never transgressed, was that there was to be no lawless activity in the Mormon country to the north of them. The Mormons and the Indians were left strickly alone, and were their friends. So were the few ranchers who lived in the area. These few traded at the stores run by the gang, and bought their supplies close to home and at cheaper prices than they could have managed elsewhere.

Ben Curry had never quite made up his mind about Kerb Perrin. He knew that Perrin was growing restive, that he was aware that Curry was aging and was eager for the power of leadership. Yet the one factor Curry couldn't be certain about was whether Perrin would stand for the taking over of the band by Mike Bastian.

Well, Mike had been well trained; it would be his problem. Ben smiled grimly. He was the old bull of the herd, and Perrin was pawing the dirt, but what would he say when a young bull stepped in? One who had not won his spurs with the gang?

That was why Curry had sent for him, for it was time Mike be groomed for leadership, time he moved out on his first job. And he had just the one. It was big, it was sudden, and it was dramatic. It would have an excellent effect on the gang if it was brought off smoothly, and he was going to let Mike plan the whole job himself.

There was a sharp knock outside, and Curry smiled a little, recognizing it.

"Come in!" he bellowed.

He watched Perrin stride into the room with his quick, nervous steps, his eyes scanning the room.

"Chief," Perrin said, "the boys are gettin' restless. It's spring, you know, and most of them are broke. Have you got anything in mind?"

"Sure, several things. But one that's good and tough! Struck me it might be a good one to break the kid in on."

"Oh?" Perrin's eyes veiled. "You mean he'll go along?"

"No, I'm going to let him run it. The whole show. It will be good for him."

Kerb Perrin absorbed that. For the first time, an element of doubt entered his mind. He had wondered before about Bastian and what his part would be in all this.

For years, Perrin had looked forward to the time when he could take over. He knew there would be trouble with Rigger Molina, but he had thought that phase of it out. He knew he could handle it. But what if Curry was planning to jump young Bastian into leadership?

Quick, hot passion surged through Perrin, and when he looked up, it was all he could do to keep his voice calm.

"You think that's wise?" he questioned. "How will the boys feel about goin' out with a green kid?"

"He knows what to do," Curry said. "They'll find he's smart as any of them, and he knows plenty. This is a big job, and a tough one."

"Who goes with him?"

"Maybe I'll let him pick them," Curry said thoughtfully. "Good practice for him."

"What's the job?" Perrin asked, voice sullen.

"The gold train!"

Perrin's fingers tightened, digging into his palms. This was the job he wanted! The shipment from the mines! It would be enormous, rich beyond anything they had done!

Months before, in talking of this job, he had laid out his plan for it before Curry. But it had been vetoed. He had recommended the killing of every manjack of them, and burial of them all, so the train would vanish completely.

"You sound like Molina," Curry had said chuckling. "Too bloody!"

"Dead men don't talk!" he had replied grimly.

"That will be tough for the kid," Perrin said now, slowly, "Mighty tough!"

Yet, even as he spoke he was thinking of something else. He was thinking of the effect of this upon the men of the outfit. He knew many of them liked Mike Bastian, and more than one of them had helped train him. In a way, many of the older men were as proud of Mike as if he had been their own son. If he stepped out now and brought off this job, he would acquire power and prestige in the gang equal to Perrin's own.

Fury engulfed Perrin. Curry had no right to do this to him! Sidetracking him for an untried kid. Shoving Bastian down all their throats!

Suddenly, the rage died and in its place came resolution. It was time he acted on his own. He would swing his own job, the one he had had in mind for so long, and that would counteract the effect of the gold-train steal. Moreover, he would be throwing the challenge into Ben Curry's teeth, for he would plan this job without consulting him. If there was going to be a struggle for leadership, it could begin here and now.

"He'll handle the job all right," Curry said confidently. "He has been trained, and he has the mind for it. He plans well. I hadn't spoken of it before, but I asked his advice on a few things without letting him know why, and he always came through with the right answers."

Kerb Perrin left the stone house filled with burning resentment but also something of triumph. At last, after years of taking orders, he was going on his own. Yet the still, small voice of fear was in him, too. What would Ben Curry do?

The thought made him quail. He had seen the cold fury of Curry when it was aroused, and he had seen him use a gun. He himself was fast, but was he as fast as Ben Curry? In his heart, he doubted it. He dismissed the thought, although storing it in his mind. Something would have to be done about Ben Curry . . .

Mike Bastian stood before Ben Curry's table and the two men stared at each other.

Ben Curry, the old outlaw chief, huge, bearlike, and mighty, his eyes fierce yet glowing with a kindly light now, and something of pride, too. Facing him, tall and lithe, his shoulders broad and mighty, was Mike Bastian, child of the Frontier grown to manhood and trained in every art of the wilds, every dishonest practice in the books, every skill with weapons. Yet educated, too, a man who could conduct himself well in any company.

"You take four men and look over the ground yourself, Mike," Ben Curry was saying, "I want you to plan this one. The gold train leaves the mines on the twentieth. There will be five wagons, the gold distributed among them, although there won't be a lot of it as far as quantity is concerned. That gold train will be worth roughly five hundred thousand dollars.

"When that job is done," he continued, "I'm going to step down and leave you in command. You knew I was planning that. I'm old, and I want to live quietly for awhile, and this outfit takes a strong hand to run it. Think you can handle it?"

"I think so," Mike Bastian said softly.

"I think so, too. Watch Perrin—he's the snaky one. Rigger is dangerous, but whatever he does will be out in the open. Not so Perrin. He's a conniver. He never got far with me because I was always one jump ahead of him. And I still am!"

The old man was silent for a few minutes, as he stared out the window.

"Mike," he said then, doubt entering his voice, "maybe I've done wrong. I meant to raise you the way I have. I ain't so sure what is right and wrong, and never was. Never gave it much thought, though.

"When I came west it was dog eat dog and your teeth had to be big. I got knocked down and kicked around some, and then I started taking big bites myself. I organized, and then I got bigger. In all these years nobody has ever touched me. If you've got a strong hand, you can do the same. Sometimes you'll have to buy men, sometimes you'll have to frighten them, and sometimes you'll have to kill."

He shook his head as if clearing it of memories past, then glanced up.

"Who will you take with you?" he asked "I mean, in scouting this layout."

Ben Curry waited, for it was judgment of men that Bastian would need most. It pleased him that Mike did not hesitate.

"Roundy, Doc Sawyer, Colley and Garlin."

Curry glanced at him, his eyes hard and curious. "Why?"

"Roundy has an eye for terrain like no man in this world," Mike said. "He says mine's as good, but I'll take him along to verify or correct my judgment. Doc Sawyer is completely honest. If he thinks I'm wrong, he'll say so. As for Colley and Garlin, they are two of the best men in the whole outfit. They will be pleased that I ask their help, which puts them on my side in a measure, and they can see how I work."

Curry nodded. "Smart—and you're right. Colley and Garlin are two of the best men, and absolutely fearless." He smiled a little. "If you have trouble with Perrin or Molina, it won't hurt to have them on your side."

Despite himself, Mike Bastian was excited. He was twenty-two years old and by Frontier standards had been a man for several years. But in all that time, aside from a few trips into the Mormon country and one to Salt Lake, he had never been out of the maze of canyons and mountains north of the Colorado.

Roundy led the way, for the trail was an old one to him. They were taking the secret route south used by the gang on their raids, and as they rode toward it, Mike stared at the country. He was always astonished by its ruggedness.

Snow still lay in some of the darker places of the forest, but as they neared the canyon the high cliffs towered even higher and the trail dipped down through a narrow gorge of rock. Countless centuries of erosion had carved the rock into grotesque figures resembling those of men and animals, colored with shades of brown, pink, gray, and red, and tapering off into a pale yellow. There were shadowed pools among the rocks, some from snow water and others from natural springs, and there were scattered clumps of oak and piñon.

In the bottom of the gorge the sun did not penetrate except at high noon, and there the trail wound along between great jumbled heaps of boulders, cracked and broken from their fall off the higher cliffs.

Mike Bastian followed Roundy, who rode hump-shouldered on a ragged, gray horse that seemed as old as he himself, but as sure-footed and mountainwide. He had substituted boots for the moccasins he usually wore, although they reposed in his saddlebags, ready at hand.

Behind them rode "Doc" Sawyer, his lean saturnine face quiet, his eyes faintly curious and interested as he scanned the massive walls of the canyon. "Tubby" Colley was short and thick-chested, and very confident—a hard jawed man who had been a first-rate ranch foreman before he shot two men and hit the outlaw trail.

"Tex" Garlin was tall, rangy, and quiet. He was a Texan, and little was known of his background, although it was said he could carve a dozen notches on his guns if he wished.

Suddenly, Roundy turned the gray horse and rode abruptly at the face of the cliff, but when close up, the sand and boulders broke and a path showed along the under-scoured rock. Following this for several hundred yards they found a canyon that cut back into the cliff itself, then turned to head toward the river.

The roar of the Colorado, high with spring freshets, was loud in their ears before they reached it. Finally they came out on a sandy bank littered with driftwood. Nearby was a small cabin and a plot of garden. The door of the house opened and a tall old man came out.

"Howdy!" he said. "I been expectin' somebody." His shrewd old eyes glanced from face to face, then hesitated at sight of Mike. "Ain't seen you before," he said pointedly.

"It's all right, Bill," Roundy said. "This is Mike Bastian."

"Ben Curry's boy?" Bill stared. "I heard a sight of you, son. I sure have! Can you shoot like they say?"

Mike flushed. "I don't know what they say," he said, grinning. "But I'll bet a lot of money I can hit the side of that mountain if it holds still."

Garlin stared at him thoughtfully, and Colley smiled a little.

"Don't take no funnin' from him," Roundy said. "That boy can shoot."

"Let's see some shootin', son," Bill suggested. "I always did like to see a man that could shoot."

Bastian shook his head. "There's no reason for shootin'," he protested. "A man's a fool to shoot unless he's got cause. Ben Curry always taught me never to draw a gun unless I meant to use it."

"Go ahead," Colley said, "show him."

Old Bill pointed. "See that black stick end juttin' up over thar? It's about fifty maybe sixty paces. Can you hit it?"

"You mean that one?" Mike palmed his gun and fired, and the black stick pulverized.

It was a movement so smooth and practiced that no one of the men even guessed he had intended to shoot, and Garlin's jaws stopped their calm chewing and he stared with his mouth open for as long as it took to draw a breath. Then he glanced at Colley.

"Wonder what Kerb would say to that?" he said, astonished. "This kid can shoot!"

"Yeah," Colley agreed, "but the stick didn't have a gun!"

Old Bill worked the ferry out of a cave under the cliff and freighted them across the swollen river in one hair-raising trip. With the river behind, they wound up through the rocks and started south.

III

The mining cowtown of Weaver was backed up near a large hill on the banks of a small creek. Colley and Garlin rode into the place at sundown, and an hour later Doc Sawyer and Roundy rode in.

Garlin and Colley were leaning on the bar having a drink, and they ignored the newcomers. Mike Bastian followed not long afterward, and walked to the bar alone.

Most of those in the saloon were Mexicans, but three tough-looking white men lounged against the bar nearby. They glanced at Mike and his buckskins, and one of them whispered something to the others, at which they all laughed.

Doc Sawyer was sitting in a poker game, and his eyes lifted. Mike leaned nonchalantly against the bar, avoiding the stares of the three toughs who stood near him. One of them moved over closer.

"Hi, stranger!" he said, "That's a right purty suit you got. Where could I get one like it?"

Garlin looked up and his face stiffened. He nudged Colley. "Look!" Garlin said quickly. "Corbus and Fletcher! An' trouble huntin'! We'd better get into this!"

Colley shook his head. "No. Let's see what the kid does."

Mike looked around, his expression mild. "You want a suit like this?" he inquired of the stranger. His eyes were innocent, but he could see the sort of man he had to deal with. These three were tough, and dangerous. "Most any Navajo could make one for you."

"Just like that?" Corbus sneered.

He was drinking and in a nagging, quarrelsome mood. Mike looked altogether too neat for his taste.

"Sure! Just like this," Mike agreed. "But I don't know what you'd want with it though. This suit would be pretty hard for you to fill."

"Huh?" Corbus' face flamed. Then this mouth tightened. "You gettin' smart with me, kid?"

"No." Mike Bastian turned and his voice cracked like a whip in the suddenly silent room. "Neither am I being hurrahed by any lame-brained, liquor-guzzling saddle tramp! You made a remark about my suit, and I answered it. Now, you can have a drink on me, all three of you, and I'm suggesting you drink up." His voice suddenly became soft. "I want to drink up because I want to be very, very sure we're friends, see?"

Corbus stared at Bastian, a cold hint of danger filtering through the normal stubbornness of his brain. Something told him this was perilous going, yet he was stubborn, too stubborn. He smiled slowly. "Kid," he drawled, "supposin' I don't want to drink with no tenderfoot brat?"

Corbus never saw what happened. His brain warned him as Mike's lcft hand moved, but he never saw the right. The left stabbed his lips and the right cracked the side of his jaw, and he lifted from his feet and hit the floor on his shoulder blades, out cold.

Fletcher and the third tough stared from Corbus to Mike. Bastian was not smiling. "You boys want to drink?" he asked. "Or do we go on from here?"

Fletcher stared at him. "What if a man drawed a gun instead of usin' his fists?" he demanded.

"I'd kill him," Bastian replied quietly.

Fletcher blinked. "I reckon you would," he agreed. He turned, said, "Let's have a drink. That Boot Hill out there's already got twenty graves in it."

Garlin glanced at Colley, his eyebrows lifted. Colley shrugged.

"I wonder what Corbus will do when he gets up?" he said.

Garlin chuckled. "Nothin today. He won't be feelin' like it!"

Colley nodded. "Reckon you're right, an' I reckon the old man raised him a wildcat! I can hardly wait to see Kerb Perrin's face when we tell him."

"You reckon," Garlin asked, "that what we heard is true? That Ben Curry figures to put this youngster into his place when he steps out?"

"Yep, that's the talk," Colley answered.

"Well, maybe he's got it. We'll sure know before this trip is over."

Noise of the stagecoach rolling down the street drifted into the saloon, and Mike Bastian strolled outside and started toward the stage station. The passengers were getting down to stretch their legs and to eat. Three of them were women.

One of them noticed Mike standing there and walked toward him. She was a pale pretty girl with large gray eyes. "How much farther to Red Wall Canyon?" she inquired.

Mike Bastian stiffened. "Why, not far. That is, you'll make it by morning if you stick with the stage. There is a crosscountry way if you had you a buckboard, though."

"Could you tell us where we could hire one? My mother is not feeling well."

He stepped down off the boardwalk and headed toward the livery stable with her. As they drew alongside the stage, Mike looked up. An older woman and a girl were standing near the stage, but he was scarcely aware of anything but the girl. Her hair was blondish, but darker than the girl who walked beside him, and her eyes, too, were gray. There the resemblance ended, for where this girl was quiet and sweet, the other was vivid.

She looked at him and their eyes met. He swept off his hat. The girl beside him spoke.

"This is my mother, Mrs. Ragan, and my sister Drusilla." She looked up at him quickly. "My name is Juliana."

Mike bowed. He had eyes only for Drusilla, who was staring at him.

"I am Mike Bastian," he said.

"He said he could hire us a rig to drive across country to Red Wall Canyon," Juliana explained. "It will be quicker that way."

"Yes," Mike agreed, "much quicker. I'll see what I can do. Just where in Red Wall did you wish to go?"

"To Voyle Ragan's ranch," Drusilla said. "The V Bar."

He had turned away, but he stopped in midstride.

"Did you say . . . Voyle Ragan's?"

"Yes. Is there anything wrong?" Drusilla stared at him. "What's the matter?"

He regained his composure swiftly. "Nothing. Only, I'd heard the name and"—he smiled—"I sort of wanted to know for sure, so if I came calling."

Juliana laughed. "Why, of course! We'd be glad to see you."

He walked swiftly away. These, then were Ben Curry's daughters! That older women would be his wife! He was their foster brother, yet obviously his name had meant nothing to them. Neither, he reflected, would their names have meant anything to him nor the destination, had it not been for what Roundy had told him only the previous day.

Drusilla, her name was. His heart pounded at the memory of her, and he glanced back through the gathering dusk at the three women standing there by the stage.

Hiring the rig was a matter of minutes. He liked the look of the driver, a lean man, tall and white-haired. "No danger on that road this time of year," the driver said. "I can have them there in no time by taking the canyon road."

Drusilla was waiting for him when Mike walked back.

"Did you find one?" she asked, then listened to his explanation and thanked him.

"Would it be all right with you," Mike said, "if I call at the V Bar?"

She looked at him, her face grave, but a dancing light in her eyes. "Why, my sister invited you, did she not?"

"Yes, but I'd like you to invite me too."

"I?" She studied him for a minute. "Of course, we'd be glad to see you. My mother likes visitors as well as Julie and I, so won't you ask her, too?"

"I'll take the invitation from you and your sister as being enough." He grinned. "If I ask your mother, I might have to ask your father!"

"Father isn't with us!" she laughed. "We'll see him at Ragan's. He's a rancher somewhere way up north in the wilds. His name is Ben Ragan. Have you heard of him?"

"Seems to me I have," he admitted, "but I wouldn't say for sure."

After they had gone Mike wandered around and stopped in the saloon, after another short talk with a man at the livery stable. Listening and asking an occasional question, he gathered the information he wanted on the gold shipment. Even as he asked the questions, it seemed somehow fantastic that he, of all people, should be planning such a thing.

Never before had he thought of it seriously, but now he did. And it was not only because the thought went against his own grain, but because he was thinking of Drusilla Ragan.

What a girl she was! He sobered suddenly. Yet, for all of that, she was the daughter of an outlaw. Did she know it? From her question, he doubted it very much.

Doc Sawyer cashed in his chips and left the poker game to join Mike at the bar.

"The twentieth, all right," he said softly. "And five of them are going to carry shotguns. There will be twelve guards in all, which looks mighty tough. The big fellow at the poker table is one of the guards, and all of them are picked men."

Staring at his drink, Mike puzzled over his problem. What Roundy had said was, of course, true. This was a turning point for him. He was still an honest man, yet when he stepped over the boundary it would make a difference. It might make a lot of difference to a girl like Dru Ragan, for instance.

The fact that her father also was an outlaw would make little difference. Listening to Sawyer made him wonder. Why had such a man, brilliant, intelligent, and well educated, ever become a criminal?

Sawyer was a gambler and a very skillful one, yet he was a doctor, too, and a fine surgeon. His education was as good as study and money could make it, and it had been under his guidance that Mike Bastian had studied.

"Doc," he said suddenly, "whatever made you ride a crooked trail?"

Sawyer glanced at him suddenly, a new expression in his eyes. "What do you mean, Mike? Do you have doubts?"

"Doubts? That seems to be all I do have these last few days."

"I wondered about that," Doc said. "You have been so quiet that I never doubted but that you were perfectly willing to go on with Ben Curry's plans for you. It means power and money, Mike—all a man could want. If it is doubt about the future for outlaws that disturbs you, don't let it. From now on it will be political connections and bribes, but with the money you'll have to work with, that should be easy."

"It should be," Mike said slowly. "Only maybe—just maybe—I don't want to."

"Conscience rears its ugly head!" Sawyer smiled ironically. "Can it be that Ben Curry's instructions have fallen on fallow ground? What started this sudden feeling? The approach of the problem? Fear?" Doc had turned toward Mike and was staring at him with aroused interest. "Or," he added, "is there a woman? A girl?"

"Would that be so strange?"

"Strange? But no! I've wondered it hasn't happened before, but then you've lived like a recluse these past years. Who is she?"

"It doesn't matter, " Mike answered. "I was thinking of this before I saw her. Wondering what I should do."

"Don't ask me," Sawyer said. "I made a mess of my own life. Partly a woman and partly the desire for what I thought was easy money. Well, there's no such a thing as easy money, but I found that out too late. You make your own decision. What was it Matthew Arnold said? I think you learned the quotation."

"'No man can save his brother's soul, or pay his brother's debt.'"

"Right! So you save your own and pay your own. There's one thing to remember, Mike. No matter which way you go, there will be killing. If you take over Ben Curry's job, you'll have to kill Perrin and Molina, if you can. And you may have to kill them, and even Ben Curry, if you step out."

"Not Dad," Mike said.

"Don't be sure. It isn't only what he thinks that matters, Mike. No man is a complete ruler or dictator. His name is only a symbol. He is the mouthpiece for the wishes of his followers, and as long as he expresses those wishes, he leads them. When he fails, he falls. Ben Curry is the boss not only because he has power in him, but also because he has organization, because he has made them money, because he has offered them safety. If you left, there would can a chink in the armor. No outlaw ever trusts another outlaw who turns honest, for he always fears betrayal."

Bastian tossed off his drink. "Let's check with Roundy. He's been on the prowl."

Roundy came to them hastily. "We've got to get out of town, quick!" he said. "Ducrow and Fernandez just blew in and they are drunk and raisin' the devil. Both of them are talkin', too, and if they see us they will spill everything!"

"All right." Mike straightened. "Get out horses. Get theirs, too, we'll take them with us."

Garlin and Colley had come to the bar. Garlin shook his head. "Ducrow's poison mean when he's drunk, and Fernandez sides him in everything," Garlin informed. "When Ducrow gets drunk he always pops off too much! The Boss forbade him weeks ago to come down here."

"He's a pal of Perrin's," Colley said, "so he thinks he can get away with it."

"Here they come now!" Roundy exclaimed.

"All right—drift!" Bastian ordered. "Make it quick with the horses."

IV

Saloon doors slammed open and the two men came in. One look, and Mike could see there was cause for worry. Tom Ducrow was drunk and ugly, and behind him was "Snake" Fernandez. They were an unpleasant pair, and they had made their share of trouble in Ben Curry's organization, though always protected by Perrin.

Bastian started forward, but he had scarcely taken a step when Ducrow saw him.

"There he is!" he bellowed loudly. "The pet! The Boss' pet!" He stared around at the people in the barroom. "You know who this man is? He's—"

"Ducrow!" Mike snapped. "Shut up and go home. Now!"

"Look who's givin' orders!" Ducrow sneered. "Gettin' big for your britches, ain't you?"

"Your horses will be outside in a minute," Mike said. "Get on them and start back fast!"

"Suppose," Ducrow sneered, "you make me!"

Mike had been moving toward him, and now with a panther-like leap he was beside the outlaw and with a quick slash from his pistol barrel, floored him.

With an oath, Snake Fernandez reached for a gun, and Mike had no choice. He shot him in the shoulder. Fernandez staggered, the gun dropping from his fingers. Mouthing curses, he reached for his left-hand gun.

But even as he reached, Garlin—who had stayed behind when the others went for the horses—stepped up behind him. Jerking the gun from the man's holster, he spun him about and shoved him through the door.

Mike pulled the groggy Ducrow to his feet and pushed him outside after Fernandez.

A big man got up hastily from the back of the room. Mike took one quick glimpse at the star on his chest.

"What goes on here?" the sheriff demanded.

"Nothing at all," Mike said affably. "Just a couple of the boys from our ranch feeling their oats a little. We'll take them out and off your hands."

The sheriff stared from Mike to Doc Sawyer and Colley, who had just come through the door.

"Who are you?" he demanded. "I don't believe I know you hombres."

"That's right, sir, you don't," Mike said. "We're from the Mogollons, riding back after driving some cattle through to California. It was a rough trip, and this liquor here got to a couple of the boys."

The sheriff hesitated, looking sharply from one to the other.

"You may be a cowhand," he said, "but that hombre"—he pointed to Sawyer—"looks like a gambler!"

Mike chuckled. "That's a joke on you, boy!" he said to Doc. Then he turned back to the sheriff. "He's a doctor, sir, and quite a good one. A friend of my boss."

A gray-haired man got up and strolled alongside the sheriff. His eyes were alive with suspicion.

"From the Mogollons?" he queried. "That's where I'm from. Who did you say your boss was?"

Doc Sawyer felt his scalp tighten, but Mike smiled.

"Jack McCardle," he said, "of the Flying M. We aren't his regular hands, just a bunch passing through. Doc, here, he being an old friend of Jack's, handles the sale of the beef."

The Sheriff looked around.

"That right, Joe?" he asked the gray-haired man. "There a Flying M over there?"

"Yes, there is." Joe was obviously puzzled. "Good man, too, but I had no idea he was shipping beef!"

The sheriff studied Bastian thoughtfully. "Guess you're all right," he said finally. "But you sure don't talk like a cowhand."

"As a matter of fact," Mike said swallowing hard, "I was studying for the ministry, but my interests began to lead me in more profane directions, so I am afraid I backslid. It seems," he said gravely, "that a leaning toward poker isn't conducive to the correct manner in the pulpit!"

"I should say not!" the sheriff chuckled. "All right, son, you take your pardners with you, let 'em sleep it off."

Mike turned, and his men followed him. Ducrow and Fernandez had disappeared. They rode swiftly out of town and took the trail for Toadstool Canyon. It wasn't until they were several miles on the road that Sawyer glanced at Mike.

"You'll do," he said. "I was never so sure of a fight in my life!"

"That's right, Boss!" Garlin said. "I was bettin' we'd have to shoot our way out of town! You sure smooth-talked 'em. Never heard it done prettier!"

"Sure did," Colley agreed. "I don't envy you havin' Ducrow an' Fernandez for enemies though."

Kerb Perrin and Rigger Molina were both in conference with Ben Curry when Mike Bastian came up the stone steps and through the door. They both looked up sharply.

"Perrin," Bastian said, "what were Ducrow and Fernandez doing in Weaver?"

"In Weaver?" Perrin straightened up slowly, nettled by Mike's tone, but puzzled, too.

"Yes, in Weaver! We nearly had to shoot our way out of town because of them. They were down there, drunk and talking too much. When I told them to get on their horses and go home, they made trouble."

Kerb Perrin was on dangerous ground. He well knew how harsh Ben Curry was about talkative outlaws, and while he had no idea what the two were doing in Weaver, he knew they were trouble-makers. He also knew they were supporters of his. Ben Curry knew it, and so did Rigger Molina.

"They made trouble?" Perrin questioned now. "How?"

"Ducrow started to tell who I was."

"What happened?"

Mike was aware that Ben Curry had tipped back in his chair and was watching him with interest.

"I knocked him down with a pistol barrel," he said.

"You what?" Perrin stared. Ducrow was a bad man to tangle with. "What about Fernandez?"

"He tried to draw on me, and I put a bullet in his shoulder."

"You should've killed him," Molina said. "You'll have to, sooner or later."

Kerb Perrin was stumped. He had not expected this, or that Mike Bastian was capable of handling such a situation. He was suddenly aware that Doc Sawyer had come into the room.

Bastian faced Ben Curry. "We got what we went after," he said, "but another bad break like Ducrow and Fernandez, and we'd walk into a trap!"

"There won't be another!" Curry said harshly.

When Mike had gone out, Doc Sawyer looked at Ben Curry and smiled.

"You should have seen him and heard him," he said as Molina and Perrin were leaving. "It would have done your heart good! He had a run-in with Corbus and Fletcher, too. Knocked Corbus out with a punch and backed Fletcher down. Oh, he'll do, that boy of yours, he'll do! The way he talked that sheriff out of it was one of the smoothest things I've seen!"

Ben Curry nodded with satisfaction. "I knew it! I knew he had it!"

Doc Sawyer smiled, and looked up at the chief from under his sunburned eyebrows. "He met a girl, too."

"A girl? Good for him! It's about time!"

"This was a very particular girl, Chief," Sawyer continued. "I thought you'd like to know. If I'm any judge of men, he fell for her and fell hard. And I'm not so sure it didn't happen both ways. He told me something about it, but I had already seen for myself."

Something in Sawyer's tone made Curry sit up a little.

"Who was the girl?" he demanded.

"A girl who came in on the stage." Doc spoke carefully, avoiding Curry's eyes now. "He got the girl and her family a rig to drive them out to a ranch. Out to the V Bar." Ben Curry's face went white. So Doc knew! It was in every line of him, every tone of his voice. The one thing he had tried to keep secret, the thing known only to himself and Roundy, was known to Doc! And to how many others?

"The girl's name," Doc continued, "was Drucilla Ragan. She's a beautiful girl."

"Well, I won't have it!" Curry said in a strained voice.

Doc Sawyer looked up, faintly curious. "You mean the foster son you raised isn't good enough for your daughter?"

"Don't say that word here!" Curry snapped, his face hard. "Who knows besides you?"

"Nobody of whom I am aware," Doc said with a shrug. "I only know by accident. You will remember the time you were laid up with that bullet wound. You were delirious, and that's why I took care of you myself—because you talked too much."

Doc lighted his pipe. "They made a nice-looking pair," he said. "And I think she invited him to Red Wall Canyon."

"He won't go! I won't have any of this crowd going there!"

"Chief, that boy's what you made him, but he's not an outlaw yet," Doc said, puffing contentedly on his pipe. "He could be, and he might be, but if he does, the crime will lie on your shoulders."

Curry shook himself and stared out the window.

"I said it, Chief: the boy has it in him," Sawyer went on. "You should have seen him throw that gun on Fernandez. The kid's fast as lightning! He thinks, too. If he takes over this gang, he'll run this country like you never ran it. I say, if."

"He'll do it," Curry said confidently, "you know he will. He always does what I tell him."

Doc chuckled. "He may, and again he may not. Mike Bastian has a mind of his own, and he's doing some thinking. He may decide he doesn't want to take over. What will you do then?"

"Nobody has ever quit this gang. Nobody ever will!"

"You'd order him killed?"

Ben Curry hesitated. This was something he had never dreamed of. Something— "He'll do what he's told!" he repeated, but he was no longer sure.

A tiny voice of doubt was arising within him, a voice that made him remember the Mike Bastian who was a quiet, determined little boy who would not cry, a boy who listened and obeyed. Yet now Curry knew and admitted it for the first time, that Mike Bastian always had a mind of his own.

Never before had the thought occurred to him that Mike might disobey, that he might refuse. And if he did, what then? It was a rule of the outlaw pack that no man could leave it and live. It was a rule essential to their security. A few had tried, and their bodies now lay in Boot Hill. But Mike, his son? No, not Mike!

Within him there was a deeper knowledge, an awareness that here his interests and those of the pack would divide. Even if he said no, they would say yes.

"Who would kill him, Chief? Kerb Perrin? Rigger Molina? You?" Doc Sawyer shook his head slowly. "You might be able to do it, maybe one of the others, but I doubt it. You've created the man who may destroy you, Chief, unless you join him."

Long after Doc Sawyer was gone, Ben Curry sat there staring out over the shadowed valley. He was getting old. For the first time he was beginning to doubt his rightness, beginning to wonder if he had not wronged Mike Bastian.

And what of Mike and Dru, his beloved, gray-eyed daughter? The girl with dash and spirit? But why not? Slowly, he thought over Mike Bastian's life. Where was the boy wrong? Where was he unfitted for Dru? By the teachings given him on his, Curry's, own suggestion? His own order? Or was there yet time?

Ben Curry heaved himself to his feet and began to pace the carpeted floor. He would have to make up his mind, for a man's life and future lay in his hands, to make or break.

What if Dru wanted him anyway, outlaw or not? Ben Curry stopped and stared into the fireplace. If it had been Julie now, he might forbid it. But Dru? He chuckled. She would laugh at him. Dru had too much of his own nature, and she had a mind of her own.

Mike Bastian was restless the day after the excitement in Weaver. He rolled out of his bunk and walked out on the terrace. Only he and Doc Sawyer slept in the stone house where Ben Curry lived. Roundy was down in town with the rest of them, but tonight Mike wanted to walk, to think.

There had been a thrill of excitment in outtalking the sheriff, in facing down Fletcher, in flattening Corbus. And there had been more of it in facing Ducrow and Fernandez. Yet, was that what he wanted? Or did he want something more stable, more worthwhile? The something he might find with Drusilla Ragan?

Already, he had won a place with the gang. He knew the story would be all over the outlaw camp now.

Walking slowly down the street of the settlement, he turned at right angles and drifted down a side road. He wanted to get away from things for a little while, to think things out. He turned again and started back into the pines, and then he heard a voice coming from a near-by house. The words halted him. ". . . at Red Wall." Mike heard the ending.

Swiftly, he glided to the house and flattened against the side. Kerb Perrin was speaking:

"It's a cinch, and we'll do it on our own without anybody's say-so. There's about two thousand cattle in the herd, and I've got a buyer for them. We can hit the place just about sunup. Right now, they have only four hands on the place, but about the first of next month they will start hiring. It's now or not at all."

"How many men will we take?" That was Ducrow speaking.

"A dozen. That will keep the divvy large enough, and they can swing it. Hell, that Ragan ranch is easy! The boss won't hear about it until too late, and the chances are he will never guess it was us."

"I wouldn't want him to," Fernandez said.

"To hell with him!" Ducrow was irritated. "I'd like a crack at that Bastian again."

"Stick with me," Perrin said, "and I'll set him up for you. Curry is about to turn things over to him. Well, we'll beat him to it."

"You said there were girls?" Ducrow suggested.

"There's two white girls and a couple of Mexican girls who work there. One older woman. I want one of those girls myself—the youngest of the Ragan sisters. What happens to the others is none of my business."

Mike Bastian's hand dropped to his gun and his lips tightened. The tone of Perrin's voice filled him with fury, and Ducrow was as bad.

"What happens if Curry does find out?" Ducrow demanded.

"What would happen?" Perrin said fiercely. "I'll kill him like I've wanted to all these years! I've hated that man like I never hated anyone in my life!"

"What about that Bastian?" Ducrow demanded.

Perrin laughed. "That's your problem! If you and Fernandez can't figure out how to handle him, then I don't know you."

"He knocked out Corbus, too," Ducrow aid. "We might get him to throw in with us, if this crowd is all afraid of old Ben Curry.

"I ain't so sure about him my ownself," said another voice, which Mike placed as belonging to an outlaw named Bayless. "He may not be so young anymore, but he's hell on wheels with a gun!"

"Forget him!" Perrin snapped. Then: "You three, and Clatt, Penelli, Monson, Kiefer, and a few others will go with us. All good men. There's a lot of dissatisfaction, anyway. Molina wants to raid the Mormons. They've a lot of rich stock and there's no reason why we can't sell it south of the river, and the other stock north of it. We can get rich!"

V

Mike Bastian waited no longer, but eased away from the wall. He was tempted to wait for Perrin and brace him when he came out. His first thought was to go to Ben Curry, but he might betray his interest in Drusilla and the time was not yet ripe for that. What would her father say if he found the foster son he had raised to be an outlaw was in love with his daughter?

It was foolish to think of it, yet he couldn't help it. There was time between now and the twentieth for him to get back to Red Wall and see her.

A new thought occured to him. Ben Curry would know the girls and their mother were here and would be going to see them! That would be his chance to learn of Ben's secret pass to the river bank, and how he crossed the Colorado.

Recalling other trips, Bastian knew the route must be a much quicker one than any he knew of, and was probably farther west and south, toward the canyon country. Already he was eager to see the girl again, and all he could think of was her trim figure, the laughter in her eyes, the soft curve of her lips.

There were other things to be considered. If there was as much unrest in the gang as Perrin said, things might be nearing a definite break. Certainly, outlaws were not the men to stand hitched for long, and Ben Curry had commanded them for longer than anyone would believe. Their loyalty was due partly to the returns from their ventures under his guidance, and partly to fear of his far-reaching power. But he was growing old, and there were those among them who feared he was losing his grip.

Mike felt a sudden urge to saddle his horse and be gone, to get away from all this potential cruelty, the conniving and hatred that lay dormant here, or was seething and ready to explode. He could ride out now by the Kaibab trail through the forest, skirt the mountains, and find his own way through the canyon. It was a question whether he could escape, whether Ben Curry would let him go.

To run now meant to abandon all hope of seeing Dru again, and Mike knew he could not do that.

Returning to his quarters in the big stone house, he stopped in front of a mirror. With deadly, flashing speed, he began to practice quick draws of his guns. Each night he did this twenty times as swiftly as his darting hands could move.

Finally he sat down on his bed thinking. Roundy first, and today Doc Sawyer. Each seemed to be hoping he would throw up the sponge and escape this outlaw life before it was too late. Doc said it was his life, but was it?

There was a light tap on the door. Gun in hand, he reached for the latch. Roundy stepped in. He glanced at the gun.

"Gettin' scary, Mike?" he queried. "Things are happenin'!"

"I know."

Mike went on to explain what he had overheard, and Roundy's face turned serious. "Mike, did you ever hear of Dave Lenaker?"

Bastian looked up. "You mean the Colorado gunman?"

"That's the one. He's headed this way. Ben Curry just got word that Lenaker's on his way to take over the Curry gang!"

"I thought he was one of Curry's ablest lieutenants?"

Roundy shrugged. "He was, Mike, but the word has gone out that the old man is losing his grip, and outlaws are quick to sense a thing like that. Lenaker never had any use for Perrin, and he's most likely afraid that Perrin will climb into the saddle. Dave Lenaker's a holy terror, too."

"Does Dad Curry know?" Mike said.

"Yeah. He's some wrought up, too," Roundy answered. "He was figurin' on bein' away for a few days, one of those trips he takes to Red Wall. Now, he can't go."

Morning came cool and clear. Mike Bastian could feel disaster in the air, and he dressed hurriedly and headed for the bunkhouse. Few of the men were eating, and those few were silent. He knew they were all aware of impending change. He was finishing his coffee when Perrin came in.

Instantly, Mike was on guard. Perrin walked with a strut, and his eyes were bright and confident. He glanced at Bastian, faintly amused, and then sat down at the table and began to eat.

Roundy came in, and then Doc Sawyer. Mike dallied over his coffee and a few minutes later was rewarded by seeing Ducrow come in with Kiefer, followed in a few minutes by "Rocky" Clatt, Monson, and Panelli.

Suddenly, with the cup half to his mouth, Mike recalled with a shock that this was the group Perrin planned to use on his raid on the Ragan ranch! That could mean the raid would come off today!

He looked up to see Roundy suddenly push back his chair and leave his breakfast unfinished. The old woodsman hurried outside and vanished.

Mike put down his own cup and got up. Then he stopped, motionless. The hard muzzle of a gun was prodding him in the back, and a voice was saying, "Don't move!"

The voice was that of Fernandez, and Mike saw Perrin smiling.

"Sorry to surprise you, Bastian," Perrin said. "But with Lenaker on the road we had to move fast. By the time he gets here I'll be in the saddle. Some of the boys wanted to kill you, but I figured you'd be a good talkin' point with the Old Man. He'd be a hard kernel to dig out of that stone shell of his without you. But with you for an argument, he'll come out all right!"

"Have you gone crazy, Perrin? You can't get away with this!"

"I am, though. You see, Rigger Molina left this morning with ten of his boys to work a little job they heard of. In fact, they are on their way to knock over the gold train."

"The gold train?" Bastina exclaimed. "Why, that was my job! He doesn't even know the plan made for it. Or the information I got."

Perrrin smiled triumphantly. "I traded with him. I told him to give me a free hand here, and he could have the gold train. I neglected to tell him about the twelve guards riding with it, or the number of shotguns. In fact, I told him only five guards would be along. I think that will take care of Rigger for me."

Perrin turned abruptly. "Take his guns and tie his hands behind his back, then shove him out into the street. I want the Old Man to see him."

"What about him?" Kiefer demanded, pointing a gun at Doc Sawyer.

"Leave him alone. We many need a doctor, and he knows where his bread is buttered."

Confused and angry, Mike Bastian was shoved into the warm morning sun, then jerked around to face up the canyon toward the stone house.

Suddenly, fierce triumph came over him. Perrin would have a time getting the old man out of the place. The sunlight was shining down the road from over the house, full into their faces. The only approach to the house was up thirty steps of stone, overlooked by an upper window of the house. From that window, and the doorway, the entire settlement could be commanded by an expert rifleman.

Ben Curry had thought of everything. The front and back doors of every building in the settlement could be commanded easily from his stronghold.

Perrin crouched behind a pile of sandbags hastily thrown up near the door of the store.

"Come on down, Curry!" he shouted. "Give yourself up or we'll kill Bastian!"

There was no answer from up the hill. Mike felt cold and sick in the stomach. Wind touched his hair and blew a strand down over his face. He stared up at the stone house and could see no movement, hear no response.

"Come on out!" Perrin roared again. "We know you're there! Come out or we'll kill your son!"

Still no reply.

"He don't hear you," Clatt said. "Maybe he's still asleep. Let's rush the place."

"You rush it," Kiefer said. "Let me watch!"

Despite his helplessness, Mike felt a sudden glow of satisfaction. Old Ben Curry was a wily fighter. He knew that once he showed himself or spoke, their threat would take force. It was useless to kill Bastian unless they knew Curry was watching them.

Perrin had been so sure Curry would come out rather than sacrifice Mike, and now they were not even sure he was hearing them! Nor, Mike knew suddenly, was anybody sure Ben would come out even if they did warn him Mike would be killed.

"Come on out!" Perrin roared. "Give yourself up and we'll give you and Bastian each a horse and a half-mile start! Otherwise, you both die! We've got dynamite!"

Mike chuckled. Dynamite wasn't going to do them much good. There was no way to get close to that stone house, backed up against the mountain as it was.

"Perrin," he said, "you've played the fool. Curry doesn't care whether I live or die. He won't come out of there, and there's no way you can get at him. All he's got to do is sit tight and wait until Dave Lenaker gets here. He will make a deal with Dave then, and where will you be?"

"Shut up!" Perrin bellowed. But for the first time he seemed to be aware that his plan was not working. "He'll come out, all right!"

"Let's open fire on the place," Ducrow suggested. "Or rush it like Clatt suggested!"

"Hell," Kiefer was disgusted. "Let's take what we can lay hands on and get out! There's two thousand head of cattle down in these bottoms. Rigger's gone, Lenaker ain't here yet, let's take what we can and get out."

"Take pennies when there's millions up there in that stone house?" Perrin demanded. His face swelled in anger and the veins stood out on his forehead. "That strong room has gold in it! Stacks of money! I know it's there. With all that at hand, would you run off with a few cattle?"

Kiefer was silent but unconvinced.

Standing in the dusty street, Mike looked up at the stone house. All the loyalty and love he felt for the old man up there in that house came back with a rush. Whatever he was, good or bad, he owed to Ben Curry. Perhaps Curry had reared him for a life of crime, for outlawry, but to Ben Curry it was not a bad life. He lived like a feudal lord, and had respect for no law he did not make himself.

Wrong he might be, but he had given the man that was Mike Bastian a start. Suddenly, Mike knew that he could never have been a outlaw, that it was not in him to steal and rob and kill. But that did not mean he could be unloyal to the old man who had reared him and given him a home when he had none.

He was suddenly, fiercely proud of the old man up there alone. Like a cornered grizzly, he would fight to the death. He, Mike Bastian, might die here in the street, but he hoped old Ben Curry would stay in his stone shell and defeat them all.

Kerb Perrin was stumped. He had made his plan quickly when he'd heard Dave Lenaker was on his way here, for he knew that if Lenaker arrived, it might well turn into a bloody four-cornered fight. But with Molina out of the way, he might take over from Ben Curry before Lenaker and the men he brought with him in an ambush.

He had been sure that Ben Curry would reply, that he might give himself up, or at least show himself, and Perrin had a sniper concealed to pick him off if he moved into the open. That he would get nothing but silence, he could not believe.

Mike Bastian stood alone in the center of the street. There was simply nothing he could do. At any moment Perrin might decide to have him killed where he stood. With his hands tied behind him, he was helpless. Mike wondered what had happened to Roundy? The old mountain man had risen suddenly from the table and vanished. Could he be in league with Perrin?

That was impossible. Roundy had always been Ben Curry's friend, and had never liked anything about Kerb Perrin. "All right," Perrin said suddenly, "we'll hold Bastian. He's still a good argument. Some men will stay here, and the rest of us will make that raid on the Ragan outfit. I've an idea that when we come back, Curry will be ready to talk business."

VI

Bastian was led back from the street and thrown into a room in the rear of the store. There his feet were tied and he was left in darkness.

His mind was in a turmoil. If Perrin's men hit the ranch now they would take Drusilla and Juliana! He well knew how swiftly they would strike, and how helpless any ordinary ranch would be against them. And here he was tied hand and foot, helpless to do anything!

He heaved his body around and fought the ropes that bound him, until sweat streamed from his body. Even then, with his wrists torn by his struggles against the rawhide throngs that made him fast, he did not stop. There was nothing to aid him—no nail, no sharp corner, nothing at all.

The room was built of thin boards nailed to two-by-fours. He rolled himself around until he could get his back against the boards, trying to remember where the nails were. Bracing himself as best he could, he pushed his back back against the wall. He bumped against it until his back was sore. But with no effect.

Outside, all was still. Whether they had gone, he did not know. Yet if Perrin had gone on his raid, he would soon be leaving. However, if he, Mike, could escape and find Curry's private route across the river, he might beat them to it.

He wondered where Doc Sawyer was. Perhaps he was afraid of what Perrin might do if he tried to help. Where was Roundy?

Just when he had all but given up, he had an idea—a solution, so simple that he cursed himself for not thinking of it before. Mike rolled over and got up on his knees and reached back with his bound hands for his spurs. Fortunately, he was wearing boots instead of the moccasins he wore in the woods. By wedging one spur against the other, he succeeded in holding the rowel almost immovable, and then he began to chafe the rawhide with the prongs of the rowel.

Desperately he sawed, until every muscle was crying for relief. As he stopped he heard the rattle of horses' hoofs. They were just going! Then he had a fighting chance if he could get free and get his hands on a gun!

He knew he was making headway for he could feel the notch he had already cut in the rawhide. Suddenly footsteps sounded outside. Fearful whoever was there would guess what he was doing, Mike rolled over on his side.

The door opened and Snake Fernandez came in, and in his hand he held a knife. His shoulder was bandaged crudely but tightly, and the knife was held in his left hand. He came in and closed the door.

Mike stared, horror mounting within him. Perrin was gone, and Snake Fernandez was moving toward him, smiling wickedly.

"You think you shoot Pablo Fernandez, eh?" the outlaw said, leering. "Now, we see who shoots! I am going to cut you to little pieces! I am going to cut you very slowly!"

Bastian lay on his shoulder and stared at Fernandez. There was murder in the breed's eyes, and all the Yaqui in him was coming to the fore. The man stooped over him and pricked him with the knife. Clamping his jaws, Mike held himself tense.

Rage mounted in the Yaqui. He leaned closer. "You do not jump, eh? I make you jump!"

He stabbed down hard with the knife, and Mike whipped over on his shoulder blades and kicked out wickedly with his bound feet. The movement caught the killer by surprise. Mike's feet hit him on the knees and knocked him rolling. With a lunge. Mike rolled over and jerked at the ropes that bound him.

Something snapped, and he jerked again. Like a cat the killer was on his feet now, circling warily. Desparately, Mike pulled at the ropes, turning on his shoulders to keep his feet toward Fernandez. Suddenly, he rolled over and hurled himself at the Mexican's legs, but Fernandez jerked back and stabbed.

Mike felt a sliver of pain run along his arms, and then he rolled to his feet and jerked wildly at the thongs. His hands came loose suddenly and he hurled himself at Fernandez's legs, grabbing one ankle.

Fernandez came down hard and Bastian jerked at the leg, then scrambled to get at him. One hand grasped the man's wrist, the other his throat. With all the power that was in him, Mike shut down on both hands.

Fernandez fought like an injured wildcat, but Mike's strength was too great. Gripping the throat with his left hand, Mike slammed the Mexican's head against the floor again and again, his throttling grip freezing tighter and tighter.

The outlaws face went dark with blood, and his struggles grew weaker. Mike let go of his throat hold suddenly and slugged him three times on the chin with his fist.

Jerking the knife from the unconscious man's hand, Mike slashed at the thongs that bound his ankles. He got to his feet shakily. Glancing down at the sprawled-out Fernandez, he hesitated. The man was not wearing a gun, but must have had one. It could be outside the door. Easing to the door, Mike opened it a crack.

The street was deserted as far as he could see. His hands felt awkward from their long constraint, and he worked his fingers to loosen them up. There was no gun in sight, so he pushed the door wider. Fernandez's gun-belts hung over the chair on the end of the porch.

He had taken two steps toward them when a man stepped out of the bunkhouse. The fellow had a toothpick lifted to his lips, but when he saw Mike Bastian he let out a yelp of surprise and went for his gun.

It was scarcely fifteen paces and Mike threw the knife underhanded, pitching it point first off the palm of his hand. It flashed in the sun as the fellow's gun came up. Then Mike could see the shaft protruding from the man's middle section.

The fellow screamed and, dropping the gun, clutched at the knife hilt in agony of fear. His breath came in horrid gasps which Mike could hear as he grabbed Fernandez's guns and belted them on. Then he lunged for the mess hall, where his own guns had been taken from him. Shoving open the door, he sprang inside, gun in hand.

Then he froze. Doc Sawyer was standing there smiling, and Doc had a shotgun on four of Perrin's men. He looked up with relief.

"I was hoping you would escape!" he said. "I didn't want to kill these men, and didn't know how to go about tying them up by myself."

Mike caught up his own guns, removed Fernandez's gunbelts and strapped his own on. Then he shoved the outlaw's guns inside the waist band of his pants.

"Down on the floor," he ordered. "I'll tie them, and fast!"

It was the work of only a few minutes to have the four outlaws bound hand and foot. He gathered up their guns.

"Where's Roundy?" he asked.

"I haven't seen him since he left here," Doc said. "I've been wondering."

"Let's go up to the house. We'll get Ben Curry, and then we'll have things under control in a hurry."

Together, they went out the back door and walked swiftly down the line of buildings. Mike took off his hat and sailed it into the brush, knowing he could be seen from the stone house and hoping that Ben Curry would recognize him. Sawyer was excited, but trying to appear calm. He had been a gambler, and while handy with guns, was not a man accustomed to violence. Always before, he had been a bystander rather than an active participant.

Side by side, gambling against a shot from someone below, they went up the stone stairs.

There was no sound from within the house. They walked into the wide living room and glanced around. There was no sign of anyone. Then Mike saw a broken box of rifle shells.

"He's been around here!" he said. Then he looked up and shouted, "Dad!"

A muffled cry reached them, and Mike was out of the room and up another staircase. He entered the room at the top, then froze in his tracks. Sawyer was behind him now.

This was the fortress room, a heavy-walled stone room that had water trickling from a spring in the wall of the cliff and running down a stone trough and out through a pipe. There was food stored here, and plenty of ammunition.

The door was heavy and could be locked and barred from within. The walls of this room were all of four feet thick, and nothing short of dynamite could have blasted a way in.

This was Ben Curry's last resort, and he was here, now. But he was sprawled on the floor, his face contorted with pain.

"Broke my leg!" he panted. "Too heavy! Tried to move too . . . fast! Slipped on the steps, dragged myself up here!" He looked up at Mike. "Good for you, son! I was afraid they had killed you. You got away by yourself?"

"Yes, Dad."

Sawyer had dropped to his knees, and now he looked up.

"This is a bad break, Mike," he said. "He won't be able to move."

"Get me on a bed where I can see out of that window." Ben Curry's strength seemed to flow back with his son's presence. "I'll stand them off. You and me, Mike, we can do it!"

"Dad," Mike said, "I can't stay. I've got to go."

Ben Curry's face went gray with shock, then slowly the blood flowed back into it. Bastian dropped down beside him.

"Dad, I know where Perrin's going. He's gone to make a raid on the Ragan ranch. He wants the cattle and the women."

The old man lunged so mightily that Sawyer cried out and tried to push him back. Before he could speak, Mike said:

"Dad, you must tell me about the secret crossing of the Colorado that you know. I must beat them to the ranch."

Ben Curry's expression changed to one of vast relief, and then quick calculation. He nodded.

"You could do it, but it'll take tall riding!" Quickly, he outlined the route, and then added, "Now listen! At the river there's an old Navajo. He keeps some horses for me, and he has six of the finest animals ever bred. You cross that river and get a horse from him. He knows all about you."

Mike got up. "Make him comfortable, Doc. Do all you can."

Sawyer stared at Mike. "What about Dave Lenaker? He'll kill us all!"

"I'll take care of Lenaker!" Curry flared. "I'm not dead by a danged sight! I'll show that renegade where he heads in. The moment he comes up that street, I'm going to kill him!" He looked at Mike again. "Son, maybe I've done wrong to raise you like I have, but if you kill Kerb Perrin or Lenaker you would be doing the West a favor. If I don't get Dave Lenaker, you may have to. So remember this: watch his left hand!"

Mike ran down the steps and stopped in his room to grab his .44 Winchester. It was the work of a minute to throw a saddle on a horse, and then he hit the trail. Ben Curry and Doc Sawyer could, if necessary, last for days in the fortresslike room—unless, somehow, dynamite was pitched into the window. He would have to get to the Ragan ranch, and then get back here as soon as possible.

Mike Bastian left the stable and wheeled the gray he was riding into the long winding trail through the strands of ponderosa and fir. The horse was in fine fettle and ready for the trail, and he let it out. His mind was leaping over the trail, turning each bend, trying to see how it must lay.

This was all new country to him, for he was heading southwest now into the wild, unknown region toward the great canyons of the Colorado, a region he had never traversed and, except for old Ben Curry, perhaps never crossed by any white man.

How hard the trail would be on the horse, Mike could not guess, but he knew he must ride fast and keep going. His route was the shorter, but Kerb Perrin had a lead on him, and would be hurrying to make his strike and return.

Patches of snow still hid themselves around the roots of the brush and in the hollows under the end of some giant deadfall. The air was crisp and chill, but growing warmer, and by afternoon it would be hot in the sunlight. The wind of riding whipped his black hair, and he ran the horse down a long path bedded deep with pine needles, and then turned at a blazed tree and went out across the arid top of a plateau.

This was the strange land that he loved, the fiery land of the sun. Riding along the crest of a long ridge, he looked out over a long valley dotted with mesquite and sagebrush. Black dots of cattle grazing offered the only life beyond the lonely, lazy swing of a high-soaring buzzard.

He saw the white rock he had been told to look for, and turned the free-running horse into a cleft that led downward. They moved slowly here, for it was a steep slide down the side of the mesa and out on the long roll of the hill above the valley.

Time and time again Mike's hand patted his guns, as if to reassure himself they were there. His thoughts leaped ahead, trying to foresee what would happen. Would he reach the ranch first? Would he arrive only to find the buildings burned and the girls gone?

He knew only that he must get there first, that he must face them, and that at all costs he must kill Kerb Perrin and Ducrow. Without them the others might run, might not choose to fight it out. Mike had an idea that without Perrin, they would scatter to the four winds.

Swinging along the hillside, he took a trail that led again to a plateau top and ran off through the sage, heading for the smoky-blue distance of the canyon.

VII

Mike's mind lost track of time and distance, leaping ahead to the river and the crossing, and beyond it to Ragan's V Bar ranch. Down steep trails through the great, broken cliffs heaped high with the piled-up stone of ages. Down through the wild, weird jumble of boulders and across the flat toplands that smelled of sage and piñon, he kept the horse moving.

Then suddenly he was once more in the forest of the Kaibab. The dark pines closed around him and he rode on in the vast stillness of virgin timber, the miles falling behind, the trail growing dim before him.

Then suddenly the forest split aside and he was on the rim of the canyon—an awful blue immensity yawning before him that made him draw the gray to a halt in gasping wonder. Far out over that vast, misty blue rose islands of red sandstone, islands that were laced and crossed by bands of purple and yellow. The sunset was gleaming on the vast plateaus and buttes and peaks with a ruddy glow, fading into the opaques of the deeper canyon.

The gray was beaten and weary, now. Mike turned the horse toward a break in the plateau and rode down it, giving the animal its head. They came out upon a narrow trail that hung above a vast gorge, its bottom lost in the darkness of gathering dusk. The gray stumbled on, seeming to know its day was almost done.

Dozing in the saddle, almost two hours later, Mike Bastian felt the horse come to a halt. He jerked his head up and opened his eyes. He could feel the dampness of the deep canyon and could hear the thundering roar of the mighty river as it charged through the rock-walled slit. In front of him was a square of light.

"Halloo, the house!" he called.

He swung down as the door opened.

"Who's there?" a voice cried out.

"Mike Bastian!" he said, moving toward the house with long, swinging strides. "For Ben Curry!"

The man backed into the house. He was an ancient Navajo, but his eyes were keen and sharp.

"I want a horse," Mike said.

"You can't cross the river tonight." The Navajo spoke English well. "It is impossible!"

"They'll be a moon later," Mike answered, "When it comes up, I'm going across."

The Indian looked at him, then shrugged.

"Then eat," he said, "you'll need it."

"There are horses?"

"Horses?" The Navajo chuckled. "The best a man ever saw! Do you suppose Ben Curry would have horses here that were not the best? But they are on the other side of the stream, and safe enough. My brother is with them."

Mike slumped into a seat. "Take care of my horse, will you? I've most killed him."

When the Indian was gone, Mike slumped over on the table, burying his head in his arms. In a moment he was asleep, dreaming wild dreams of a mad race over a strange misty-blue land with great crimson islands, riding a splendid black horse and carrying a girl in his arms. He awakened with a start. The old Indian was sitting by the fireplace, and he looked up.

"You'd better eat," he said. "The moon is rising."

They went out together walking, down the path to the water's edge. As the moon shone down into the canyon, Mike stared at the tumbling stream in consternation. Nothing living could swim in that water! It would be impossible.

"How do you cross?" he demanded. "No horse could swim that! And a boat wouldn't get fifty feet before it would be dashed to pieces!"

The Indian chuckled. "That isn't the way we cross it. You are right in saying no boat could cross here, for there is no landing over there, and the canyon is so narrow that the water piles up back of the narrows and comes down with a great rush."

Mike looked at him again. "You talk like an educated man," he said. "I don't understand."

The Navajo shrugged. "I was for ten years with a missionary, and after traveling with him as an interpreter he took me back to the States, where I stayed with him for two years. Then I lived in Santa Fe."

He was leading the way up a steep path that skirted the cliff but was wide enough to walk comfortably. Opposite them, the rock wall of the canyon lifted and the waters of the tumbling river roared down through the narrow chasm.

"Ben Curry does things well, as you shall see," the guide said. "It took him two years of effort to get this bridge built."

Mike stared. "Across there?"

"Yes. A bridge for a man with courage. It is a rope bridge, made fast to iron rings sunk in the rock."

Mike Bastian halted on the rocky ledge at the end of the trail and looked out across the gorge. In the pale moonlight he could see two slim threads trailing across the canyon high above the tumbling water. Just two ropes, and one of them four feet above the other.

"You mean," he said, "that Ben Curry crossed on that?"

"He did. I have seen him cross that bridge a dozen times, at least."

"Have you crossed it?"

The Navajo shrugged. "Why should I? The other side is the same as this, is it not? There is nothing over there that I want."

Mike looked at the slender strands, and then he took hold of the upper rope and tentatively put a foot on the lower one. Slowly, carefully, he eased out above the raging waters. One slip and he would be gone, for no man could hope to live in those angry flood waters. He slid his foot along, then the other, advancing his handholds as he moved. Little by little, he worked his way across the canyon.

He was trembling when he got his feet in the rocky cavern on the opposite side, and so relieved to be safely across that he scarcely was aware of the old Indian who sat there awaiting him.

The Navajo got up, and without a word started down the trail. He quickly led Mike to a cabin built in the opening of a dry, branch canyon, and tethered before the door of the cabin was a large bay stallion.

Waving at the Indian, Mike swung into the saddle and the bay turned, taking to the trail as if eager to be off.

Would Perrin travel at night? Mike doubted it, but it was possible, so he kept moving himself. The trail led steadily upward, winding finally out of the canyon to the plateau.

The bay stallion seemed to know the trail; it was probable that Curry had used this horse himself. It was a splendid animal, big and very fast. Letting the horse have his head, Mike felt the animal gather his legs under him. Then he broke into a long swinging lope that literally ate up the space. How long the horse could hold the speed he did not know, but it was a good start.

It was at least a ten-hour ride to the Ragan V-Bar ranch.

The country was rugged and wild. Several times startled deer broke and ran before him, and there were many rabbits. Dawn was breaking faintly in the east now, and shortly after daybreak he stopped near a pool of melted snow water and made coffee. Then he remounted the rested stallion and raced on.

Drusilla Ragan brushed her hair thoughtfully, and then pinned it up. Outside, she could hear her mother moving about, and the Mexican girls who helped around the house whenever they were visiting. Julie was up, she knew, and had been for hours. She was outside talking to that blond cowhand from New Mexico, the one Voyle Ragan had hired to break horses.

Suddenly she heard Julie's footsteps, and then the door opened.

"Aren't you ready yet?" Julie asked. "I'm famished!"

"I'll be along in a minute." Then as Julie turned to go. "What did you think of him, Julie? That cowboy who got the buckboard for us? Wasn't he the handsomest thing?"

"Oh, you mean that Mike Bastian?" Julie said. "I was wondering why you were mooning around in here. Usually you're the first one up. Yes, I expect he is good looking. But did you see the way he looked when you mentioned Uncle Voyle? He acted so strange!"

"I wonder if Uncle Voyle knows anything about him? Let's ask!"

"You ask," Julie replied, laughing. "He's your problem!"

Voyle Ragan was a tall man, but lean and without Ben Curry's weight. He was already seated at the table when they came in, and Dru was no sooner in her seat than she put her question. Voyle's face became a mask.

"Mike Bastian?" he said thoughtfully. "I don't know. Where'd you meet him?"

The girls explained, and he nodded.

"In Weaver?" Voyle Ragan knew about the gold train, and his eyes narrowed. "I think I know who he is, but I never saw him that I heard of. You probably won't see him again, because most of those riders from up in the Strip stay there most of the time. They are a wild bunch."

"On the way down here," Julie said, "the man who drove was telling us that outlaws live up there."

"Could be. It's wild enough." Voyle Ragan lifted his head, listening. For a moment he had believed he heard horses. But it was too soon for Ben to be coming. If anyone else came, he would have to get rid of them, and quickly.

He heard it again, and then saw the cavalcade of horsemen riding into the yard. Voyle came to his feet abruptly.

"Stay here!" he snapped.

His immediate thought was of a posse, and then he saw Kerb Perrin. He had seen Perrin many times, although Perrin had never met him. Slowly, he moved up to the door, uncertain of his course. These were Ben's men, but Ben had always told him that none of them was aware that he owned this ranch or that Voyle was his brother.

"Howdy!" Voyle said. "What can I do for you?"

Kerb Perrin swung down from his horse. Monson, Ducrow, and Kiefer were getting down.

"You can make as little trouble as you know how," Perrin said, his eyes gleaming. "All you got to do is stay out of the way. Where's the girls? We want them, and we want your cattle."

"What is this?" Voyle demanded. He wasn't wearing a gun; it was hanging from a clothes-tree in the next room. "You men can't get away with anything here!"

Perrin's face was ugly as he strode toward the door. "That's what you think!" he sneered.

The tall old man blocked his way, and Perrin shoved him aside. Perrin had seen the startled faces of the girls inside and knew the men behind him were spreading out.

Ragan swung suddenly and his fist struck Perrin in the mouth. The gunman staggered, his face went white with fury.

A Mexican started from the corral toward the house and Ducrow wheeled, firing from the hip. The man cried out and sprawled over on the hardpacked earth, moaning out his agony.

Perrin had drawn back slowly, his face ugly with rage, a slow trickling of blood from his lips. “For that, I’ll kill you!” he snarled at Ragan.

“Not yet, Perrin!”

The voice had a cold ring of challenge, and Kerb Perrin went numb with shock. He turned slowly, to see Mike Bastian standing at the corner of the corral.

Kerb Perrin was profoundly shocked. He had left Bastian a prisoner at Toadstool Canyon. Since he was free now, it could mean that Ben Curry was back in the saddle. It could mean a lot of things. An idea came to kill Mike Bastian, and kill him now!

“You men have made fools of yourselves!” Bastian’s voice was harsh. He stood there in his gray buckskins, his feet a little apart, his black hair rippled by the wind. “Ben Curry’s not through! And this place is under his protection. He sent me to stop you, and stop you I shall! Now, any of you who don’t want to fight Ben Curry, get out while the getting is good!”

“Stay where you are!” Perrin snapped. “I’ll settle with you, Bastian, right now!”

His hand darted down in the sweeping, lightning-fast draw for which he was noted. His lips curled in sneering contempt. Yet, as his gun lifted, he saw flame blossom from a gun in Bastian’s hand and a hard object slugged him. Perplexed and disturbed, he took a step backward. Whatever had hit him had knocked his gun out of line. He turned it toward Bastian again. The gun in Mike’s hand blasted a second time, and a third.

Perrin could not seem to get his own gun leveled. His mind wouldn’t function right, and he felt a strangeness in the stomach. His legs— Suddenly he was on his knees. He tried to get up and saw a dark pool forming near his knees. He must have slipped, he must have— That was blood.

It was his blood!

From far off he heard shouts, then a scream, then the pound of horses' hoofs. Then the thunder of those hoofs seemed to sweep through his brain and he was lying face down in the dirt. And then he knew: Mike Bastian had shot him three times. Mike Bastian had killed him!

He started to scream a protest—and then he just laid there on his face, his cheek against the bloody ground, his mouth half open.

Kerb Perrin was dead.

In that instant that Perrin had reached for his gun, Ducrow suddenly cut and ran toward the corner of the house. Kiefer, seeing his leader gunned down then, made a wild grab for his own weapon. The old man in the doorway killed him with a hastily caught-up rifle.

The others broke for their horses. Mike rushed after them and got off one more shot as they raced out of the yard. It was then he heard the scream, and whirled.

Ducrow had acted with suddenness. He had come to the ranch for women, and women he intended to have. Even as Bastian was killing Perrin, he had rushed for the house. Darting around the corner where two saddle horses were waiting, he was just in time to see Juliana, horrified at the killing, run back into her bedroom. The bedroom window opened beside Ducrow, and the outlaw reached through and grabbed her.

Julie went numb with horror. Ducrow threw her across Perrin's saddle, and with a piggin string, which he always carried from his days as a cowhand, he jerked her ankles together under the horse's belly.

Instantly, he was astride the other horse. Julie screamed, then. Wheeling, he struck her across the mouth with a backhand blow. He caught up the bridle of her horse, drove in spurs to his own mount, and they went out of the ranch yard at a dead run.

Mike hesitated only an instant when he heard Julie scream, then ran for the corner of the house. By the time he rounded the corner, gun in hand, the two horses were streaking into the piñons. In the dust, he could only catch a glimpse of the riders. He turned and walked back.

That had been a woman's scream, but Dru was in the doorway and he had seen her. Only then did he recall Julie. He sprinted for the doorway.

"Where's Julie?" he shouted to Drusilla. "Look through the house!"

He glanced around quickly. Kerb Perrin, mouth agape, lay dead on the hard earth of the ranch yard. Kiefer lay near the body of the Mexican Ducrow had killed. The whole raid had been a matter of no more than two or three minutes.

Voyle Ragan dashed from the house. "Julie's gone!" he yelled hoarsely. "I'll get a horse!"

Bastian caught his arm. His own dark face was tense and his eyes wide.

"You'll stay here!" he said harshly. "Take care of the women and the ranch. I'll go after Julie."

Dru ran from the house. "She's gone, Mike, she's gone! They have her!"

Mike walked rapidly to his horse, thumbing shells into his gun. Dru Ragan started to mount another horse.

"You go back to the house!" he ordered.

Dru's chin can up. In that moment she remided him of Ben Curry.

"She's my sister!" Dru cried. "When we find her, she may need a woman's care!"

"All right," Mike said, "but you'll have to do some riding!"

He wheeled the big bay around. The horse Dru had mounted was one of Ben Curry's beautiful horses, bred not only for speed but for staying power.

Mike's mind leaped ahead. Would Ducrow get back with the rest of them? Would he join Monson and Clatt? If he did, it was going to be a problem. Ducrow was a handy man with a six-gun, but the three of them, or more if they were all together, would be nothing less than suicide.

He held the bay horse's pace down. He had taken a swift glance at the hoofmarks of the horses he was trailing, and knew them both.

Would Drew head back for Toadstool Canyon? Bastian considered that as he rode, and decided he would not. Ducrow did not know that Julie was Ben Curry's daughter. But from what Mike had said, Ducrow had cause to believe that Ben was back in the saddle again. And men who went off on rebel raids were not lightly handled by Curry.

Besides, he would want, if possible, to keep the girl for himself.

Mike had been taught by Roundy that there was more to trailing a man than following his tracks, for you trailed him down the devious paths of mind as well. He tried to put himself in Ducrow's place.

The man could not have much food, yet on his many outlaw forays he must have learned the country and would know where there was water. Also, there were many ranch hangouts of the outlaws that Ducrow would know. He would probably go to one of them. Remembering the maps that Ben Curry had shown him and made him study, Mike knew the locations of all those places.

The trail turned suddenly off through the chaparral, and Mike turned to follow. Drusilla had said nothing since they started. Once he had glanced at her. Even now, with her face dusty and tear-streaked, she was lovely. Her eyes were fastened on the trail, and he noted with a little thrill of satisfaction that she had brought her rifle along.

Dru certainly was her father's daughter, and the fit companion for any man.

Bastian turned his attention to the trail. Despite the small lead he had, Ducrow had vanished. That taught Mike something of the nature of the man he was tracing; his years of outlawry had taught him how to disappear when need be. The method was simple. Turning off into the thicker desert growth, he had ridden down into a sandy wash.

Here, due to the deep sand and the tracks of horses and cattle, it was a problem and it took Mike several minutes to decide whether Ducrow had gone up or down the wash. Then he caught a hoofprint, and they were off, winding up the sandy wash. Yet Mike knew they would not be in that sand for long. Ducrow would wish to save his horses' strength.

True enough, the trail soon turned out. From then on, it was a nightmare. Ducrow ran off in a straitway, then turned at right angles, weaving about in the sandy desert. Several times he had stopped to brush out portions of his trail, but Roundy had not spent years of training in vain and Mike Bastian hung to the trail like a bloodhound.

Dru, riding behind him, saw him get off and walk, saw him pick up sign where she could see nothing.

Hours passed and the day slowly drew toward an end. Dru, her face pale, realized night would come before they found her sister. She was about to speak, when Mike looked up at her.

"You wanted to come," he said, "so you'll have to take the consequences. I'm not stopping because of the darkness."

"How can you trail them?"

"I can't," he shrugged. "But I think I know where they are going. We'll take a chance."

Darkness closed around them. Mike's shirt stuck to his body with sweat, and a chill wind of the higher plateaus blew down through the trees. He rode on, his face grim and his body weary with long hours in the saddle. The big bay kept on, seemingly unhurt by the long hours of riding. Time and again he patted the big horse, and Dru could hear him talking to it in a low voice. Suddenly at the edge of a clearing, he reined in.

"Dru," he said, "there's a ranch ahead. It's an outlaw hangout. There may be one or more men there. Ducrow may be there. I am going up to find out."

"I'll come too," the girl said impulsively.

"You'll stay here!" His voice was flat. "When I whistle, then you come. Bring my horse along."

He swung down and, slipping off his boots, pulled on his moccasins. Then he went forward into the darkness. Alone, she watched him vanish toward the dark bulk of the buildings. Suddenly a light came on—too soon for him to have arrived.

Mike weaved his way through sage and mesquite to the corral, and worked his way along the bars. Horses were there but it was too dark to make them out. One of them stood near, and he put his hand through the bars, touching the horse's flank. It was damp with sweat.

His face tightened.

The horse stepped away, snorting. As if waiting for just that sound, a light went on in the house: a lamp had been lighted. By that time Mike was at the side of the house, flattened against the wall peering in.

He saw a heavy, square-faced man with a pistol in his hand. The man put the gun under a towel on the table, then began pacing around the room, waiting. Mike smiled grimly, walked around the house and stepped up on the porch. In his moccasins, he made no sound. He opened the door suddenly and stepped into the room.

VIII

Obviously the man had been waiting for the sound of boots, of horses, or the jingle of spurs. Even a knock. Mike Bastian's sudden appearance startled him, and he straightened up from the table, his hand near the towel that covered the gun.

Bastian closed the door behind him. The man stared at the black-haired young man who faced him, stared with puckered brow. This man didn't lool like a sheriff to him. Not those tied down guns, or that gray buckskin stained with travel, and no hat.

"You're Walt Sutton," Mike snapped. "Get your hands off that table before I blow you wide open! Get 'em off!"

He jammed the muzzle of the gun into Sutton's stomach with such force that it doubled the man up.

Then he swept the towel from the gun.

"You fool!" he said sharply. "If you'd tried that, I'd have killed you!"

Sutton staggered back, his face gray. He had never even seen Mike's hand move.

"Who are you?" he gasped, struggling to get his wind back.

"I'm Mike Bastian, Ben Curry's foster son. He owns this ranch. He set you up here, gave you stock to get started with, now you double-cross him! Where's Ducrow?"

Sutton swallowed. "I ain't seen him!" he protested.

"You're a liar, Sutton! His horses are out in that corral. I could pistol-whip you, but I'm not going to. You're going to tell me where he is, and now, or I'm going to start shooting!"

Walt Sutton was unhappy. He knew Ducrow as one of Ben Curry's men who had come here before for fresh horses. He had never seen this man who called himself Mike Bastian, yet so far as he knew, no one but Curry himself had ever known the true facts about his ranch. If this man was lying, how could he know?

"Listen, mister," he protested, "I don't want no trouble—least of all with old Ben. He did set me up here. Sure, I seen Ducrow, but he told me the law was after him."

"Do I look like the law?" Mike snapped. "He's kidnapped the daughter of a friend of Curry's, niece of Voyle Ragan. I've got to find him."

"Kipnapped Voyle's niece? Gosh, mister, I wondered why he wanted two saddle horses!"

Mike whistled sharply. "Where'd he go?" he demanded then.

"Darned if I know," Sutton answered. "He came in here maybe an hour ago, wanted two saddle horses and a pack horse loaded with grub. He took two canteens, then, and lit out."

Drusilla appeared in the doorway, and Walt Sutton's eyes went to her.

"I know you," he said. "You're one of Voyle Ragan nieces."

"She is," Mike said. "Ducrow kidnapped the other one. I'm going to find him. Get us some grub, but fast!"

Mike paced restlessly while Sutton filled a pack and strapped it behind the saddle of one of the fresh horses he furnished them. The horses were some of those left at the ranch by Ben Curry's orders, and were good.

"No pack horses," Mike had said. "We're travelling fast."

Now, he turned to Sutton again. "You got any idea where Ducrow might be going?"

"Well"— Sutton licked his lips —"he'd kill me if he knowed I said anything, but he did say something about Peach Meadow Canyon."

"Peach Meadow?" Bastian stared at Sutton. The canyon was almost a legend in Coconino country. "What did he ask you?"

"If I knowed the trail in there, an' if it was passable."

"What did you say?"

Sutton shrugged. "Well, I've heard tell of that there canyon ever since I been in this country, an' ain't seen no part of it. I've looked, all right. Who wouldn't look, if all they say is true?"

When they were about to mount their horses, Mike turned to the girl and put his hand under her arm.

"Dru," he said, "It's going to be rough, so if you want to go back, say so."

"I wouldn't think of it!" she said firmly.

"Well, I won't say I'm sorry, because I'm not. I'll sure like having you beside me. In fact"—he hesitated, then went on—"it will be nice having you."

That was not what he had started to say, and Dru knew it. She looked at Mike for a moment, her eyes soft. He was tired now, and she could see how drawn his face was. She knew only a little of the ride he had made to reach them before Perrin's outlaws came.

When they were in the saddle, Mike explained a little of what he had in mind. "I doubt Ducrow will stop for anything now," he said. "There isn't a good hiding place within miles, so he'll head right for the canyon country. He may actually know something about Peach Meadow Canyon. If he does, he knows a perfect hideaway. Outlaws often stumble across places in their getaways that a man couldn't find if he looked for it for years."

"What is Peach Meadow Canyon?" Dru asked.

"It's supposed to be over near the river in one of the deep canyons that branch off from the Colorado. According to the story, a fellow found the place years ago, but the Spanish had been there before him, and the Indians before them. There are said to be old Indian ruins in the place, but no way to get into it from the plateau. The Indians found a way through some caves in the Coconino sandstone, and the Spanish are suppposed to have reached it by boat."

"Anyway," he continued, "this prospector who found it said the climate was tropical, or almost. That it was in a branch canyon, that there was fresh water and a nice meadow. Somebody had planted some fruit trees, and when he went back he took a lot of peach pits and was supposed to have planted an orchard.

"Nobody ever saw him or it again," Mike went on, "so the place exists only on his say-so. The Indians alive now swear they have never heard of it. Ducrow might be trying to throw us off, or he might honestly know something."

For several miles the trail was a simple thing. They were riding down the floor of a high-walled canyon from which there was no escape. Nevertheless, from time to time Bastian stopped and examined the sandy floor with matches. Always the tracks were there, and going straight down the canyon.

This was new country to Mike. He knew the altitude was gradually lessening, and believed they would soon emerge on the desert plateau that ran toward the canyon and finally lost itself on the edge of the pine forest.

When they had traveled about seven miles, the canyon ended abruptly and they emerged in a long valley. Mike reined in and swung down.

"Like it or not," he said, "here's where we stop. We can't have a fire, because from here it could be seen for miles. We don't want Ducrow to believe we stopped."

Mike spread his poncho on the sand and handed Dru a blanket. She was feeling the chill and gathered it close around her.

"Aren't you cold?" she said suddenly. "If we sat close together, we could share the blanket."

He hesitated, then sat down alongside her and pulled the blanket across his shoulders, grateful for the warmth. Leaning back against the rock, warmed by proximity and the blanket, they dozed a little.

Mike had loosened his girths and ground-hitched the horses. He wasn't worried about them straying off.

When the sky was just faintly gray, he opened his eyes. Dru's head was on his shoulder and she was sleeping. He could feel the rise and fall of her breathing against his body. He glanced down at her face, amazed that this could happen to him—that he, Mike Bastian, foster son of an outlaw, could be sitting alone in the desert with this girl sleeping on his shoulder!

Some movement of his must have awakened her, for her breath caught, and then she looked up. He could see the sleepy smile in her eyes and on her mouth.

"I was tired!" She whispered the words, and made no effort to move her head from his shoulder. "You've nice shoulders," she said. "If we were riding anywhere else, I'd not want to move at all."

"Nor I." He glanced at the stars. "We'd better get up. I think we can chance a very small fire and a quick cup of coffee."

While he was breaking dried mesquite and greasewood, Dru got the pack open and dug out the coffee and some bread. There was no time for anything else.

The fire made but little light, shielded by the rocks and kept very small, and there was less glow now due to the grayness of the sky. They ate quickly.

When they were in the saddle again, he turned down the trail left by the two saddle horses and the pack horse he was following. Sign was dim, but could be followed without dismounting.

Dawn broke, and the sky turned red and gold, then blue. The sun lifted and began to take some of the chill from their muscles.

The trail crossed the valley, skirting an alkali lake, and then dipped into the rocky wilderness that preceded the pine forest. He could find no signs of a camp. Julie, who lacked the fire and also the strength of Dru, must be almost dead with weariness, for Ducrow was not stopping. Certainly, the man had more than a possible destination before him. In fact, the farther they rode, the more confident Mike was that the outlaw knew exactly where he was headed.

The pines closed around them and the trail became more difficult to follow. It was slow going, and much of it Mike Bastian walked. Suddenly he stopped, scowling. The trail, faint as it had been, had vanished into thin air!

"Stay where you are," he told Dru. "I've got to look around a bit."

Mike studied the ground carefully. Then he walked back to the last tracks he had seen. Their own tracks did not cover them, as he had avoided riding over them in case he needed to examine the hoofprints once more.

Slowly, Mike paced back and forth over the pine needles. Then he stopped and studied the surrounding timber very carefully. It seemed to be absolutely uniform in appearance. Avoiding the trail ahead, he left the girl and circled into the woods, describing a slow circle around the horses.

There were no tracks.

He stopped, his brow furrowed. It was impossible to lose them after following so far—yet they were gone, and they had left no trail. He walked back to the horses again, and Dru stared at him, her eyes wide.

"Wait a minute," he said as she began to speak. "I want to think."

He studied, inch by inch, the woods on his left, the trail ahead, and then the trail on his right. Nothing offered a clue. The tracks of three horses had simply vanished as though the animals and their riders had been swallowed into space.

On the left the pines stood thick, and back inside the woods the brush was so dense as to allow no means of passing through it. That was out, then. He had studied that brush and had walked through those woods, and if a horseman did turn that way there would be no place to go.

The trail ahead was trackless, so it had to be on the right. Mike turned and walked again to the woods on his right. He inched over the ground, yet there was nothing, no track, no indication that anything heavier than a rabbit had passed that way. It was impossible, yet it happened.

"Could they have backtracked?" Dru asked suddenly. "Over the same trail?"

Mike shook his head. "There were no tracks," he said, "but those going ahead, I think—I'm a fool! A darned fool!" He grinned at her. "Lend me your hat."

Puzzled, she removed her sombrero and handed it to him. He turned and using the hat for a fan, began to wave it over the ground to let the wind disturb the surface needles. Patiently, he worked over the area around the last tracks seen, and then to the woods on both sides of the trail. Suddenly, he stopped.

"Got it!" he said. "Here they are!"

Dru ran to him. He pointed to a track, then several more.

"Ducrow was smart," Mike explained. "He turned at right angles and rode across the open space, and then turned back down the way he had come, riding over on the far side. Then he dismounted and, coming back, gathered pine needles from somewhere back in the brush and came along here, pressing the earth down and scattering the needles to make it seem there had been no traces at all!"

Mounting again, they started back, and from time to time he dismounted to examine the trail. Suddenly the tracks ended and turned off into thick woods. Leading their horses, they followed.

"Move quietly as you can," Mike said softly "We may be close, now. Or he may wait and try to ambush us."

"You think he knows we're following him?" Dru asked.

"Sure! And he knows I'm a tracker. He'll use every trick in the books, now."

For awhile, the trail was not difficult to follow and they rode again. Mike Bastian could not take his mind from the girl who rode with him. What would she think when she discovered her father was an outlaw? That he was the mysterious leader of the outlaws?

IX

Pine trees thinned out, and before them was the vast blue and misty distance of the canyon. Mike slid to the ground and walked slowly forward on mocassined feet. There were pines and the cracked and splintered rim of the canyon, breaking sharply off to fall away into the vast depths. Carefully, he scouted the edge of the canyon, and when he saw the trail he stopped flat-footed and stared, his heart in his mouth.

Had they gone down there? He knelt on the rock. Yes, there was the scar of a horse's hoof. He walked out a little farther, looking down.

The cliff fell away for hundreds of feet without even a hump in the wall, then just a little farther along was the trial. It was a rocky ledge scarcely three feet wide that ran steeply down the side of the rock from the canyon's rim. On the left the wall, on the right the vast, astonishing emptiness of the canyon.

Thoughtfully, he walked back and explained.

"All right, Mike," Dru nodded, "if you're ready, I am."

He hesitated to bring the horses, but decided it would be the best thing. He drew his rifle from the saddle scabbard and jacked a shell into the chamber.

Dru looked at him, steady-eyed. "Mike, maybe he'll be waiting for us," she said. "We may get shot. Especially you."

Bastian nodded. "That could be," he agreed.

She came toward him. "Mike, who are you, what are you? Uncle Voyle seemed to know you, or about you, and that outlaw, Perrin. He knew you. Then I heard you say Ben Curry had sent you to stop them from raiding the ranch. Are you an outlaw, Mike?"

For as long as a man might have counted a slow ten, Mike stared out over the canyon, trying to make up his mind. Now at this stage, there was only one thing he could say.

"No, Dru, not exactly, but I was raised by an outlaw," he explained. "Ben Curry brought me up like his own son, with the idea that I would take over the gang when he stepped out."

"You lived with them in their hideout?"

"When I wasn't out in the woods." He nodded. "Ben Curry had me taught everything—how to shoot, to track, to ride, even to open safes and locks."

"What's he like, this Ben Curry?" Dru asked.

"He's quite a man!" Mike Bastian said, smiling. "When he started outlawing, everybody was rustling a few cows, and he just went a step further and robbed banks and stages, or planned the robberies and directed them. I don't expect he really figured himself bad. He might have done a lot of other things, for he has brains. But he killed a man—and then in getting away, he killed another. The first one was justified. The second one— Well, he was in a hurry."

"Are you apologizing for him?" Dru said quickly. "After all, he was an outlaw and a killer."

He glanced at her. "He was, yes. And I am not making any apologies for him, nor would he want them. He's a man who always stood on his own two feet. Maybe he was wrong, but there were the circumstances. And he was mighty good to me. I didn't have a home, no place to go, and he took me in and treated me right."

"Was he a big man, Mike? A big old man?"

He did not look at her. She knew, then?

"In many ways," he said, "he is one of the biggest men I know. We'd better get started."

It was like stepping off into space, yet the horses took it calmly enough. They were mountain bred and would go anywhere as long as they could get a foothold on something.

The red maw of the canyon gaped to receive them and they went down, following the narrow, switchback trail that seemed to be leading them into the very center of the earth.

It was late afternoon before they started down, and now the shadows began to creep up the canyon walls, reaching with ghostly fingers for the vanished sunlight. Overhead the red blazed with the setting sun's reflection and seemed to be hurling arrows of flame back into the sky. The depths of the canyon seemed to chill after the sun on the plateau, and Mike walked warily, always a little ahead of the horse he was leading.

Dru was riding, and when he glanced back once, she smiled brightly at him, keeping her eyes averted from the awful depths below.

Mike had no flair for making love, for his knowledge of women was slight. He wished now that he knew more of their ways, knew the things to say that would appeal to a girl.

A long time later they reached the bottom, and far away on their right they could hear the river rushing through the canyon. Mike knelt, and striking a match, he studied the trail. The tracks turned back into a long canyon that led back from the river.

He got into the saddle then, his rifle across his saddle, and rode forward.

At the end, it was simple. The long chase had led to a quiet meadow, and he could smell the grass before he reached it, could hear the babble of a small stream. The canyon walls flared wide and he saw, not far away, the faint sparkle of a fire.

Dru came alongside him. "Is . . . that them?" she asked, low-voiced.

"It couldn't be anyone else." Her hand was on his arm and he put his own hand over it. "I've got to go up there alone, Dru. I'll have to kill him, you know."

"Yes," she said, simply, "but don't you be killed!"

He started to ride forward and she caught his arm.

"Mike, why have you done all this?" she asked. "She isn't your sister."

"No." He looked very serious in the vague light. "She's yours."

He turned his head and spoke to the horse. The animal started forward.

When, shortly, he stopped the mount, he heard a sound nearby. Dru Ragan was close behind him.

"Dru," he whispered, "you've got to stay back! Hold my horse. I'm going up on foot."

He left her like that and walked steadily forward. Even before he got to the fire, he could see them. The girl, her head slumped over her arms, half dead with weariness, and Ducrow bending over the fire. From time to time Ducrow glanced at the girl. Finally, he reached over and cuffed her on the head.

"Come on, get some of this coffee into you!" he growled.

"This is where we stay—in Peach Meadow Canyon. Might as well give up seein' that sister of yours, because you're my woman, now." He sneered. "Monson and them, they ran like scared foxes! No bottom to them. I come for a woman, and I got one!"

"Why don't you let me go?" Juliana protested. "My father will pay you well. He has lots of money."

"Your pa?" Ducrow stared at her. "I thought Voyle Ragan was your uncle?"

"He is. I mean Ben Ragan. He ranches up north of the canyon."

"North of the canyon?" Ducrow laughed "Not unless he's a Mormon, he don't. What's he look like, this pa of yours?"

"He's a great big man, with iron-gray hair, a heavy jaw—" She stopped, staring at Ducrow. "What's the matter with you?"

Ducrow got slowly to his feet. "Your Pa—Ben Ragan? A big man with gray hair, an' maybe a scar on his jaw—that him?"

"Oh yes! Take me to him! He'll pay you well!"

Suddenly, Ducrow let out a guffaw of laughter. He slapped his leg and bellowed. "Man, oh, man! Is that a good one! You're Ben Curry's daughter! Why that old—" He sobered. "What did you call him? Ragan? Why, honey, that old man of yours is the biggest outlaw in the world! Or was until today! Well, of all the—"

"You've laughed enough, Ducrow!"

As Mike Bastian spoke, he stepped to the edge of the firelight. "You leave a tough trail, but I followed it."

Ducrow turned, half crouching, his cruel eyes glaring at Bastian.

"Roundy was right," he snarled. "You could track a snake across a flat rock! Well, now that you're here, what are you goin' to do?"

"That depends on you, Ducrow. You can drop your gun and I'll take you in for a trial. Or you can shoot it out."

"Drop my guns?" Ducrow chuckled. "You'd actually take me in, too! You're too soft, Bastian. You'd never make the boss man old Ben Curry was. He would never even of said yes, or no, he would have seen me and gone to blastin'! You got a sight to learn, youngster. Too bad you ain't goin' to live long enough to learn it."

Ducrow lifted one hand carelessly and wiped it across the tobacco-stained stubble of his beard. His right hand swept down for his gun even as his left touched his face. His gun came up, spouting flame.

Mike Bastian palmed his gun and momentarily held it rigid, then he fired.

Ducrow winced like he had been slugged in the chest, and then he lifted on his tiptoes. His gun came level again.

"You're . . . fast!" he gasped. "Devilish fast!"

He fired, and then Mike triggered his gun once more. The second shot spun Ducrow around and he fell, face down at the edge of the fire.

Dru came running, her rifle in her hand, but when she saw Mike still standing, she dropped the rifle and ran to him.

"Oh, Mike!" she sobbed. "I was so frightened! I thought you were killed!"

Julie started to rise, then fell headlong into a faint. Dru rushed to her side.

Mike Bastian absently thumbed shells into his gun and stared down at the fallen man. He had killed a third man. Suddenly, and profoundly, he wished with all his heart he would never have to kill another.

He holstered his weapon, and gathered up the dead man, carried him away from the fire. He would bury him here, in Peach Meadow Canyon.

X

Sunlight lay upon the empty street of the settlement in Toadstool Canyon when Mike Bastian, his rifle crosswise on his saddle, rode slowly into the lower end of the town.

Beside him, sitting straight in her saddle, rode Dru Ragan. Julie had stayed at the ranch, but Dru flatly refused. Ben Curry was her father, and she was going to him, outlaw camp or not.

If Dave Lenaker had arrived, Mike thought, he was quiet enough, for there was no sound. No horses stood at the hitchrails, and the door of the saloon stood wide open.

Something fluttered on the ground and Mike looked at it quickly. It was a torn bit of cloth on a man's body. The man was a stranger. Dru noticed it, and her face paled.

His rifle at ready, Mike rode on, eyes shifting from side to side. A man's wrist lay in sight across a window sill, his pistol on the porch outside. There was blood on the stoop of another house.

"There's been a fight," Mike said, "and a bad one. You'd better get set for the worst."

Dru said nothing, but her mouth held firm. At the last building, the mess hall, a man lay dead in a doorway. They rode on, then drew up at the foot of the stone steps and dismounted. Mike shoved his rifle back in the saddle scabbard and loosened his six-guns.

"Let's go!" he said.

The wide veranda was empty and still, but when he stepped into the huge living room, he stopped in amazement, five men sat about a table playing cards.

Ben Curry's head came up and he waved at them.

"Come on in, Mike!" he called. "Who's that with you? Dru, by all that's holy!"

Doc Sawyer, Roundy, Garlin, and Colley were there. Garlin's head was bandaged, and Colley had one foot stretched out stiff and straight, as did Ben Curry. But all were smiling.

Dru ran to her father and fell on her knees beside him.

"Oh, Dad!" she cried. "We were so scared!"

"What happened here?" Mike demanded. "Don't sit there grinning! Did Dave Lenaker come?"

"He sure did, and what do you think?" Doc said. "It was Rigger Molina got him! Rigger got to Weaver and found out Perrin had double-crossed him before he ever pulled the job. He discovered that Perrin had lied about the guards, so he rushed back. When he found out that Ben was crippled, and that Kerb Perrin had run out, he waited for Lenaker himself.

"He was wonderful, Mike," Doc continued. "I never saw anything like it! He paced the veranda out there like a bear in a cage, swearing and waiting for Lenaker. Muttered, 'Leave you in the lurch, will they? I'll show 'em! Lenaker thinks he can gun you down because you're gettin' old, does he? Well, killer I may be, but I can kill him!' And he did, Mike. They shot it out in the street down there. Dave Lenaker, as slim and tall as you, and that great bear of a Molina.

"Lenaker beat him to the draw," Doc went on. "He got two bullets into the Rigger, but Molina wouldn't go down. He stood there spraddle-legged in the street and shot until both guns were empty. Lenaker kept shooting, and must have hit Molina five times, but when he went down, Rigger walked over to him and spat in his face. 'That for double-crossers!' he said. He was magnificent!"

"They fooled me, Mike," Roundy said. "I seen trouble a-comin' an' figured I'd better get to old Ben. I never figured they'd slip in behind you, like they done. Then the news of Lenaker comin' got me. I knowed him an' was afraid of him, so I figured to save Ben Curry I'd get down the road and drygulch him. Never killed a white man in my life, Mike, but I was sure aimin' to! But he got by me on another trail. After Molina killed Lenaker, his boys and some of them from here started after the gold they'd figured was in this house."

"Doc here," Garlin said, "is some fighter! I didn't know he had it in him."

"Roundy, Doc, Garlin, an' me," Colley said, "we sided Ben Curry. It was a swell scrap while it lasted. Garlin got one through his scalp, and I got two bullets in the leg. Aside from that, we came out all right."

Briefly, then, Mike explained all that transpired, how he had killed Perrin, and then had trailed Ducrow to Peach Meadow Canyon and the fight there.

"Where's the gang?" he demanded now. "All gone?"

"All the live ones." Ben Curry nodded grimly. "There's a few won't go anywhere. Funny, the only man who ever fooled me was Rigger Molina. I never knew the man was that loyal, yet he stood by me when I was in no shape to fight Lenaker. Took that fight right off my hands. He soaked up lead like a sponge soaks water!"

Ben Curry looked quickly at Dru. "So you know you're the daughter of an outlaw? Well, I'm sorry, Dru. I never aimed for you to know. I was gettin' shut of this business, and planned to settle down on a ranch with your mother and live out the rest of my days plumb peaceful."

"Why don't you?" Dru demanded.

He looked up at her, his admiring eyes taking in her slim, well-rounded figure. "You reckon she'll have me?" he asked. "She looked a sight like you when she was younger, Dru."

"Of course, she'll have you! She doesn't know—or didn't know until Julie told her. But I think she guessed. I knew. I saw you talking with some men once, and later heard they were outlaws, and then I began hearing about Ben Curry."

Curry looked thoughtfully from Dru to Mike.

"Is there something between you two? Or am I an old fool?"

Mike flushed, and kept his eyes away from Dru.

"He's a fine man, Dru," Doc Sawyer said. "And well educated, if I do say so—who taught him all he knows."

"All he knows!" Roundy stared at Doc with comtempt. "Book learnin'! Where would that gal be but for what I told him? How to read sign, how to foller a trail? Where would she be?"

Mike took Dru out to the veranda then.

"I can read sign, all right," he said, "but I'm no hand at reading the trail to a woman's heart. You would have to help me, Dru."

She laughed softly, and her eyes were bright as she slipped her arm through his. "Why, Mike, you've been blazing a trail over and back and up again, ever since I met you in the street at Weaver!"

Suddenly, she sobered. "Mike, let's get some cattle and go back to Peach Meadow Canyon. You said you could make a better trail in, and it would be a wonderful place! Just you and I and—"

"Sure," he said, "in Peach Meadow Canyon."

Roundy craned his head toward the door, then he chuckled.

"That youngster," he said, "he may not know all the trails, but he sure gets where he's goin', he sure does!"

RIDE, YOU TONTO RAIDERS!

CHAPTER ONE:
The Seventh Man

The rain, which had been falling steadily for three days, had turned the trail into a sloppy river of mud. Peering through the slanting downpour, Mathurin Sabre cursed himself for the quixotic notion that impelled him to take this special trail to the home of the man that he had gunned down.

Nothing good could come of it, he reflected, yet the thought that the young widow and child might need the money he was carrying had started him upon the long ride from El Paso to the Mogollons. Certainly, neither the bartender nor the hangers-on in the saloon could have been entrusted with that money, and nobody was taking that dangerous ride to the Tonto Basin for fun.

Matt Sabre was no trouble hunter. At various times he had been many things, most of them associated with violence. By birth and inclination he was a Western man, although much of his adult life had been lived far from his native country. He had been a buffalo hunter, a prospector, and for a short time, a two-gun marshal of a tough cattle town. It was his stubborn refusal either to back up or back down that kept him in constant hot water.

Yet some of his trouble derived from something more than that. It stemmed from a dark and bitter drive toward violence—a drive that lay deep within him. He was aware of this drive, and held it in restraint, but at times it welled up and he went smashing into trouble—a big, rugged, and dangerous man who fought like a Viking gone berserk, except that he fought coldly and shrewdly.

He was a tall man, heavier than he appeared, and his lean, dark face had a slightly patrician look with high cheekbones and green eyes. His eyes were usually quiet and reserved. He had a natural affinity for horses and weapons. He understood them and they understood him. It had been love of a good horse that brought him to his first act of violence.

He had been buffalo hunting with his uncle, and had interfered with another hunter who was beating his horse. At sixteen a buffalo hunter was a man and expected to stand as one. Matt Sabre stood his ground and shot it out, killing his first man. Had it rested there, all would have been well, but two of the dead man's friends had come hunting Sabre. Failing to find him, they had beaten his ailing uncle and stolen the horses. Matt Sabre trailed them to Mobeetie and killed them both in the street, taking his horses home.

Then he left the country, to prospect in Mexico, fight a revolution in Central America, and join the Foreign Legion in Morocco, from which he deserted after two years. Returning to Texas, he drove a trail herd up to Dodge, then took a job as marshal of a town. Six months later in El Paso he became engaged in an altercation with Billy Curtin, and Curtin called him a liar and went for his gun.

With that incredible speed that was so much a part of him, Matt drew his gun and fired. Curtin hit the floor. An hour later he was summoned to the dying man's hotel room.

Billy Curtin, his dark, tumbled hair against a folded blanket, his face drawn and deathly white, was dying. They told him outside the door that Curtin might live an hour or even two. He could not live longer.

Tall, straight, and quiet, Sabre walked into the room and stood by the dying man's bed. Curtin held a packet wrapped in oilskin. "Five thousand dollars," he whispered. "Take it to my wife—to Jenny, on the Pivotrock, in the Mogollons. She's in—in—trouble."

It was a curious thing, that this dying man should place a trust in the hands of the man who had killed him. Sabre stared down at him, frowning a little.

"Why me?" he asked. "You trust me with this? And why should I do it?"

"You—you're a gentleman. I trust—you help her, will you? I—I was a hot—headed fool. Worried—impatient. It wasn't your fault."

The reckless light was gone from the blue eyes, and the light that remained was fading.

"I'll do it, Curtin. You've my word—you've got the word of Matt Sabre."

For an instant then, the blue eyes blazed wide and sharp with knowledge. "You—Sabre?"

Matt nodded, but the light had faded, and Billy Curtin had bunched his herd.

It had been a rough and bitter trip, but there was little further to go. West of El Paso there had been a brush with marauding Apaches. In Silver City two strangely familiar riders had followed him into a saloon and started a brawl. Yet Matt was too wise in the ways of thieves to be caught by so obvious a trick and he had slipped away in the darkness after shooting out the light.

The roan slipped now on the muddy trail, scrambled up, and moved on through the trees. Suddenly, in the rain-darkened dusk there was one light, then another.

"Yellowjacket," Matt said, with a sigh of relief. "That means a good bed for us, boy. A good bed and a good feed."

Yellowjacket was a jumping-off place. It was a stage station and a saloon, a livery stable and a ramshackle hotel. It was a cluster of 'dobe residences and some false-fronted stores. It bunched its buildings in a corner of Copper Creek.

It was Galusha Reed's town, and Reed owned the Yellowjacket Saloon and the Rincon Mine. Sid Trumbull was town marshal, and he ran the place for Reed. Wherever Reed rode, Tony Sikes was close by, and there were some who said that Reed in turn was owned by Prince McCarran who owned the big PM brand in the Tonto Basin country.

Matt Sabre stabled his horse and turned to the slope-shouldered liveryman. "Give him a bail of corn. Another in the morning."

"Corn?" Simpson shook his head. "We've no corn."

"You have corn for the freighters' stock, and corn for the stage horses. Give my horse corn."

Sabre had a sharp ring of authority in his voice and before he realized it, Simpson was giving the big roan his corn. He thought about it, and stared after Sabre. The tall rider was walking away, a light, long step, easy and free, on the balls of his feet. And he carried two guns, low hung and tied down.

Simpson stared, then shrugged. "A bad one," he muttered. "Wish he'd kill Sid Trumbull!"

Matt Sabre pushed into the door of the Yellowjacket and dropped his saddlebags to the floor. Then he strode to the bar. "What have you got, Man? Anything but rye?"

"What's the matter? Ain't rye good enough for you?" Hobbs was sore himself. No man should work so many hours on feet like his.

"Have you brandy? Or some Irish whiskey?"

Hobbs stared. "Mister, where do you think you are? New York?"

"That's all right, Hobbs. I like a man who knows what he likes. Give him some of my cognac."

Matt Sabre turned and glanced at the speaker. He was a tall man, immaculate in black broadcloth, with blond hair slightly wavy, and a rosy complexion. He might have been thirty or older. He wore a pistol on his left side, high up.

"Thanks," Sabre said briefly. "There's nothing better than cognac on a wet night."

"My name is McCarran. I run the PM outfit, east of here. Northeast, to be exact."

Sabre nodded. "My name is Sabre, I run no outfit, but I'm looking for one. Where's the Pivotrock?"

He was a good poker player, men said. His eyes were fast from using guns, and so he saw the sudden glint and the quick caution in Prince McCarran's eyes.

"The Pivotrock? Why, that's a stream over in the Mogollons. There's an outfit over there, all right? A one-horse affair. Why do you ask?"

Sabre cut him off short. "Business with them."

"I see. Well, you'll find it a lonely ride. There's trouble up that way now, some sort of a cattle war."

Matt Sabre tasted his drink. It was good cognac. In fact, it was the best, and he had found none west of New Orleans.

McCarran, his name was. He knew something, too. Curtin had asked him to help his widow. Was the Pivotrock outfit in the war? He decided against asking McCarran, and they talked quietly of the rain and of cattle, then of cognac. "You never acquired a taste for cognac in the West. May I ask where?"

"Paris," Sabre replied, "Marseilles, Fez, and Marrakesh."

"You've been around then. Well, that's not uncommon." The blond man pointed toward a heavy-shouldered young man who slept with his head on his arms. "See that chap? Calls himself Camp Gordon. He's a Cambridge man, quotes the classics when he's drunk—which is over half the time—and is one of the best cowhands in the country when he's sober.

"Keys over there, playing the piano, studied in Weimar. He knew Strauss, in Vienna, before he wrote The Blue Danube. There's all sorts of men in the West, from belted earls and remittance men to vagabond scum from all corners of the world. They are here a few weeks and they talk the lingo like veterans. Some of the biggest ranches in the West are owned by Englishmen."

Prince McCarran talked to him a few minutes longer, but he learned nothing. Sabre was not evasive, but somehow he gave out no information about himself or his mission. McCarran walked away very thoughtfully. Later, after Matt Sabre was gone, Sid Trumbull came in.

"Sabre?" Trumbull shook his head. "Never heard of him. Keys might know. He knows about ever'body. What's he want on the Pivotrock?"

Lying on his back in bed, Matt Sabre stared up into the darkness and listened to the rain on the window and on the roof. It rattled hard, skeleton fingers against the glass, and he turned restlessly in his bed, frowning as he recalled that quick, guarded expression in the eyes of Prince McCarran.

Who was McCarran, and what did he know? Had Curtin's request that he help his wife been merely the natural request of a dying man, or had he felt that there was a definite need of help? Was something wrong here?

He went to sleep vowing to deliver the money and ride away. Yet even as his eyes closed the last time, he knew he would not do it if there was trouble.

It was still raining, but no longer pouring, when he awakened. He dressed swiftly and checked his guns, his mind taking up his problems where they had been left the previous night.

Camp Gordon, his face puffy from too much drinking and too sound a sleep, staggered down the stairs after him. He grinned woefully at Sabre. "I guess I really hung one on last night," he said. "What I need is to get out of town."

They ate breakfast together, and Gordon's eyes sharpened suddenly at Matt's query of directions to the Pivotrock. "You'll not want to go there, man. Since Curtin ran out they've got their backs to the wall. They are through! Leave it to Galusha Reed for that."

"What's the trouble?"

"Reed claims title to the Pivotrock. Bill Curtin's old man bought it from a Mex who had it from a land grant. Then he made a deal with the Apaches, which seemed to cinch his title. Trouble was, Galusha Reed shows up with a prior claim. He says Fernandez had no grant. That his man Sonoma had a prior one. Old Man Curtin was killed when he fell from his buckboard, and young Billy couldn't stand the gaff. He blew town after Tony Sikes buffaloed him."

"What about his wife?"

Gordon shook his head, then shrugged. Doubt and worry struggled on his face. "She's a fine girl, Jenny Curtin is. The salt of the earth. It's too bad Curtin hadn't a tenth of her nerve. She'll stick, and she swears she'll fight."

"Has she any men?"

"Two. An old man who was with her father-in-law, and a half-breed Apache they call Rado. It used to be Silerado."

Thinking it over, Sabre decided there was much left to be explained. Where had the five thousand dollars come from? Had Billy really run out, or had he gone away to get money to put up a battle? And how did he get it?

"I'm going out," Sabre got to his feet. "I'll have a talk with her."

"Don't take a job there. She hasn't a chance!" Gordon said grimly. "You'd do well to stay away."

"I like fights when one side doesn't have a chance," Matt replied lightly. "Maybe I will ask for a job. A man's got to die sometime, and what better time than fighting when the odds are against him?"

"I like to win," Gordon said flatly. "I like at least a chance."

Matt Sabre leaned over the table, aware that Prince McCarran had moved up behind Gordon, and that a big man with a star was standing near him. "If I decide to go to work for her," Sabre's voice was easy, confident, "then you'd better join us. Our side will win."

"Look here, you!" The man wearing the star, Sid Trumbull, stepped forward. "You either stay in town or get down the trail! There's trouble enough in the Mogollons. Stay out of there."

Matt looked up. "You're telling me?" His voice cracked like a whip. "You're town marshal, Trumbull, not a United States marshal or a sheriff, and if you were a sheriff, it wouldn't matter. It is out of this county. Now suppose you back up and don't step into conversations unless you're invited."

Trumbull's head lowered and his face flushed red. Then he stepped around the table, his eyes narrow and mean. "Listen, you!" His voice was thick with fury. "No two-by-twice cowpoke tells me—!"

"Trumbull," Sabre spoke evenly, "you're asking for it. You aren't acting in line of duty now. You're picking trouble, and the fact that you're marshal won't protect you."

"Protect me?" His fury exploded. "Protect me? Why, you—!"

Trumbull lunged around the table, but Matt sidestepped swiftly and kicked a chair into the marshal's path. Enraged, Sid Trumbull had no chance to avoid it and fell headlong, bloodying his palms on the slivery floor.

Kicking the chair away, he lunged to his feet, and Matt stood facing him, smiling. Camp Gordon was grinning, and Hobbs was leaning his forearms on the bar, watching with relish.

Trumbull stared at his torn palms, then lifted his eyes to Sabre's. Then he started forward, and suddenly, in midstride, his hand swept for his gun.

Sabre palmed his Colt and the gun barked even as it lifted. Stunned, Sid Trumbull stared at his numbed hand. His gun had been knocked spinning, and the .44 slug, hitting the trigger guard, had gone by to rip off the end of Sid's little finger. Dumbly, he stared at the slow drip of blood.

Prince McCarran and Gordon were only two of those who stared, not at the marshal, but at Matt Sabre.

"You throw that gun mighty fast, stranger," McCarran said. "Who are you, anyway? There aren't half a dozen men in the country who can throw a gun that fast. I know most of them by sight."

Sabre's eyes glinted coldly. "No? Well, you know another one now. Call it seven men." He spun on his heel and strode from the room. All eyes followed him.

CHAPTER TWO:
Coyote Trouble

Matt Sabre's roan headed up Shirt Tail Creek, crossed Bloody Basin and Skeleton Ridge and made the Verde in the vicinity of the hot springs. He bedded down that night in a corner of a cliff near Hardscrabble Creek. It was late when he turned in, and he had lighted no fire.

He had chosen his position well, for behind him the cliff towered, and on his left there was a steep hillside that sloped away toward Hardscrabble Creek. He was almost at the foot of Hardscrabble Mesa, with the rising ground of Deadman Mesa before him. The ground in front sloped away to the creek, and there was plenty of dry wood. The overhang of the cliff protected it from the rain.

Matt Sabre came suddenly awake. For an instant, he lay very still. The sky had cleared, and as he lay on his side he could see the stars. He judged that it was past midnight. Why he had awakened he could not guess, but he saw that the roan was nearer, and the big gelding had his head up and ears pricked.

"Careful, boy!" Sabre warned.

Sliding out of his bed roll he drew on his boots and got to his feet. Feeling out in the darkness, he drew his Winchester near.

He was sitting in absolute blackness due to the cliff's overhang. He knew the boulders and the clumps of cedar were added concealment. The roan would be lost against the blackness of the cliff, but from where he sat he could see some thirty yards of the creek bank and some open ground.

There was subdued movement below and whispering voices. Then silence. Leaving his rifle, Sabre belted on his guns and slid quietly out of the overhang and into the cedars.

After a moment, he heard the sound of movement, and then a low voice: "He can't be far! They said he came this way, and he left the main trail after Fossil Creek."

There were two of them. He waited, standing there among the cedars, his eyes hard and his muscles poised and ready. They were fools. Did they think he was that easy?

He had fought Apaches and Kiowas, and he had fought the Tauregs in the Sahara and the Riffs in the Atlas Mountains. He saw them then, saw their dark figures, moving up the hill, outlined against the pale gravel of the slope.

That hard, bitter thing inside him broke loose, and he could not stand still. He could not wait. They would find the roan, and then they would not leave until they had him. It was now or never. He stepped out, quickly, silently.

"Looking for somebody?"

They wheeled, and he saw the starlight on a pistol barrel, and heard the flat, husky cough of his own gun. One went down, coughing and gasping. The other staggered, then turned and started off in a stumbling run, moaning half in fright, half in pain. He stood there, trying to follow the man, but he lost him in the brush.

He turned back to the fellow on the ground, but did not go near him. He circled wide instead, returning to his horse. He quieted his roan, then lay down. In a few minutes he was dozing.

Daybreak found him standing over the body. The roan was already saddled for the trail. It was one of the two he had seen in Silver City, a lean, dark-faced man with deep lines in his cheeks and a few gray hairs at the temples. There was an old scar, deep and red, over his eye.

Sabre knelt and went through his pockets, taking a few letters and some papers. He stuffed them into his own pockets, then mounted. Riding warily, he started up the creek. He rode with his Winchester across his saddle, ready for whatever came. Nothing did.

The morning drew on, the air warm and still after the rain. A fly buzzed around his ears, and he whipped it away with his hat. The roan had a long striding, space-eating walk. It moved out swiftly and surely toward the far purple ranges, dipping down through grassy meadows lined with pines and aspens, with here and there the whispering leaves of a tall cotton wood.

It was a land to dream about, a land perfect for the grazing of either cattle or sheep, a land for a man to live in. Ahead and on his left he could see the towering Mogollon Rim, and it was beyond this Rim, up on the plateau, that he would find the Pivotrock. He skirted a grove of rustling aspen and looked down a long valley.

For the first time he saw cattle—fat, contented cattle, fat from the rich grass of these bottomlands. Once, far off, he glimpsed a rider, but he made no effort to draw near, wanting only to find the trail to the Pivotrock.

A wide-mouthed canyon opened from the northeast and he turned the roan and started up the creek that ran down it. Now he was climbing, and from the look of the country he would climb nearly three thousand feet to reach the Rim. Yet he had been told there was a trail ahead and he pushed on.

The final eight hundred feet to the Rim was by a switchback trail that had him climbing steadily, yet the air on the plateau atop the Rim was amazingly fresh and clear. He pushed on, seeing a few scattered cattle, and then he saw a crude wooden sign by the narrow trail. It read:

PIVOTROCK . . . 1 MILE

The house was low and sprawling, lying on a flat-topped knoll with the long barns and sheds built on three sides of a square. The open side faced the Rim and the trail up which he was riding. There were cottonwoods, pine, and fir backing up the buildings. He could see the late afternoon sunlight glistening on the coats of the saddlestock in the corral.

An old man stepped from the stable with a carbine in his hands. "All right, stranger. You stop where you are. What you want here?"

Matt Sabre grinned. Lifting his hand carefully, he pushed back his flat-brimmed hat. "Huntin' Mrs. Jenny Curtin," he said. "I've got news." He hesitated. "Of her husband."

The carbine muzzle lowered. "Of him? What news would there be of him?"

"Not good news," Sabre told him. "He's dead."

Surprisingly, the old man seemed relieved. "Right," he said briefly. "I reckon we figured he was dead. How'd it happen?"

Sabre hesitated. "He picked a fight in a saloon in El Paso, then drew too slow."

"He was never fast." The old man studied him. "My name's Tom Judson. Now, you sure didn't come all the way here from El Paso to tell us Billy was dead. What did you come for?"

"I'll tell Mrs. Curtin that. However, they tell me down the road you've been with her a long time, so you might as well know. I brought her some money. Bill Curtin gave it to me on his death bed, asked me to bring it to her. It's five thousand dollars."

"Five thousand?" Judson stared. "Reckon Bill must have set some store by you to trust you with it. Know him long?"

Sabre shook his head. "Only a few minutes. A dying man hasn't much choice."

A door slammed up at the house, and they both turned. A slender girl was walking toward them, and the sunlight caught the red in her hair. She wore a simple cotton dress, but her figure was trim and neat. Ahead of her dashed a boy who might have been five or six. He lunged at Sabre, then slid to a stop and stared up at him, then at his guns.

"Howdy, Old Timer!" Sabre said, smiling. "Where's your spurs?"

The boy was startled and shy. He drew back, surprised at the question. "I—I've got no spurs!"

"What? A cowhand without spurs? We'll have to fix that." He looked up. "How are you, Mrs. Curtin? I'm Mathurin Sabre, Matt for short. I'm afraid I've some bad news for you."

Her face paled a little, but her chin lifted. "Will you come to the house, Mr. Sabre? Tom, put his horse in the corral, will you?"

The living room of the ranch house was spacious and cool. There were Navajo rugs upon the floor, and the chairs and the divan were beautifully tanned cowhide. He glanced around appreciatively, enjoying the coolness after his hot ride in the Arizona sun, liking the naturalness of this girl, standing in the home she had created.

She faced him abruptly. "Perhaps you'd better tell me now, there's no use pretending or putting a bold face on it when I have to be told."

As quickly and quietly as possible, he explained. When he was finished her face was white and still. "I—I was afraid of this. When he rode away I knew he would never come back. You see, he thought—he believed he had failed me, failed his father."

Matt drew the oilskin packet from his pocket. "He sent you this. He said it was five thousand dollars. He said to give it to you."

She took it, staring at the package, and tears welled into her eyes. "Yes." Her voice was so low that Matt scarcely heard it. "He would do this. He probably felt it was all he could do for me, for us. You see," Jenny Curtin's eyes lifted, "we're in a fight, and a bad one. This is war money.

"I—guess Billy thought—well, he was no fighter himself, and this might help, might compensate. You're probably wondering about all this."

"No," he said. "I'm not. And maybe I'd better go out with the boys now. You'll want to be alone."

"Wait!" Her fingers caught his sleeve. "I want you to know, since you were with him when he died, and you have come all this way to help us. There was no trouble with Billy and me. It was—well, he thought he was a coward. He thought he had failed me.

"We've had trouble with Galusha Reed in Yellowjacket. Tony Sikes picked a fight with Billy. He wanted to kill him, and Billy wouldn't fight. He—he backed down. Everybody said he was a coward, and he ran. He went—away."

Matt Sabre frowned thoughtfully, staring at the floor. The boy who picked a fight with him, who dared him, who went for his gun, was no coward. Trying to prove something to himself? Maybe. But no coward.

"Ma'am," he said abruptly, "you're his widow. The mother of his child. There's something you should know. Whatever else he was, I don't know. I never knew him long enough. But that man was no coward. Not even a little bit!

"You see," Matt hesitated, feeling the falseness of his position, not wanting to tell this girl that he had killed her husband, yet not wanting her to think him a coward; "I saw his eyes when he went for his gun. I was there, Ma'am, and saw it all. Bill Curtin was no coward."

Hours later, lying in his bunk, he thought of it, and the five thousand was still a mystery. Where had it come from? How had Curtin come by it?

He turned over and after a few minutes, went to sleep. Tomorrow he would be riding.

The sunlight was bright the next morning when he finally rolled out of bed. He bathed and shaved, taking his time, enjoying the sun on his back, and feeling glad he was footloose again. He was in the bunkhouse belting on his guns when he heard the horses. He stepped to the door and glanced out.

Neither the dark-faced Rado nor Judson were about, and there were three riders in the yard. One of them he recognized as a man from Yellowjacket, and the tallest of the riders was Galusha Reed. He was a big man, broad and thick in the body without being fat. His jaw was brutal.

Jenny Curtin came out on the steps. "Ma'am," Reed said abruptly, "we're movin' you off this land. We're goin' to give you ten minutes to pack, an' one of my boys'll hitch the buckboard for you. This here trouble's gone on long enough, an' mine's the prior claim to this land. You're gettin' off!"

Jenny's eyes turned quickly toward the stable, but Reed shook his head. "You needn't look for Judson or the breed. We watched until we seen them away from here, an' some of my boys are coverin' the trail. We're try in' to get you off here without any trouble."

"You can turn around and leave, Mr. Reed. I'm not going!"

"I reckon you are," Reed said patiently. "We know that your man's dead. We just can't put up with you squattin' on our range."

"This happens to be my range, and I'm staying."

Reed chuckled. "Don't make us put you off, Ma'am. Don't make us get rough. Up here," he waved a casual hand, "we can do anything we want, and nobody the wiser. You're leavin', as of now."

Matt Sabre stepped out of the bunkhouse and took three quick steps toward the riders. He was cool and sure of himself, but he could feel the jumping invitation to trouble surging up inside him. He fought it down, and held himself still for an instant. Then he spoke.

"Reed, you're a fat-headed fool and a bully. You ride up here to take advantage of a woman because you think she's helpless. Well, she's not. Now you three turn your horses—turn 'em mighty careful—and start down the trail. And don't you ever set foot on this place again!"

Reed's face went white, then dark with anger. He leaned forward a little. "So you're still here? Well, we'll give you a chance to run. Get goin'!"

Matt Sabre walked forward another step. He could feel the eagerness pushing up inside him, and his eyes held the three men, and he saw the eyes of one widen with apprehension.

"Watch it, Boss! Watch it!"

"That's right, Reed. Watch it. You figured to find this girl alone. Well, she's not alone. Furthermore, if she'll take me on as a hand, I'll stay. I'll stay until you're out of the country or dead. You can have it either way you want.

"There's three of you. I like that. That evens us up. If you want to feed buzzards, just edge that hand another half inch toward your gun and you can. That goes for the three of you."

He stepped forward again. He was jumping with it now—that old drive for combat welling up within him. Inside he was trembling, but his muscles were steady and his mind was cool and ready. His fingers spread and he moved forward again.

"Come on, you mangy coyotes! Let's see if you've got the nerve. Reach!"

Reed's face was still and cold. His mouth looked pinched, and his eyes were wide. Some sixth sense warned him that this was different. This was death he was looking at, and Galusha Reed suddenly realized he was no gambler when the stakes were so high.

He could see the dark eagerness that was driving this cool man; he could see beyond the coolness on his surface the fierceness of his readiness; inside he went sick and cold at the thought.

"Boss!" the man at his side whispered hoarsely, "let's get out of here. This man's poison!"

Galusha Reed slowly eased his hand forward to the pommel of the saddle. "So, Jenny, you're hiring gunfighters? Is that the way you want it?"

"I think you hired them first," she replied coolly. "Now you'd better go."

"On the way back," Sabre suggested, "you might stop in Hardscrabble Canyon and pick up the body of one of your killers. He guessed wrong last night."

Reed stared at him. "I don't know what you mean," he flared. "I sent out no killer."

Matt Sabre watched the three men ride down the trail and he frowned. There had been honest doubt in Reed's eyes, but if he had not sent the two men after him, who had? Those men had been in Silver City and El Paso, yet they also knew this country, and knew someone in Yellowjacket. Maybe they had not come after him, but had first followed Bill Curtin.

He turned and smiled at the girl. "Coyotes," he said, shrugging. "Not much heart in them."

She was staring at him strangely. "You—you'd have killed them, wouldn't you? Why?"

He shrugged. "I don't know. Maybe it's because—well, I don't like to see men take advantage of a woman alone. Anyway," he smiled, "Reed doesn't impress me as a good citizen."

"He's a dangerous enemy." She came down from the steps. "Did you mean what you said, Mr. Sabre? I mean about staying here and working for me? I need men, although I must tell you that you've small chance of winning, and it's rather a lonely fight."

"Yes, I meant it." Did he mean it? Of course. He remembered the old Chinese proverb: if you save a person's life he becomes your responsibility. That wasn't the case here, but he had killed this girl's husband, and the least he could do would be to stay until she was out of trouble.

Was that all he was thinking of? "I'll stay," he said. "I'll see you through this. I've been fighting all my life and it would be a shame to stop now. And I've fought for lots less reasons."

CHAPTER THREE:
Hot Night in Yellowjacket

Throughout the morning he worked around the place. He worked partly because there was much to be done and partly because he wanted to think.

The horses in the remuda were held on the home place, and were in good shape. Also, they were better than the usual ranch horses, for some of them showed a strong Morgan strain. He repaired the latch on the stable door, and walked around the place, sizing it up from every angle, studying all the approaches.

With his glasses he studied the hills and searched the notches and canyons wherever he could see them. Mentally, he formed a map of all that terrain within reach of his glass.

It was mid-afternoon before Judson and Rado returned, and they had talked with Jenny before he saw them.

"Howdy," Judson was friendly, but his eyes studied Sabre with care. "Miss Jenny tells me you ran Reed off. That you're aimin' to stay on here."

"That's right. I'll stay until she's out of trouble, if she'll have me. I don't like being pushed around."

"No, neither do I." Judson was silent for several minutes, and then he turned his eyes on Sabre. "Don't you be gettin' any ideas about Miss Jenny. She's a fine girl."

Matt looked up angrily. "And don't you be getting any ideas," he said coldly. "I'm helping her, the same as you are, and we'll work together. As to personal things, leave them alone. I'll only say that when this fight is over, I'm hitting the trail."

"All right," Judson said mildly. "We can use help."

Three days passed smoothly. Matt threw himself into the work of the ranch, and he worked feverishly. Even he could not have said why he worked so desperately hard. He dug postholes and fenced an area in the long meadow near the seeping springs in the bottom.

Then, working with Rado, he rounded up the cattle nearest the Rim and pushed them back behind the fence. The grass was thick and deep there and would stand a lot of grazing, for the meadow wound back up the canyon for some distance. He carried a running iron and branded stock wherever he found it required.

As the ranch had been short-handed for a year, there was much to do. Evenings, he mended gear and worked around the place, and at night he slept soundly. During all this time he saw nothing of Jenny Curtin.

He saw nothing of her, but she was constantly in his thoughts. He remembered her as he had seen her that first night, standing in the living room of the house, listening to him, her eyes, wide and dark, upon his face. He remembered her facing Galusha Reed and his riders from the steps.

Was he staying on because he believed he owed her a debt, or because of her?

Here and there around the ranch, Sabre found small, intangible hints of the sort of man Curtin must have been. Judson had liked him, and so had the halfbreed. He had been gentle with horses. He had been thoughtful. Yet he had hated and avoided violence. Slowly, rightly or wrongly Matt could not tell, a picture was forming in his mind of a fine young man who had been totally out of place.

Western birth, but born for peaceful and quiet ways, he had been thrown into a cattle war and had been aware of his own inadequacy. Matt was thinking of that, and working at a rawhide riata, when Jenny came up.

He had not seen her approach or he might have avoided her, but she was there beside him before he realized it.

"You're working hard, Mr. Sabre."

"To earn my keep, Ma'am. There's a lot to do, I find, and I like to keep busy." He turned the riata and studied it.

"You know, there's something I've been wanting to talk to you about. Maybe it's none of my affair, but young Billy is going to grow up, and he's going to ask questions about his Dad. You aren't going to be able to fool him. Maybe you know what this is all about and maybe I'm mounting on the off-side, but it seems to me that Bill Curtin went to El Paso to get that money for you.

"I think he realized he was no fighting man, and that the best thing he could do was to get that money so he could hire gun-fighters. It took nerve to do what he did, and I think he deliberately took what Sikes handed him because he knew that if Sikes killed him you'd never get that money.

"Maybe along the way to El Paso he began to wonder, and maybe he picked that fight down there with the idea of proving to himself that he did have the nerve to face a gun."

She did not reply, but stood there, watching his fingers work swiftly and evenly, plaiting the leather.

"Yes," she said finally, "I thought of that. Only I can't imagine where he got the money. I hesitate to use it without knowing."

"Don't be foolish," he said irritably. "Use it. Nobody would put it to better use, and you need gun-hands."

"But who would work for me?" Her voice was low and bitter. "Galusha Reed has seen to it that no one will."

"Maybe if I rode in I could find some men." He was thinking of Camp Gordon, the Shakespeare-quoting English cowhand. "I believe I know one man."

"There's a lot to be done. Jud tells me you've been doing the work of three men."

Matt Sabre got to his feet. She stepped back a little, suddenly aware of how tall he was. She was tall for a girl, yet she came no farther than his lips. She drew back a little at the thought. Her eyes dropped to his guns. He always wore them, always low and tied down.

"Judson said you were a fast man with a gun. He said you had the mark of the—of the gunfighter."

"Probably." He found no bitterness at the thought. "I've used guns. Guns and horses, they are about all I've known."

"Where were you in the Army? I've watched you walk and ride and you show military training."

"Oh, several places. Africa mostly."

"Africa?" She was amazed. "You've been there?"

He nodded. "Desert and mountain country. Morocco and the Sahara, all the way to Timbuktu and Lake Chad, fighting most of the time." It was growing dark in the shed where they were standing. He moved out into the dusk. A few stars had already appeared, and the red glow that was in the west beyond the Rim was fading.

"Tomorrow I'll ride in and have a look around. You'd better keep the other men close by."

Dawn found him well along on the trail to Yellowjacket. It was a long ride, and he skirted the trail most of the time, having no trust in well-traveled ways at such a time. The air was warm and bright, and he noticed a few head of Pivotrock steers that had been overlooked in the rounding up of cattle along the Rim.

He rode ready for trouble, his Winchester across his saddle bows, his senses alert. Keeping the roan well back under the trees, he had the benefit of the evergreen needles that formed a thick carpet and muffled the sound of his horse's hoofs.

Yet as he rode, he considered the problem of the land grant. If Jenny were to retain her land and be free of trouble, he must look into the background of the grant, and see which had the prior and best claim, Fernandez or Sonoma.

Next, he must find out, if possible, where Bill Curtin had obtained that five thousand dollars. Some might think that the fact he had it was enough, and that now his wife had it, but it was not enough if Bill had sold any rights to water or land on the ranch, or if he had obtained the money in some way that would reflect upon Jenny or her son.

When those things were done he could ride on about his business, for by that time he would have worked out the problem of Galusha Reed.

In the few days he had been on the Pivotrock he had come to love the place, and while he had avoided Jenny, he had not avoided young Billy. The youngster had adopted him, and had stayed with him hour after hour.

To keep him occupied, Matt had begun teaching him how to plait rawhide, and so as he mended riatas and repaired bridles, the youngster had sat beside him, working his fingers clumsily through the intricacies of the plaiting.

It was with unease that he recalled his few minutes alone with Jenny. He shifted his seat in the saddle and scowled. It would not do for him to think of her as anything but Curtin's widow. The widow, he reflected bitterly, of the man he had killed.

What would he say when she learned of that? He avoided the thought, yet it remained in the back of his mind, and he shook his head, wanting to forget it. Sooner or later she would know. If he did not finally tell her himself, then he was sure that Reed would let her know.

Avoiding the route by way of Hardscrabble, Matt Sabre turned due south, crossing the eastern end of the mesa and following an old trail across Whiterock and Polles Mesa, crossing the East Verde at Rock Creek. Then he cut through Boardinghouse Canyon to Bullspring, crossing the main stream of the Verde near Tangle Peak. It was a longer way around by a few miles, but Sabre rode with care, watching the country as he travelled. It was very late when he walked his roan into the parched street of Yellowjacket.

He had a hunch and he meant to follow it through. During his nights in the bunkhouse he had talked much with Judson, and from him heard of Pepito Fernandez, a grandson of the man who sold the land to Old Man Curtin.

Swinging down from his horse at the livery stable, he led him inside. Simpson walked over to meet him, his eyes searching Sabre's face. "Man, you've a nerve with you. Reed's wild. He came back to town blazing mad, and Trumbull's telling everybody what you can expect."

Matt smiled at the man. "I expected that. Where do you stand?"

"Well," Simpson said grimly, "I've no liking for Trumbull. He carries himself mighty big around town, and he's not been friendly to me and mine. I reckon, Mister, I've rare been so pleased as when you made a fool of him in yonder. It was better than the killing of him, although he's that coming, sure enough."

"Then take care of my horse, will you? And a slip knot to tie him with."

"Sure, and he'll get corn, too. I reckon any horse you ride would need corn."

Matt Sabre walked out on the street. He was wearing dark jeans and a gray wool shirt. His black hat was pulled low, and he merged well with the shadows. He'd see Pepito first, and then look around a bit. He wanted Camp Gordon.

Thinking of that, he turned back into the stable. "Saddle Gordon's horse, too. He'll be going back with me."

"Him?" Simpson stared. "Man, he's dead drunk and has been for days!"

"Saddle his horse. He'll be with me when I'm back, and if you know another one or two, good hands who would use a gun if need be, let them know I'm hiring and there's money to pay them. Fighting wages if they want . . ."

In the back office of the Yellowjacket, three men sat over Galusha Reed's desk. There was Reed himself, Sid Trumbull, and Prince McCarran.

"Do you think Tony can take him?" Reed asked. "You've seen the man draw, Prince."

"He'll take him. But it will be close—too close. I think what we'd better do is have Sid posted somewhere close by."

"Leave me out of it." Sid looked up from under his thick eyebrows. "I want no more of the man. Let Tony have him."

"You won't be in sight," McCarran said dryly, "or in danger. You'll be upstairs over the hotel, with a Winchester."

Trumbull looked up and touched his thick lips with his tongue. Killing was not new to him, yet the way this man accepted it always appalled him a little.

"All right," he agreed, "like I say, I've no love for him."

"We'll have him so you'll get a flanking shot. Make it count and make it the first time. But wait until the shooting starts."

The door opened softly and Sikes stepped in. He was a lithe, dark-skinned man who moved like an animal. He had graceful hands, restless hands. He wore a white buckskin vest worked with red quills and beads. "Boss, he's in town. Sabre's here." He had heard them.

Reed let his chair legs down, leaning forward. "Here? In town?"

"That's right. I just saw him outside the Yellowjacket." Sikes started to build a cigarette. "He's got nerve. Plenty of it."

The door sounded with a light tap, and at a word, Keys entered. He was a slight man with gray hair and a quiet, scholar's face.

"I remember him now, Prince," he said. "Matt Sabre. I'd been trying to place the name. He was marshal of Mobeetie for awhile. He's killed eight or nine men."

"That's right!" Trumbull looked up sharply. "Mobeetie! Why didn't I remember that? They say Wes Hardin rode out of town once when Sabre sent him word he wasn't wanted."

Sikes turned his eyes on McCarran. "You want him now?"

McCarran hesitated, studying the polished toe of his boot. Sabre's handling of Trumbull had made friends in town, and also his championing of the cause of Jenny Curtin. Whatever happened must be seemingly above board and in the clear, and he wanted to be where he could be seen at the time, and Reed also.

"No, not now. We'll wait." He smiled. "One thing about a man of his courage and background, if you send for him, he'll always come to you."

"But how will he come?" Keys asked softly. "That's the question."

McCarran looked around irritably. He had forgotten Keys was in the room and had said far more than he had intended. "Thanks, Keys. That will be all. And remember—nothing will be said about anything you've heard here."

"Certainly not," Keys smiled and walked to the door and out of the room.

Reed stared after him. "I don't like that fellow, Prince. I wouldn't trust him."

"Him? He's interested in nothing but that piano and enough liquor to keep himself mildly embalmed. Don't worry about him."

CHAPTER FOUR:
Fugitive

Matt Sabre turned away from the Yellowjacket after a brief survey of the saloon. Obviously, something was doing elsewhere for none of the men were present in the big room. He hesitated, considering the significance of that, and then turned down a dark alleyway and walked briskly along until he came to an old rail fence.

Following this past rustling cottonwoods and down a rutted road, he turned past a barn and cut across another road toward a 'dobe where the windows glowed with a faint light.

The door opened to his knock and a dark, Indianlike face showed briefly. In rapid Spanish, he asked for Pepito. After a moment's hesitation, the door widened and he was invited inside.

The room was large, and at one side a small fire burned in the blackened fireplace. An oilcloth-covered table with a coal oil light stood in the middle of the room, and on a bed at one side a man snored peacefully.

A couple of dark-eyed children ceased their playing to look up at him. The woman called out and a blanket pushed aside and a slender, dark-faced youth entered the room, pulling his belt tight.

"Pepito Fernandez? I am Matt Sabre."

"I have heard of you, señor."

Briefly, he explained why he had come, and Pepito listened, then shook his head. "I do not know, señor. The grant was long ago, and we are no longer rich. My father," he shrugged, "he liked the spending of money when he was young."

He hesitated, considering that. Then he said carelessly, "I, too, like the spending of money. What else is it for? But no, señor, I do not think there are papers. My father, he told me much of the grant, and I am sure the Sonomas had no strong claim."

"If you remember anything, will you let us know?" Sabre asked. Then a thought occured to him. "You're a vaquero? Do you want a job?"

"A job?" Pepito studied him thoughtfully. "At the Señora Curtin's ranch?"

"Yes. As you know, there may be much trouble. I am working there, and tonight I shall take one other man back with me. If you would like the job, it is yours."

Pepito shrugged. "Why not? Señor Curtin, the old one, he gave me my first horse. He gave me a rifle, too. He was a good one, and the son also."

"Better meet me outside of town where the trail goes between the Buttes. You know the place?"

"Si, señor. I will be there."

Keys was idly playing the piano when Matt Sabre opened the door and stepped into the room. His quick eyes placed Keys, Hobbs at the bar, Camp Gordon fast asleep with his head on a table, and a half dozen other men. Yet as he walked to the bar, a rear door opened and Tony Sikes stepped into the room.

Sabre had never before seen the man, yet he knew him from Judson's apt and careful description. Sikes was not as tall as Sabre, yet more slender. He had the wiry, stringy build that is made for speed, and quick, smooth-flowing fingers. His muscles were relaxed and easy, but knowing such men, Matt recognized danger when he saw it. Sikes had seen him at once, and he moved to the bar nearby.

All eyes were on the two of them, for the story of Matt's whipping of Trumbull and his defiance of Reed had swept the country. Yet Sikes merely smiled and Matt glanced at him. "Have a drink?"

Tony Sikes nodded. "I don't mind if I do." Then he added, his voice low, and his dark, yellowish eyes on Matt's with a faintly sardonic, faintly amused look, "I never mind drinking with a man I'm going to kill."

Sabre shrugged. "Neither do I." He found himself liking Sikes' direct approach. "Although perhaps I have the advantage. I choose my own time to drink and to kill. You wait for orders."

Tony Sikes felt in his vest pocket for cigarette papers and began to roll a smoke. "You will wait for me, compadre. I know you're the type."

They drank, and as they drank, the door opened and Galusha Reed stepped out. His face darkened angrily when he saw the two standing at the bar together, but he was passing without speaking when a thought struck him. He stopped and turned.

"I wonder," he said loudly enough for all in the room to hear, "what Jenny Curtin will say when she finds out her new hand is the man who killed her husband?"

Every head came up, and Sabre's face whitened. Where the faces had been friendly or noncomittal, now they were sharp-eyed and attentive. Moreover, he knew that Jenny was well liked, as Curtin had been. Now, they would be his enemies.

"I wonder just why you came here, Sabre? After killing the girl's husband, why would you come to her ranch? Was it to profit from your murder? To steal what little she has left? Or is it for the girl herself?"

Matt struggled to keep his temper. After a minute he said casually, "Reed, it was you ordered her off her ranch today. I'm here for one reason, and one alone. To see that she keeps her ranch and that no yellow-bellied thievin' lot of coyotes ride over and take it away from her!"

Reed stood flat-footed, facing Sabre. He was furious, and Matt could feel the force of his rage. It was almost a physical thing pushing against him. Close beside him was Sikes. If Reed chose to go for a gun, Sikes could grab Matt's left arm and jerk him off-balance. Yet Matt was ready even for that, and again that black force was rising within him, that driving urge toward violence.

He spoke again and his voice was soft and almost purring. "Make up your mind, Reed. If you want to die, you can right here. You make another remark to me and I'll drive every word of it back down that fat throat of yours! Reach and I'll kill you. If Sikes wants in on this, he's welcome!"

Tony Sikes spoke softly, too. "I'm out of it, Sabre. I only fight my own battles. When I come after you, I'll be alone."

Galusha Reed hesitated. For an instant, counting on Sikes, he had been tempted. Now he hesitated, then turned abruptly and left the room.

Ignoring Sikes, Sabre downed his drink and crossed to Camp Gordon. He shook him. "Come on, Camp, I'm puttin' you to bed."

Gordon did not move. Sabre stooped and slipped an arm around the big Englishman's shoulders and, hoisting him to his feet, started for the door. At the door, he turned. "I'll be seeing you, Sikes!"

Tony lifted his glass, his hat pushed back, "Sure," he said. "And I'll be alone."

It was not until after he had said it that he remembered Sid Trumbull and the plans made in the back room. His face darkened a little and his liquor suddenly tasted bad. He put his glass down carefully on the bar and turned, walking through the back door.

Prince McCarran was alone, idly riffling the cards and smoking. "I won't do it, Prince," Sikes said. "You've got to leave that killing to me and me alone."

Matt Sabre, with Camp Gordon lashed to the saddle of a led horse, met Pepito in the darkness of the space between the Buttes. Pepito spoke softly, and Sabre called back to him. As the Mexican rode out he glanced once at Gordon, and then the three rode on together. It was late the following morning when they reached the Pivotrock. All was quiet—too quiet.

Camp Gordon was sober and swearing, "Shanghaied!" His voice exploded with violence. "You've a nerve, Sabre. Turn me loose so I can start back. I'm having no part of this."

Gordon was tied to his horse so he would not fall off, but Matt only grinned. "Sure, I'll turn you loose. But you said you ought to get out of town awhile, and this was the best way. I've brought you here," he said gravely, but his eyes were twinkling, "for your own good. It's time you had some fresh, mountain air, some cold milk, some—"

"Milk?" Gordon exploded. "Milk, you say? I'll not touch the stuff! Turn me loose and give me a gun and I'll have your hide!"

"And leave this ranch for Reed to take? Reed and McCarran?"

Gordon stared at him from bloodshot eyes, eyes that were suddenly attentive. "Did you say McCarran? What's he got to do with this?"

"I wish I knew. But I've a hunch he's in up to his ears. I think he has strings on Reed."

Gordon considered that. "He may have." He watched Sabre undoing the knots. "It's a point I hadn't considered. But why?"

"You've known him longer than I have. Somebody had two men follow Curtin out of the country to kill him, and I don't believe Reed did it. Does that make sense?"

"No." Gordon swung stiffly to the ground. He swayed a bit, clinging to the stirrup leather. He glanced sheepishly at Matt.

"I guess I'm a mess." A surprised look crossed his face. "Say, I'm hungry! I haven't been hungry in weeks."

With four hands besides himself, work went on swiftly. Yet Matt Sabre's mind would not rest. The five thousand dollars was a problem, and also there was the grant. Night after night he led Pepito to talk of the memories of his father and grandfather, and little by little, he began to know the men. An idea was shaping in his mind, but as yet there was little on which to build.

In all this time there was no sign of Reed. On two occasions riders had been seen, apparently scouting. Cattle had been swept from the Rim edge and pushed back, accounting for all or nearly all the strays he had seen on his ride to Yellowjacket.

Matt was restless, sure that when trouble came it would come with a rush. It was like Reed to do things that way. By now he was certainly aware that Camp Gordon and Pepito Fernandez had been added to the roster of hands at Pivotrock.

"Spotted a few head over near Baker Butte," Camp said one morning. "How'd it be if I drifted that way and looked them over?"

"We'll go together," Matt replied. "I've been wanting to look around there, and there's been no chance."

The morning was bright and they rode swiftly, putting miles behind them, alert to all the sights and sounds of the high country above the Rim. Careful as they were, they were no more than a hundred yards from the riders when they saw them. There were five men, and in the lead rode Sid Trumbull and a white-mustached stranger.

There was no possibility of escaping unnoticed. They pushed on toward the advancing riders who drew up and waited. Sid Trumbull's face was sharp with triumph when he saw Sabre.

"Here's your man, Marshal!" he said, with satisfaction. "The one with the black hat is Sabre."

"What's this all about?" Matt asked quietly. He had already noticed the badge the man wore. But he noticed something else. The man looked to be a competent, upstanding officer.

"You're wanted in El Paso. I'm Rafe Collins, Deputy United States Marshal. We're making an inquiry into the killing of Bill Curtin."

Camp's lips tightened and he looked sharply at Sabre. When Reed had brought out this fact in the saloon, Gordon had been dead drunk.

"That was a fair shooting, Marshal. Curtin picked the fight and drew on me."

"You expect us to believe that?" Trumbull was contemptuous. "Why, he hadn't the courage of a mouse! He backed down from Sikes only a few days before. He wouldn't draw on any man with two hands!"

"He drew on me." Matt Sabre realized he was fighting two battles here—one to keep from being arrested, the other to keep Gordon's respect and assistance. "My idea is that he only backed out of a fight with Sikes because he had a job to do, and knew Sikes would kill him."

"That's a likely yarn!" Trumbull nodded to him. "There's your man. It's your job, Marshal."

Collins was obviously irritated. That he entertained no great liking for Trumbull was obvious. Yet he had his duty to do. Before he could speak, Sabre spoke again.

"Marshal, I've reason to believe that some influence has been brought to bear to discredit me and to get me out of the country for awhile. Can't I give you my word that I'll report to El Paso when things are straightened out? My word is good, and that there are many in El Paso who know that."

"Sorry." Collins was regretful. "I've my duty and my orders."

"I understand that," Sabre replied. "I also have my duty. It is to see that Jenny Curtin is protected from those who are trying to force her off her range. I intend to do exactly that."

"Your duty?" Collins eyed him coldly but curiously. "After killing her husband?"

"That's reason enough, sir!" Sabre replied flatly. "The fight was not my choice. Curtin pushed it, and he was excited, worried, and overwrought. Yet he asked me on his death bed to deliver a package to his wife and to see that she was protected. That duty, sir," his eyes met those of Collins, "comes first."

"I'd like to respect that," Collins admitted. "You seem like a gentleman, sir, and it's a quality that's too rare. Unfortunately, I have my orders. However, it should not take long to straighten this out if it was a fair shooting."

"All these rats need," Sabre replied, "is a few days!" He knew there was no use arguing. His horse was fast, and dense pines bordered the road. He needed a minute, and that badly.

As if divining his thought, Camp Gordon suddenly pushed his gray between Matt and the marshal, and almost at once, Matt lashed out with his toe and booted Trumbull's horse in the ribs. The bronc went to bucking furiously. Whipping his horse around, Matt slapped the spurs to his ribs and in two startled jumps he was off and deep into the pines running like a startled deer.

Behind him a shot rang out, and then another. Both cut the brush over his head, but the horse was running now, and he was mounted well. He had started into the trees at right angles, but swung his horse immediately and headed back toward the Pivotrock. Corduroy Wash opened off to his left and he turned the black and pushed rapidly into the mouth of the wash.

Following it for almost a mile, he came out and paused briefly in the clump of trees that crowned a small ridge. He stared back.

A string of riders stretched out on his back trail, but they were scattered out, hunting for tracks. A lone horseman sat not far from them, obviously watching. Matt grinned, that would be Gordon, and he was all right.

Turning his horse, Matt followed a shelf of rock until it ran out, rode off it into thick sand, and then into the pines with their soft bed of needles that left almost no tracks.

Cinch Hook Butte was off to his left, and nearer, on his right, Twenty-Nine Mile Butte. Keeping his horse headed between them, but bearing steadily northwest, he headed for the broken country around Horsetank Wash. Descending into the canyon he rode northwest, then circled back south and entered the even deeper Calfpen Canyon.

Here, in a nest of boulders, he staked out his horse on a patch of grass. Rifle across his knees, he rested. After an hour, he worked his way to the ledge at the top of the canyon, but nowhere could he see any sign of pursuit. Nor could he hear the sound of hoofs.

There was water in the bottom of Calfpen, not far from where he had left his horse. Food was something else again. He shucked a handful of chia seeds and ate a handful of them, along with the nuts of a piñon.

Obviously, the attempted arrest had been brought about by either the influence of Galusha Reed or Prince McCarran. In either case he was now a fugitive. If they went on to the ranch, Rafe Collins would have a chance to talk to Jenny Curtin. Matt felt sick when he thought of the marshal telling her that it was he who had killed her husband. That she must find out sooner or later, he knew, but he wanted to tell her himself, in his own good time.

CHAPTER FIVE:
Bushwhack Bait

When dusk had fallen he mounted the black and worked his way down Calfpen toward Fossil Springs. As he rode, he was considering his best course. Whether taken by Collins or not, he was not now at the ranch and they might choose this time to strike. With some reason they might believe he had left the country. Indeed, there was every chance that Reed actually believed he had come here with some plan of his own to get the Curtin ranch.

Finally, he bedded down for the night in a draw above Fossil Springs and slept soundly until daylight brought a sun that crept over the rocks and shone upon his eyes. He was up, made a light breakfast of coffee and jerked beef, and then saddled up.

Wherever he went now he could expect hostility. Doubt or downright suspicion would have developed as a result of Reed's accusation in Yellowjacket, and the country would know the United States Marshal was looking for him.

Debating his best course, Matt Sabre headed west through the mountains. By nightfall the following day, he was camped in the ominous shadow of Turret Butte where only a few years before Major Randall had ascended the peak in darkness to surprise a camp of Apaches.

Awakening at the break of dawn Matt scouted the vicinity of Yellowjacket with care.

There was some movement in town—more than usual at that hour. He observed a long line of saddled horses at the hitch rails. He puzzled over this, studying it narrow-eyed from the crest of a ridge through his glasses. Marshal Collins could not yet have returned, hence this must be some other movement. That it was organized was obvious.

He was still watching when a man wearing a faded red shirt left the back door of a building near the saloon, went to a horse carefully hidden in the rear, and mounted. At this distance there was no way of seeing who he was. The man rode strangely. Studying him through the glasses—a relic of Sabre's military years—Matt suddenly realized why the rider seemed strange. He was riding Eastern fashion!

This was no Westerner, slouched and lazy in the saddle, nor yet sitting upright as a cavalryman might. This man rode forward on his horse, a poor practice for the hard miles of desert or mountain riding. Yet it was his surreptitious manner rather than his riding style that intrigued Matt. It required but a few minutes for Matt to see that the route the rider was taking away from town would bring him by near the base of the promontory where he watched.

Reluctant as he was to give over watching the saddled horses, Sabre was sure this strange rider held some clue to his problems. Sliding back on his belly well into the brush, Matt got to his feet and descended the steep trail and took up his place among the boulders beside the trail.

It was very hot here out of the breeze, yet he had waited only a minute until he heard the sound of the approaching horse. He cleared his gun from its holster and moved to the very edge of the road. Then the rider appeared. It was Keys.

Matt's gun stopped him. "Where you ridin', Keys?" Matt asked quietly. "What's this all about?"

"I'm riding to intercept the marshal," Keys said sincerely. "McCarran and Reed plan to send out a posse of their own men to hunt you, then under cover of capturing you, they intend to take the Pivotrock and hold it."

Sabre nodded. That would be it, of course, and he should have guessed it before. "What about the marshal? They'll run into him on the trail."

"No, they're going to swing south of his trail. They know how he's riding because Reed is guiding him."

"What's your stake in this? Why ride all the way out there to tell the marshal?"

"It's because of Jenny Curtin," he said frankly. "She's a fine girl, and Bill was a good boy. Both of them treated me fine, as their father did before them. It's little enough to do, and I know too much about the plotting of that devil McCarran."

"Then it is McCarran. Where does Reed stand in this?"

"He's stupid!" Keys said contemptuously. "McCarran is using him and he hasn't the wit to see it. He believes they are partners, but Prince will get rid of him like he does anyone who gets in his way. He'll be rid of Trumbull, too."

"And Sikes?"

"Perhaps. Sikes is a good tool, to a point."

Matt Sabre shoved his hat back on his head. "Keys," he said suddenly, "I want you to have a little faith in me. Believe me, I'm doing what I can to help Jenny Curtin. I did kill her husband, but he was a total stranger who was edgy and started a fight.

"I'd no way of knowing who or what he was, and the gun of a stranger kills as easy as the gun of a known man. But he trusted me. He asked me to come here, to bring his wife five thousand and to help her."

"Five thousand?" Keys stared. "Where did he get that amount of money?"

"I'd like to know," Sabre admitted. Another idea occurred to him. "Keys, you know more about what's going on in this town than anyone else. What do you know about the Sonoma Grant?"

Keys hesitated, then said slowly: "Sabre, I know very little about that. I think the only one who has the true facts is Prince McCarran. I think he gathered all the available papers on both grants and is sure that no matter what his claim, the Grant cannot be substantiated. Nobody knows but McCarran."

"Then I'll go to McCarran," Sabre replied harshly. "I'm going to straighten this out if it's the last thing I do."

"You go to McCarran and it will be the last thing you do. The man's deadly. He's smooth-talking and treacherous. And then there's Sikes."

"Yes," Sabre admitted. "There's Sikes."

He studied the situation, then looked up. "Look, don't you bother the Marshal. Leave him to me. Every man he's got with him is an enemy to Jenny Curtin, and they would never let you talk. You circle them and ride on to Pivotrock. You tell Camp Gordon what's happening. Tell him of this outfit that's saddled up. I'll do my job here, and then I'll start back."

Long after Keys had departed, Sabre watched. Evidently the posse was awaiting some word from Reed. Would McCarran ride with them? He was too careful. He would wait in Yellowjacket. He would be, as always, an innocent bystander. . . .

Keys, riding up the trail some miles distant, drew up suddenly. He had forgotten to tell Sabre of Prince McCarran's plan to have Sid Trumbull cut him down when he tangled with Sikes. For a long moment Keys sat his horse, staring worriedly and scowling. To go back now would lose time; moreover, there was small chance that Sabre would be there. Matt Sabre would have to take his own chances.

Regretfully, Keys pushed on into the rough country ahead. . . .

Tony Sikes found McCarran seated in the back room at the saloon. McCarran glanced up quickly as he came in, and then nodded.

"Glad to see you, Sikes. I want you close by. I think we'll have visitors today or tomorrow."

"Visitors?" Sikes searched McCarran's face.

"A visitor, I should say. I think we'll see Matt Sabre."

Tony Sikes considered that, turning it over in his mind. Yes, Prince was right. Sabre would not surrender. It would be like him to head for town, hunting Reed. Aside from three or four men, nobody knew of McCarran's connection with the Pivotrock affair. Reed or Trumbull were fronting for him.

Trumbull, Reed, and Sikes and Keys. Keys was a shrewd man. He might be a drunk and a piano player, but he had a head on his shoulders.

Sikes' mind leaped suddenly. Keys was not around. This was the first time in weeks that he had not encountered Keys in the bar.

Keys was gone.

Where would he go—to warn Jenny Curtin of the posse? So what? He had nothing against Jenny Curtin. He was a man who fought for hire. Maybe he was on the wrong side in this. Even as he thought of that, he remembered Matt Sabre. The man was sharp as a steel blade, trim, fast. Now that it had been recalled to his mind, he remembered all that he had heard of him as Marshal of Mobeetie.

There was in Tony Sikes a drive that forbade him to admit any man was his fighting superior. Sabre's draw against Trumbull was still the talk of the town—talk that irked Sikes, for folks were beginning to compare the two of them. Many thought Sabre might be faster. That rankled.

He would meet Sabre first, and then drift.

"Don't you think he'll get here?" McCarran asked, looking up at Tony.

Sikes nodded. "He'll get here, all right. He thinks too fast for Trumbull or Reed. Even for that marshal."

Sikes would have Sabre to himself. Sid Trumbull was out of town. Tony Sikes wanted to do his own killing.

Matt Sabre watched the saddled horses. He had that quality of patience so long associated with the Indian. He knew how to wait, and how to relax. He waited now, letting all his muscles rest. With all his old alertness for danger, his sixth sense that warned him of climaxes, and he knew this situation had reached the explosion point.

The marshal would be returning. Reed and Trumbull would be sure that he did not encounter the posse. And that body of riders, most of whom were henchmen or cronies of Galusha Reed, would sweep down on the Pivotrock and capture it, killing all who were there under the pretense of searching for Matt Sabre.

Keys would warn them, and in time. Once they knew of the danger, Camp Gordon and the others would be wise enough to take the necessary precautions. The marshal was one tentacle, but here in Yellowjacket was the heart of the trouble.

If Prince McCarran and Tony Sikes were removed, the tentacles would shrivel and die. Despite the danger out at Pivotrock, high behind the Mogollon Rim, the decisive blow must be struck right here in Yellowjacket.

He rolled over on his stomach and lifted the glasses. Men were coming from the Yellowjacket Saloon and mounting up. Lying at his ease, he watched them go. There were at least thirty, possibly more. When they had gone he got to his feet and brushed off his clothes. Then he walked slowly down to his horse and mounted.

He rode quietly, one hand lying on his thigh, his eyes alert, his brain relaxed and ready for impressions.

Marshal Rafe Collins was a just man. He was a frontiersman, a man who knew the West and the men it bred. He was no fool. Shrewd and careful, rigid in his enforcement of the law, yet wise in the ways of men. Moreover, he was Southern in the oldest of Southern traditions, and being so, he understood what Matt Sabre meant when he said it was because he had killed her husband that he must protect Jenny Curtin.

Matt Sabre left his horse at the livery stable. Simpson looked up sharply when he saw him.

"You better watch yourself," he warned. "The whole country's after you, an' they are huntin' blood!"

"I know. What about Sikes? Is he in town?"

"Sure! He never leaves McCarran." Simpson searched his face. "Sikes is no man to tangle with, Sabre. He's chain lightin'."

"I know." Sabre watched his horse led into a shadowed stall. Then he turned to Simpson. "You've been friendly, Simpson. I like that. After today there's goin' to be a new order of things around here, but today I could use some help. What do you know about the Pivotrock deal?"

The man hesitated, chewing slowly. Finally he spat and looked up. "There was nobody to tell until now," he said, "but two things I know. That grant was Curtin's all right, an' he wasn't killed by accident. He was murdered."

"Murdered?"

"Yeah." Simpson's expression was wry. "Like you he liked fancy drinkin' liquor when he could get it. McCarran was right friendly. He asked Curtin to have a drink with him that day, an' Curtin did.

"On'y a few minutes after that he came in here an' got a team to drive back, leavin' his horse in here because it had gone lame. I watched him climb into that rig, an' he missed the step an' almost fell on his face. Then he finally managed to climb in."

"Drunk?" Sabre's eyes were alert and interested.

"Him?" Simpson snorted. "That old coot could stow away more liquor than a turkey could corn. He had only one drink, yet he could hardly walk."

"Doped, then?" Sabre nodded. That sounded like McCarran. "And then what?"

"When the team was brought back after they ran away with him, an' after Curtin was found dead, I found a bullet graze on the hip of one of those broncs."

So that was how it had been. A doped man, a skittish team of horses, and a bullet to burn the horse just enough to start it running. Prince McCarran was a thorough man.

"You said you knew that Curtin really owned that grant. How?"

Simpson shrugged. "Because he had that other claim investigated. He must have heard rumors of trouble. There'd been no talk of it that I heard, an' here a man hears everythin'!

"Anyway, he had all the papers with him when he started back to the ranch that day. He showed 'em to me earlier. All the proof."

"And he was murdered that day? Who found the body?"

"Sid Trumbull. He was ridin' that way, sort of accidental-like."

The proof Jenny needed was in the hands of Prince McCarran. By all means, he must call on Prince.

CHAPTER SIX:
"Stand Up—and Die!"

Matt Sabre walked to the door and stood there, waiting a moment in the shadow before emerging into the sunlight.

The street was dusty and curiously empty. The rough-fronted gray buildings of unpainted lumber or sand-colored adobe faced him blankly from across and up the street. The hitch rail was deserted, the water trough overflowed a little, making a darkening stain under one end.

Somewhere up the street but behind the buildings a hen began proclaiming her egg to the hemispheres. A single white cloud hung lazily in the blue sky. Matt stepped out. Hitching his gun belts a little, he looked up the street.

Sikes would be in the Yellowjacket. To see McCarran, he must see Sikes first. That was the way he wanted it. One thing at a time.

He was curiously quiet. He thought of other times when he had faced such situations—of Mobeetie, of that first day out on the plains hunting buffalo, the first time he had killed a man, of a charge the Riffs made on a small desert patrol out of Taudeni long ago.

A faint breeze stirred an old sack that lay near the boardwalk, and further up the street near the water trough, a long gray rat slipped out from under a store and headed toward the drip of water from the trough. Matt Sabre started to walk, moving up the street.

It was not far, as distance goes, but there is no walk so long as the gunman's walk, no pause so long as the pause before gunfire. On this day Sikes would know, instantly, what his presence here presaged. McCarran would know too.

Prince McCarran was not a gambler. He would scarcely trust all to Tony Sikes, no matter how confident he might be. It always paid to have something to back up a facing card. Trust Prince to keep his hole card well covered. But on this occasion he would not be bluffing. He would have a hole card, but where? How? What? And when?

The last was not hard. When—the moment of the gun battle.

He had walked no more than thirty yards when a door creaked and a man stepped into the street. He did not look down toward Sabre, but walked briskly to the center of the street, then faced about sharply like a man on a parade ground.

Tony Sikes.

He wore this day a faded blue shirt that stretched tight over his broad, bony shoulders and fell slack in front where his chest was hollow and his stomach flat. It was too far yet to see his eyes, but Matt Sabre knew what they looked like.

The thin, angular face, the mustache, the high cheek bones, and the long, restless fingers. The man's hips were narrow, and there was little enough to his body. Tony Sikes lifted his eyes and stared down the street. His lips were dry, but he felt ready. There was a curious lightness within him, but he liked it so, and he liked the setup. At that moment he felt almost an affection for Sabre.

The man knew so well the rules of the game. He was coming as he should come, and there was something about him—an edged quality, a poised and alert strength.

No sound penetrated the clear globe of stillness. The warm air hung still, with even the wind poised, arrested by the drama in the street. Matt Sabre felt a slow trickle of sweat start from under his hat band. He walked carefully, putting each foot down with care and distinction of purpose. It was Tony Sikes who stopped first, some sixty yards away.

"Well, Matt, here it is. We both knew it was coming."

"Sure." Matt paused too, feet wide apart, hands swinging wide. "You tied up with the wrong outfit, Sikes."

"We'd have met, anyway," Sikes looked along the street at the tall man standing there, looked and saw his bronzed face, hard and ready. It was not in Sikes to feel fear of a man with guns. Yet this was how he would die. It was in the cards. He smiled suddenly. Yes, he would die by the gun—but not now.

His hands stirred, and as if their movement was a signal to his muscles, they flashed in a draw. Before him the dark, tall figure flashed suddenly. It was no more than that, a blur of movement and a lifted gun, a movement suddenly stilled, and the black sullen muzzle of a sixgun that steadied on him even as he cleared his gun from his open top holster.

He had been beaten—beaten to the draw.

The shock of it triggered Sikes' gun, and he knew even as the gun bucked in his hand that he had missed, and then suddenly, Matt Sabre was running! Running toward him, gun lifted, but not firing!

In a panic, Sikes saw the distance closing and he fired as fast as he could pull the trigger, three times in a thundering cascade of sound. And even as the hammer fell for the fourth shot, he heard another gun bellow.

But where? There had been no stab of flame from Sabre's gun. Sabre was running, a rapidly moving target, and Sikes had fired too fast, upset by the sudden rush, by the panic of realizing he had been beaten to the draw.

He lifted his right-hand gun, dropped the muzzle in a careful arc, and saw Sabre's skull over the barrel. Then Sabre skidded to a halt and his gun hammered bullets.

Flame leaped from the muzzle, stabbing at Sikes, burning him along the side, making his body twitch and the bullet go wild. He switched guns and then something slugged him in the wind and the next he knew he was on the ground.

Matt Sabre had heard that strange shot, but that was another thing. He could not wait now, he could not turn his attention. He saw Sikes go down, but only to his knees, and the gunman had five bullets and the range now was only fifteen yards.

Sikes' gun swung up and Matt fired again. Sikes lunged to his feet, and then his features writhed with agony and breathlessness, and he went down, hard to the ground, twisting in the dust.

Then another bullet bellowed, and a shot kicked up dust at his feet. Matt swung his gun and blasted at an open window, then started for the saloon door. He stopped, hearing a loud cry behind him.

"Matt! Sabre?"

It was Sikes, his eyes flared wide. Sabre hesitated, glanced swiftly around, then dropped to his knees in the silent street.

"What is it, Tony? Anything I can do for you?"

"Behind—behind—the desk—you—you—" His faltering voice faded, then strength seemed to flood back and he looked up. "Good man! Too—too fast!"

And then he was dead, gone just like that, and Matt Sabre was striding into the Yellowjacket.

The upstairs room was empty; the stairs were empty; there was no one in sight. Only Hobbs stood behind the bar when he came down. Hobbs, his face set and pale.

Sabre looked at him, eyes steady and cold. "Who came down those stairs?"

Hobbs licked his lips. He choked, then whispered hoarsely. "Nobody—but there's—there's a back stairs."

Sabre wheeled and walked back in quick strides, thumbing shells into his gun. The office door was open and Prince McCarran looked up as he framed himself in the door.

He was writing, and the desk was rumpled with papers, the desk of a busy man. Nearby was a bottle and a full glass.

McCarran lay down his pen. "So? You beat him? I thought you might."

"Did you?" Sabre's gaze was cold. If this man had been running, as he must have run, he gave no evidence of it now. "You should hire them faster, Prince."

"Well," McCarran shrugged, "he was fast enough until now. But this wasn't my job, anyway. He was workin' for Reed."

Sabre took a step inside the door, away from the wall, keeping his hands free. His eyes were on those of Prince McCarran, and the Prince watched him, alert, interested.

"That won't ride with me," Matt said. "Reed's a stooge, a perfect stooge. He'll be lucky if he comes back alive from this trip. A lot of that posse you sent out won't come back, either."

McCarran's eyelids tightened at the mention of the posse. "Forget it," he waved his hand. "Sit down and have a drink. After all, we're not fools, Sabre. We're grown men, and we can talk. I never liked killing, anyway."

"Unless you do it, or have it done." Sabre's hands remained where they were. "What's the matter, Prince? Yellow? Afraid to do your own killin'?"

McCarran's face was still and his eyes were wide now. "You shouldn't have said that. You shouldn't have called me yellow."

"Then get on your feet. I hate to shoot a sittin' man."

"Have a drink and let's talk."

"Sure." Sabre was elaborately casual. "You have one, too." He reached his hand for the glass that had already been poured, but McCarran's eyes were steady. Sabre switched his hand and grasped the other glass, and then, like a striking snake, Prince McCarran grasped his right hand and jerked him forward, off-balance.

At the same time, McCarran's left flashed back to the holster high on his left side, butt forward, and the gun jerked up and free. Matt Sabre, instead of trying to jerk his right hand free, let his weight go forward, following and hurling himself against McCarran. The chair went over with a crash and Prince tried to straighten, but Matt was riding him back. He crashed into the wall and Sabre broke free.

Prince swung his gun up, and Sabre's left palm slapped down, knocking the gun aside and gripping the hand across the thumb. His right hand came up under the gun barrel, twisting it back over and out of McCarran's hands. Then he shoved him back and dropped the gun, slapping him across the mouth with his open palm.

It was a free swing and it cracked like a pistol shot. McCarran's face went white from the blow and he rushed, swinging, but Sabre brought up his knee in the charging man's groin. Then, he smashed him in the face with his elbow, pushing him over and back. McCarran dove past him, blood streaming from his crushed nose, and grabbed wildly at the papers. His hand came up with a bulldog .41.

Matt saw the hand shoot for the papers and even as the .41 appeared his own gun was lifting. He fired first, three times, at a range of four feet.

Prince McCarran stiffened, lifted to his tiptoes, then plunged over on his face and lay still among the litter of papers and broken glass.

Sabre swayed drunkenly. He recalled what Sikes had said about the desk. He caught the edge and jerked it aside, swinging the desk away from the wall. Behind it was a small panel with a knob. It was locked, but a bullet smashed the lock. He jerked it open. A thick wad of bills, a small sack of gold coins, a sheaf of papers.

A glance sufficed. These were the papers Simpson had mentioned. The thick parchment of the original grant, the information on the conflicting Sonoma grant, and then . . . He glanced swiftly through them, then at a pound of horses' hoofs, he stuffed them inside his shirt. He stopped, stared. His shirt was soaked with blood.

Fumbling, he got the papers into his pocket, then stared down at himself. Sikes had hit him. Funny, he had never felt it. Only a shock, a numbness. Now Reed was coming back.

Catching up a sawed-off express shotgun, he started for the door, weaving like a drunken man. He never even got to the door.

The sound of galloping horses was all he could hear—galloping horses, and then a faint smell of something that reminded him of a time he had been wounded in North Africa. His eyes flickered open and the first thing he saw was a room's wall with the picture of a man with mutton chop whiskers and spectacles.

He turned his head and saw Jenny Curtin watching him. "So? You've decided to wake up. You're getting lazy, Matt. Mr. Sabre. On the ranch you always were the first one up."

He stared at her. She had never looked half so charming, and that was bad. It was bad because it was time to be out of here and on a horse.

"How long have I been here?"

"Only about a day and a half. You lost a lot of blood."

"What happened at the ranch? Did Keys get there in time?"

"Yes, and I stayed. The others left right away."

"You stayed?"

"The others," she said quietly, "went down the road about two miles. There was Camp Gordon, Tom Judson, Pepito, and Keys. And Rado, of course. They went down the road while I stood out in the ranchyard and let them see me. The boys ambushed them."

"Was it much of a fight?"

"None at all. The surprise was so great that they broke and ran. Only three weren't able, and four were badly wounded."

"You found the papers? Including the one about McCarran sending the five thousand in marked bills to El Paso?"

"Yes," she said simply. "We found that. He planned on having Billy arrested and charged with theft. He planned that, and then if he got killed, so much the better. It was only you he didn't count on."

"No," Matt Sabre stared at his hands, strangely white now. "He didn't count on me."

So it was all over now. She had her ranch, she was a free woman, and people would leave her alone. There was only one thing left. He had to tell her. To tell her that he was the one who had killed her husband.

He turned his head on the pillow. "One thing more," he began. "I—"

"Not now. You need rest."

"Wait. I have to tell you this. It's about—about Billy."

"You mean that you—you were the one who—?"

"Yes, I—" he hesitated, reluctant at last to say it.

"I know. I know you did, Matt. I've known from the beginning, even without all the things you said."

"I talked when I was delirious?"

"A little. But I knew, Matt. Call it intuition, anything you like, but I knew. You see, you told me how his eyes were when he was drawing his gun. Who could have known that but the man who shot him?"

"I see." His face was white. "Then I'd better rest. I've got some travelling to do."

She was standing beside him. "Travelling? Do you have to go on, Matt? From all you said last night, I thought—I thought—" her face flushed—"maybe you—didn't want to travel any more. Stay with us, Matt, if you want to. We would like to have you, and Billy's been asking for you. He wants to know where his spurs are."

After awhile, he admitted carefully, "Well, I guess I should stay and see that he gets them. A fellow should always make good on his promises to kids, I reckon."

"You'll stay then? You won't leave?"

Matt stared up at her. "I reckon," he said quietly, "I'll never leave unless you send me away."

She smiled and touched his hair. "Then you'll be here a long time, Mathurin Sabre, a very long time."

TRAIL TO PIE TOWN

Dusty Barron turned the steel-dust stallion down the slope toward the wash. He was going to have to find water soon or the horse and himself would be done for. If Emmett Fisk and Gus Mattis had shown up in the street at any other time it would have been all right.

As it was, they appeared just as he was making a break from the saloon, and they had blocked the road to the hill country and safety. Both men had reached for their guns when they saw him, and he had wheeled his horse and hit the desert road at a dead run. With Dan Hickman dead in the saloon it was no time to argue or engage in gun pleasantries while the clan gathered.

It had been a good idea to ride to Jarilla and make peace talk, only the idea hadn't worked. Dan Hickman had called him yellow and then gone for a gun. Dan was a mite slow, a fact that had left him dead on the saloon floor.

There were nine Hickmans in Jarilla, and there were Mattis and three Fisk boys. Dusty's own tall brothers were back in the hills southwest of Jarilla, but with his road blocked he had headed the steel-dust down the trail into the basin.

The stallion had saved his bacon. No doubt about that. It was only the speed of the big desert-bred horse, and its endurance, that had got him away from town before the Hickmans could catch him. The big horse had given him lead enough until night had closed in, and after that it was easier.

Dusty had turned at right angles from his original route. They would never expect that, for the turn took him down the long slope into the vast, empty expanse of the alkali basin where no man of good sense would consider going.

For him it was the only route. At Jarilla they would be watching for him, expecting him to circle back to the hill country and his own people. He should have listened to Allie when she had told him it was useless to try to settle the old blood feud.

He had been riding now, with only a few breaks, for hours. Several times he had stopped to rest the stallion, wanting to conserve its splendid strength against what must lie ahead. And occasionally he had dismounted and walked ahead of the big horse.

Dusty Barron had only the vaguest idea of what he was heading into. It was thirty-eight miles across the basin, and he was heading down the basin. According to popular rumor there was no water for over eighty miles in that direction. And he had started with his canteen only half full.

For the first hour he had taken his course from a star. Then he had sighted a peak ahead and to his left, and used that for a marker. Gradually, he had worked his way toward the western side of the basin.

Somewhere over the western side was Gallo Gap, a green meadow high in the peaks off a rocky and rarely used pass. There would be water there if he could make it, yet he knew of the Gap only from a story told him by a prospector he had met one day in the hills near his home.

Daybreak found him a solitary black speck in a vast wilderness of white. The sun stabbed at him with lances of fire, and then rising higher bathed the great alkali basin in white radiance and blasting furnace heat. Dusty narrowed his eyes against the glare. It was at least twelve miles to the mountains.

He still had four miles to go through the puffing alkali dust when he saw the tracks. At first he couldn't believe the evidence of his eyes. A wagon—here!

While he allowed the steel-dust to take a blow, he dismounted and examined the tracks. It had been a heavy wagon pulled by four mules or horses. In the fine dust he could not find an outlined track to tell one from the other.

The tracks had come out of the white distance to the east and had turned north exactly on the route he was following. Gallo Gap, from the prospector's story, lay considerably north of him, and a bit to the west.

Had the driver of the wagon known of the Gap? Or had he merely turned on impulse to seek a route through the mountains. Glancing in first one and then the other direction, Dusty could see no reason why the driver should choose either direction. Jarilla lay southwest, but from here there was no indication of it, and no trail.

Mounting again, he rode on, and when he came to the edge of the low hills fronting the mountains, he detected the wagon trail running along through the scattered rocks, parched bunch grass, and greasewood. It was still heading north. Yet when he studied the terrain before him he could see nothing but dancing heat waves and an occasional dust devil.

The problem of the wagon occupied his mind to forgetfulness of his own troubles. It had come across the alkali basin from the east. That argued it must have come from the direction of Manzano unless the wagon had turned into the trail somewhere further north on the road to Conejos.

Nothing about it made sense. This was Apache country and no place for wagon travel. A man on a fast horse, yes, but even then it was foolhardy to travel alone. Yet the driver of the wagon had the courage of recklessness to come across the dead white expanse of the basin, a trip that to say the least was miserable.

Darkness was coming again, but he rode on. The wagon interested him, and with no other goal in mind now that he had escaped the Hickmans, he was curious to see who the driver was and to learn what he had in mind. Obviously the man was a stranger to this country.

It was then, in the fading light, that he saw the mule. The steel-dust snorted and shied sharply, but Dusty kneed it closer for a better look. It had been a big mule and a fine animal, but it was dead now. It bore evidence of that brutal crossing of the basin, and here, on the far side, the animal had finally dropped dead of heat and exhaustion.

Only then did he see the trunk. It was sitting between two rocks, partly concealed. He walked over to it and looked it over. Cumbersome and heavy, it had evidently been dumped from the wagon to lighten the load. He tried to open it, but could not. It was locked tight. Beside it were a couple of chairs and a bed.

"Sheddin' his load," Dusty muttered thoughtfully. "He'd better find some water for those other mules or they'll die, too."

Then he noticed the name on the trunk, D. C. LOWE, ST. LOUIS, MO.

"You're a long way from home," Dusty remarked. He swung a leg over the saddle and rode on. He had gone almost five miles before he saw the fire.

At first, it might have been a star, but as he drew nearer he could see it was too low down, although higher than he was. The trail had been turning gradually deeper into the hills and had begun to climb a little. He rode on, using the light for a beacon.

When he was still some distance off he dismounted and tied the stallion to a clump of greasewood and walked forward on foot.

The three mules were hitched to the back of the wagon, all tied loosely, and lying down. A girl was bending over a fire, and a small boy, probably no more than nine years old, was gathering sticks of dried mesquite for fuel. There was no one else in sight.

Marveling, he returned to his horse and started back. When he was still a little distance away he began to sing. His throat was dry and it was a poor job, but he didn't want to frighten them. When he walked his horse into the firelight the boy was staring up at him, wide eyed, and the girl had an old Frontier Model Colt.

"It's all right, ma'am," he said, swinging down, "I'm just a passin' stranger an' don't mean any harm."

"Who are you?" she demanded.

"Name of Dusty Barron, ma'am. I've been followin' your trail."

"Why?" Her voice was sharp and a little frightened. She could have been no more than seventeen or eighteen.

"Mostly because I was headed this-away an' was wonderin' what anybody was doin' down here with a wagon, or where you might be headed."

"Doesn't this lead us anywhere?" she asked.

"Ma'am," Dusty replied, "if you're lookin' for a settlement there ain't none thisaway in less'n a hundred miles. There's a sort of town then, place they call Pie Town."

"But where did you come from?" Her eyes were wide and dark. If she was fixed up, he reflected, she would be right pretty.

"Place they call Jarilla," he said, "but I reckon this was a better way if you're travellin' alone. Jarilla's a Hickman town, an' they sure are a no-account lot."

"My father died," she told him, putting the gun in a holster hung to the wagon bed, "back there. Billy an' I buried him."

"You come across the basin alone?" He was incredulous.

"Yes. Father died in the mountains on the other side. That was three days ago."

Dusty removed his hat and began to strip the saddle and bridle from the stallion while the girl bent over her cooking. He found a hunk of bacon in his saddle pockets. "Got plenty of bacon?" he asked. "I most generally pack a mite along."

She looked up, brushing a strand of hair away from her face. She was flushed from the fire. "We haven't had any bacon for a week." She looked away quickly, and her chin quivered a little, then became stubborn. "Nor much of anything else, but you're welcome to join us."

He seated himself on the ground and leaned back on his saddle while she dished up the food. It wasn't much. A few dry beans and some corn bread. "You got some relatives out here somewheres?"

"No," she handed him a plate, but he was too thirsty to eat more than a few mouthfuls. "Father had a place out here. His lungs were bad and they told him the dry air would be good for him. My mother died when Billy was born, so there was nothing to keep us back in Missouri. We just headed west."

"You say your father had a place? Where is it?"

"I'm not sure. Father loaned some man some money, or rather, he provided him with money with which to buy stock. The man was to come west and settle on a place, stock it, and then send for dad."

Dusty ate slowly, thinking that over. "Got anything to show for it?"

"Yes, father had an agreement that was drawn up and notarized. It's in a leather wallet. He gave the man five thousand dollars. It was all we had."

When they had eaten, the girl and boy went to sleep in the wagon box while Dusty stretched out on the ground nearby. "What a mess!" he told himself. "Those kids comin' away out here, all by themselves now, an' the chances are that money was blowed in over a faro layout long ago!"

In the morning Dusty hitched up the mules for them. "You foller me," he advised, and turned the stallion up the trail to the north.

It was almost noon before he saw the thumblike butte that marked the entrance to Gallo Gap. He turned toward it, riding ahead to scout the best trail, and at times dismounting to roll rocks aside so the wagon could get through.

Surmounting the crest of a low hill, he looked suddenly into Gallo Gap. His red-rimmed eyes stared greedily at the green grass and trees. The stallion smelled water and wanted to keep going, so waving the wagon on, he rode down into the Gap.

Probably there were no more than two hundred acres here, but it was waist deep in rich green grass, and the towering yellow pines were tall and very old. It was like riding from desolation into a beautiful park. He found the spring by the sound of running water, crystal clear and beautiful, the water rippling over the rocks to fall into a clear pond at least an acre in extent. Nearby space had been cleared for a cabin, then abandoned.

Dusty turned in the saddle as his horse stood knee deep in the water. The wagon pulled up. "This is a little bit of heaven!" he said, grinning at the girl. "Say, what's your name, anyway?"

"Ruth Grant," she said, shyly.

All the weariness seemed to have fled from her face at the sight of the water and trees. She smiled gaily, and a few minutes later as he walked toward the trees with a rifle in the crook of his elbow he heard laughter, and then her voice, singing. He stopped suddenly, watching some deer, feeding a short distance off, and listening to her voice. It made a lump of loneliness rise in his throat.

That night after they had eaten steaks from a fat buck he'd killed, their first good meal in days, he looked across the fire at her. "Ruth," he said, "I think I'll locate me a home right here. I've been lookin' for a place of my own.

"I reckon what we better do is for you all to stay here with me until you get rested up. I'll build a cabin, and those mules of yours can get some meat on their bones again. Then I'll ride on down to Pie Town and locate this hombre your father had dealin's with, an' see how things look."

That was the way they left it, but in the days that followed Dusty Barron had never been happier. He felled trees on the mountain side and built a cabin, and in working around he found ways of doing things he had never tried before. Ruth was full of suggestions about the house, sensible, knowing things that helped a lot. He worked the mules a little, using only one at a time and taking them turn about.

He hunted a good deal for food. Nearby he found a salt lick and shot an occasional antelope, and several times, using a shot-gun from the wagon, he killed blue grouse. In a grove of trees he found some ripe black cherries similar to those growing wild in the Guadalupe Mountains of West Texas, There was also some Mexican plum.

When the cabin was up and there was plenty of meat on hand he got his gear in shape. Then he carefully oiled and cleaned his guns.

Ruth noticed them, and her face paled a little. "You believe there will be trouble?" she asked quickly. "I don't want you to—"

"Forget it," he interrupted. "I've got troubles of my own." He explained about the killing of Dan Hickman and the long standing feud between the families.

He left at daybreak. In his pocket he carried the leather wallet containing the agreement Roger Grant had made with Dick Lowe. It was a good day's ride from Gallo Gap to Aimless Creek where Dusty camped the first night. The following day he rode on into Pie Town. From his talks with Ruth he knew something of Lowe, and enough of the probable location of the ranch, if there was one.

A cowhand with sandy hair and crossed eyes was seated on the top rail of the corral. Dusty reined in and leaned his forearm on the saddlehorn and dug for the makings. After he had rolled a smoke he passed them on to the cross-eyed rider.

"Know anything about an' hombre name of Dick Lowe?" he asked.

"Reckon so." They shared a match, and looking at each other through the smoke decided they were men of a kind. "He's up there in the Spur Saloon now."

Dusty made no move. After a few drags on the cigarette, he glanced at the fire end. "What kind of hombre is he?"

"Salty." The cowhand puffed for a moment on his cigarette. "Salty, an' mean. Plumb poison with a shootin' iron, an' when you ride for him, he pays you what he wants to when you quit. If you don't think you got a square deal you can always tell him so, but when you do you better reach."

"Like that, huh?"

"Like that." He smoked quietly for a few minutes. "Four hombres haven't liked what he paid 'em. He buried all four of 'em in his own personal boothill, off to the north of the ranchhouse."

"Sounds bad. Do all his own work or does he have help?"

"He's got help. Cat McQuill an' Bugle Nose Bender. Only nobody calls him Bugle Nose to his face."

"What about the ranch? Nice place?"

"Best around here. He come in here with money, had near five thousand dollar. He bought plenty of cattle an' stocked his range well."

The cross-eyed cowhand looked at him, squinting through the smoke. "My name's Blue Riddle. I rode for him once."

"I take it you didn't argue none," Barron said, grinning.

"My maw never raised no foolish children!" Riddle replied wryly. "They had me in a cross fire. Been Lowe alone, I'd maybe of took a chance, but as it was, they would have cut me down quick. So I come away, but I'm stickin' around, just waiting. I told him I aimed to have my money, an' he just laughed."

Dusty dropped his hand back and loosened his left-hand gun. Then he swung his leg back over the saddle and thrust his toe in the stirrup. "Well," he said, "I got papers here that say I speak for a gal that owns half his layout. I'm goin' up an' lay claim to it for her."

Riddle looked up cynically. "Why not shoot yourself and save the trouble? They'll gun you down."

Then he sized Barron up again. "What did you say your name was?"

Dusty grinned. "I didn't say, but its Dusty Barron."

Blue Riddle slid off the corral rail. "One of the Barron's from Castle Rock?" He grinned again. "This I gotta see!"

Dusty was looking for a big man, but Dick Lowe, whom he spotted at once on entering the saloon, was only a bit larger than himself, and he was the only small man among the Barrons.

Lowe turned to look at him as he entered. The man's features were sharp, and his quick eyes glanced from Dusty Barron to Riddle, then back again. Dusty walked to the bar, and Riddle loitered near the door.

The man standing beside Lowe at the bar must be Cat McQuill. The reason for the nickname was obvious for there was something feline about the man's facial appearance.

"Lowe?" Dusty inquired.

"That's right," Lowe turned toward him slowly, "something you want?"

"Yeah," Dusty leaned nonchalantly on the bar and ordered a drink. "I'm representin' your partner."

Dick Lowe's face blanched, then turned hard as stone, His eyes glinted. However, he managed a smile with his thin lips. "Partner? I have no partner."

Dusty leaned on the bar watching his drink poured. He took his time.

Lowe watched him, slowly growing more and more angry. "Well," he said sharply, "if you've got something to say, say it!"

Dusty looked around, simulating surprise. "Why, I was just givin' you time to remember, Lowe! You can't tell me you can draw up an agreement with a man, have it properly notarized, and then take five thousand dollars of his money to stock a ranch and not remember it!"

Dusty was pointedly speaking loudly and the fact angered Lowe. "You have such an agreement?" Lowe demanded.

"Sure I got it."

"Where's the party this supposed agreement belongs to? Why doesn't he speak for himself?"

"He's dead. He was a lunger an' died on his way west."

Lowe's relief was evident. "I'm afraid," he said, "that this is all too obvious an attempt to get some money out of me. It won't work."

"It's nothing of the kind. Grant's dead, but he left a daughter and a son. I aim to see they get what belongs to 'em, Mr. Lowe. I hope we can do it right peaceable."

Lowe's face tightened, but he forced a smile. He was aware he had enemies in Pie Town and did not relish their overhearing this conversation. He was also aware that it was pretty generally known that he had come into Pie Town with five thousand in cash and brought cattle when everyone on the range was impoverished.

"I reckon this'll be easy settled," he said. "You bring the agreement to the ranch, an' if it's all legal I reckon we can make a deal."

"Sure!" Dusty agreed. "See you tomorrow!"

On the plank steps of the hotel, he waited until Riddle caught up with him. "You ain't actually goin' out there, are you?" Blue demanded. "That's just askin' for trouble!"

"I'm goin' out," Dusty agreed. "I want a look at the ranch myself. If I can ride out there I can get an idea what kind of stock he's got and what shape the ranch is in. I've got a hunch if we make a cash settlement Lowe isn't goin' to give us much more chance to look around if he can help it.

"Besides, I've talked in front o' the folks here in town, and rough as some of them may be they ain't goin' to see no orphans get gypped. No Western crowd would stand for that unless it's some outlaws like Lowe and his two pals."

Riddle walked slowly away shaking his head with doubt. Dusty watched him go and then went on inside.

He was throwing a saddle on the steel-dust next morning when he heard a low groan. Gun in hand he walked around the corner of the corral. Beyond a pile of poles he saw Blue Riddle pulling himself off the ground. "What happened?" Dusty demanded.

"Bender an' McQuill. They gave me my walkin' papers. Said I'd been in town too long, which didn't bother Lowe none till I took up with you. They gave me till daybreak to pull my freight."

He staggered erect, holding a hand to his head. "Then Bender bent a gun over my noggin."

Barron's eyes narrowed. "Play rough, don't they?" He looked at Riddle. "What are you goin' to do?"

"You don't see me out here runnin' down the road, do you?" Riddle said. "I'm sittin' tight!"

"Wash your face off, then," Dusty suggested, "an we'll eat!"

"You go ahead," Riddle replied. "I'll be along." Dusty glanced back over his shoulder as he left and saw Blue Riddle hiking toward the Indian huts that clustered outside of Pie Town.

When he rode out of town an hour later Dusty Barron was not feeling overly optimistic. Riddle had stayed behind only at Dusty's insistence, but now that Dusty was headed toward Lowe's ranch he no longer felt so confident. Dick Lowe was not a man to give up easily, nor to yield his ranch or any part of it without a fight. The pistol whipping of Riddle had been ample evidence of the lengths to which he was prepared to go.

The range through which Dusty rode was good. This was what he had wanted to see. How they might have bargained in town he was not sure. He doubted if anyone there would interfere if a deal was made by him. It was his own problem to see that Ruth and Billy Grant got a fair deal, and that could not be done unless he knew something, at least, of the ranch and the stock.

Dusty was quite sure now that Lowe had never expected the consumptive Roger Grant to come west and claim his piece of the ranch. Nor had he planned to give it to him if he had. He knew very well that he, himself, was riding into the lion's mouth, but felt he could depend on his own abilities and that Lowe would not go too far after his talk before the bystanders who had been in the saloon. By now Lowe would know that the story would be known to all his enemies in Pie Town.

Cat McQuill was loafing on the steps when Dusty rode up, and the gunman's eyes gleamed with triumph at seeing him. "Howdy!" he said affably. "Come on in! The boss is waitin' for you!"

Bugle Nose Bender was leaning against the fireplace and Lowe was seated at his desk. "Here he is, Boss!" McQuill said as they entered.

Lowe glanced up sharply. "Where's the agreement?" he asked, holding out his hand.

Barron handed it to him, and the rancher opened it, took a quick look, then glanced up. "This is it, Cat!"

Too late Dusty heard the slide of gun on leather, and whirled to face McQuill, but the pistol barrel crashed down over the side of his head and he hit the floor. Even as he fell he realized what a fool he had been, yet he had been so sure they would talk a little, at least, try to run a blazer or to buy him off cheap.

Bender lunged toward him and kicked him in the ribs, then Lowe reached over and jerking him to his knees, struck him three times in the face. The pistol barrel descended again and drove him down into a sea of blackness.

How long they had pounded him he had no idea. When he opened his eyes, he struggled, fighting his way to realization of where he was. It took him several minutes to understand that he was almost standing on his head in the road, one foot caught in the stallion's stirrup!

The steel-dust, true to his training, was standing rigid in the road, his head turned to look at his master. "Easy boy!" Dusty groaned. "Easy does it!" Twisting his foot in the stirrup, he tried to free it, but to no avail.

He realized what they had planned. After beating him they had brought him out here, wedged his foot in the stirrup, struck the horse and when he started to move, had ridden hastily away before they could be seen. Most horses, frightened by the unfamiliar burden in the stirrup, would have raced away over the desert and dragged him to death. In fact, it had happened to more than one unwary cowhand.

They had reckoned without the steel-dust. The stallion had been reared by Dusty Barron from a tiny colt, and the two had never been long apart. The big horse knew instantly that something was radically wrong, and had gone only a little way, then stopped. His long training told him to stand, and he stood stock still.

Dusty twisted his foot again but couldn't get loose. Nor could he pull himself up and get hold of the stirrup and so into the saddle. He was still trying this when hoof-beats sounded on the road.

He looked around wildly, fearful of Lowe's return. Then a wave of relief went over him. It was Blue Riddle!

"Hey!" Blue exclaimed. "What the heck happened?" He swung down from his horse and hastily extricated Dusty from his predicament.

Barron explained. "They wanted me killed so it would look like I was dragged to death! Lucky they got away from here in a hurry, afraid they might be seen!"

"But they got the agreement!" Riddle protested.

"Uh uh." Barron grinned, then gasped as his bruised face twinged with pain. "That was a copy. I put the agreement down an' traced over it. He took a quick look and thought it was the real thing. Now we got to get to town before he realizes what happened."

Despite his battered and bruised body and the throbbing of his face, Dusty crawled into the saddle and they raced up the road to Pie Town.

Two men were standing on the hotel porch as they rode up. One of them glanced at Dusty Barron. "Howdy. Young woman inside wants to see you."

Dusty rushed into the lobby and stopped in surprised. Facing him was Ruth Grant, holding Billy by the hand, but her smile fled when she saw his face. "Oh!" she cried. "What's happened to you?"

Briefly, he explained. Then demanded, "How'd you get here?"

"After you left," Ruth told him, "I was worried. After father's death and the trouble we had before you came there was no time to think of anything, and I had to always be thinking of where we would go and what we would do. Then I remembered a comment father made once.

"You see, Mr. Lowe left a trunk with us to bring west or send to him later. It wasn't quite full, so father opened it to pack some other things in it. He found something there that worried him a great deal, and he told me several times that he was afraid he might have trouble when we got out here.

"From all he said I had an idea what he found, so after you were gone we searched through the trunk and found some letters and a hand bill offering a five thousand dollar reward for Lowe. Why he kept them I can't imagine, but the sheriff says some criminals are very vain, and often keep such things about themselves."

"And then you rode on here?"

She nodded. "We met two men who were trailing you, and as they had extra horses with them so they could travel fast, we joined them."

Dusty's face tightened. "Men looking for me?"

Riddle interrupted. "Dick Lowe's ridin' into town now!"

Dusty Barron turned, loosening his guns. He started for the door.

"I'm in on this, too!" Riddle said, trailing him.

They walked out on the porch and stepped down into the street, spreading apart. Dick Lowe and his two henchmen had dismounted and were starting into the saloon when something made them glance up the street.

"Lowe!" Dusty yelled. "You tried to kill me, an I'm comin' for you!"

Dick Lowe's hard face twisted with fury as he wheeled, stepping down into the dust.

He stopped in the street, and Cat McQuill and Bender moved out to either side.

Dusty Barron walked steadily down the street, his eyes on Dick Lowe. All three men were dangerous, but Lowe was the man he wanted, and Lowe was the man he intended to get first.

"This man's an outlaw!" he said, speaking to Bender and McQuill. "He's wanted for murder in St. Louis! If you want out, get out now!"

"You're lying!" Bender snarled.

Dusty Barron walked on. The sun was bright in the street and little puffs of dust arose at every step. There were five horses tied to the hitch-rail behind the three men. He found himself hoping none of them would be hit by a stray shot. To his right was Blue Riddle, walking even with him, his big hands hovering over his guns.

His eyes clung to Dick Lowe, riveted there as though he alone lived in the world. He could see the man drop into a half-crouch, noticed the bulge of the tobacco sack in his breast pocket, the buttons down the two sides of his shirt. Under the brim of the hat he could see the straight bar of the man's eyebrows, and the hard gleam of the eyes beneath, and then suddenly the whole tableau dissolved into flaming, shattering action.

Lowe's hand flashed for his gun and Dusty's beat him by a hair's breadth, but Dusty held his fire, lifting the gun slowly. Lowe's quick shot flamed by his ear, and he winced inwardly at the proximity of death. Then the gunman fired again and the bullet tugged impatiently at his vest. He drew a long breath and squeezed off a shot, then another.

Lowe rose on tip-toes, opened his mouth wide as if to gasp for breath, and seemed to hold himself there for a long moment, then pitched over into the street.

Dusty's gun swung with his eyes and he saw Bender was down on his knees and so he opened up on McQuill. The Cat man jerked convulsively, then began to back away, his mouth working and his gun hammering. The man's gun stopped firing, and he stared at it, pulled the trigger again, and then reached for a cartridge from his belt.

Barron stood spraddle legged in the street and saw Cat's hand fumble at his belt. The fingers came out with a cartridge and moved toward the gun, and then his eyes glazed and he dropped his iron. Turning, as though the whole affair had slipped his mind, he started for the saloon. He made three steps, then lifted his foot, seemed to feel for the saloon step, then fell like a log across the rough board porch.

Blue Riddle was on his knees, blood staining a trouser leg. Bender was sprawled out in the dust, a darkening pool forming beneath him.

Suddenly the street was filled with people. Ruth ran up to Dusty and he slid his arm around her. With a shock, he remembered. "You said two men were looking for me. Who?"

"Only us."

He turned, staring. Two big men were facing him, grinning. "Buck and Ben! How in tarnation did you two find me?"

Buck Barron grinned. "We was wonderin' what happened to you. We come to town and had a mite of a ruckus with the Hickmans. What was left of them headed for El Paso in a mighty hurry—both of 'em.

"Then an Injun kid come ridin' up on a beat-up hoss and said you all was in a sight of trouble so we figgered we'd come along and see how you made out."

"An Injun?" Dusty was puzzled.

"Yeah," Riddle told him, "that was my doin'. I figgered you was headed for trouble, so I sent an Injun kid off after your brothers. Heck, if I'd knowed what you was like with a six-gun I'd never have sent for 'em!"

Ben Barron grinned and rubbed at the stubble of whiskers. "An' if we'd knowed there was on'y three, we'd never have come!" He looked from Dusty to Ruth. "Don't look like you'd be comin' home right soon with that place at Gallo Gap an' what you've got your arm around. But what'll we tell Allie?"

"Allie?" Ruth drew away from him, eyes wide. "Who's Allie? You didn't tell me you had a girl!"

Dusty winked at his brothers. "Allie? She's war chief of the Barron tribe! Allie's my ma!"

He turned to Riddle. "Blue, how's about you sort of keepin' an eye on that Gap place for me for a week or so? I reckon I'd better take Ruth home for a spell. Allie, she sure sets a sight of store by weddin's!"

Ruth's answering pressure on his arm was all the answer he needed.

LIT A SHUCK FOR TEXAS

The Sandy Kid slid the roan down the steep bank into the draw and fast walked it over to where Jasper Wald sat his big iron-gray stallion. The Kid, who was nineteen and new to this range, pulled up a short distance from his boss. That gray stallion was mighty near as mean as Wald himself.

"Howdy, Boss! Look what I found back over in that rough country east of here."

Wald scowled at the rock the rider held out. "I ain't payin' yuh to hunt rocks," he declared. "You get back there in the breaks roundin' up strays like I'm payin' yuh for."

"I figgered yuh'd be interested. I reckon this here's gold."

"Gold?" Wald's laugh was sardonic, and he threw a contemptuous glance at the cowhand. "In this country? Yuh're a fool!"

The Sandy Kid shoved the rock back in his chaps pocket and swung his horse back toward the brush, considerably deflated. Maybe it was silly to think of finding gold here, but that rock sure enough looked it, and it was heavy. He reckoned he'd heard somewhere that gold was a mighty heavy metal.

When he was almost at the edge of the badlands, he saw a steer heading toward the thick brush, so he gave the roan a taste of the diggers and spiked his horse's tail after the steer. That old ladino could run like a deer, and it headed out for those high rocks like a tramp after a chuckwagon, but when it neared the rocks, the mossy-horn ducked, and head down, cut off at right angles, racing for the willows.

Beyond the willows was a thicket of brush, rock, and cactus that made riding precarious and roping almost suicidal, and once that steer got into the tangle beyond he was gone.

The Kid shook out a loop and hightailed it after the steer, but it was a shade far for good roping when he made his cast. Even at that, he'd have made it but just as his rope snagged the steer, the roan's hoof went into a gopher hole, and the Sandy Kid sailed right off over the roan's ears.

As he hit the ground all in a lump, he caught a glimpse of the ladino. Wheeling around, head down with about four or five feet of horn, it started for him.

With a yelp, the Kid grabbed for his gun, but it was gone, so he made a frantic leap for a cleft in the ground. Even as he rolled into it, he felt the hot breath of the steer, or thought he did.

The steer went over the cleft, scuffing dust down on the cowboy. When the Kid looked around, he saw he was lying in a crack that was about three feet wide and at least thirty feet deep. He had landed on a ledge that all but closed off the crack for several feet.

Warily he eased his head over the edge, then jerked back with a gasp, for the steer was standing, red-eyed and mean, not over ten feet away, and staring right at him.

Digging out the makings, the Kid rolled a cigarette. After all, why get cut up about it? The steer would go away after a while, and then it would be safe to come out. In the meantime it was mighty cool here and pleasant enough, what with the sound of falling water and all.

The thought of water reminded the Kid that he was thirsty. He studied the situation and decided that with care he could climb to the bottom without any danger. Once down where the water was, he could get a drink. He was not worried, for when he had looked about he had seen his horse, bridle reins trailing, standing not far away. The roan would stand forever that way.

His six-gun, which had been thrown from his holster when he fell, also lay up there on the grass. It was not over twenty feet from the rim of the crevice, and once it was in his hand, it would be a simple thing to knock off that steer. Getting the pistol was quite another thing. With that steer on the prod, it would be suicide to try.

When he reached the bottom of the crevice he peered around in the vague light. At noon, or close to that, it would be bright down here but at any other time it would be thick with shadows. Kneeling by the thin trickle of water, the Kid drank his fill. Lifting his face from the water, he looked down stream and almost jumped out of his skin when he saw a grinning skull.

The Sandy Kid was no pilgrim. He had fought Apaches and Comanches, and twice he had been over the trail to Dodge. But seeing a skull grinning at him from a distance of only a few feet did nothing to make him feel comfortable and at ease.

"By grab, looks like I ain't the first to tumble into this place," he said. "That hombre must have broken a leg and starved to death."

Yet when he walked over and examined the skeleton, he could see he was wrong. The man had been shot through the head.

Gingerly, the Kid moved the skull. There was a hole on the other side, too, and a bullet flattened against the rock.

He was astonished.

"Well now! Somebody shot this hombre while he laid here," the Kid decided.

Squatting on his haunches, the Sandy Kid puffed his cigarette and studied the situation. Long experience in reading signs had made it easy for his eyes to see what should be seen. A few things he noticed now. This man, already wounded, had fallen or been pushed into the crack, and then a man with a gun had leaned over the edge above and shot him through the head!

There was a notch in his belt that must have been cut by a bullet, and one knee had been broken by a bullet for the slug was still there, embedded in the joint.

The Kid was guessing about the notch, but from the look of things, and the way the man was doubled up, it looked like he had been hurt pretty bad aside from the knee.

The shirt was gone except for a few shreds, and among the rocky debris there were a few buttons, an old pocket knife, and some coins. The boots, dried and stiff, were not a horseman's boots, but the high-topped, flat-heeled type that miners wear. A rusted six-shooter lay a bit further down stream, and the Kid retrieved it. After a few minutes he determined that the gun was still fully loaded.

"Prob'ly never got a shot at the skunk," the Sandy Kid said thoughtfully. "Well, now! Ain't this a purty mess?"

When he studied the skeleton further, he noticed something under the ribs that he had passed over, thinking it a rock. Now he saw it was a small leather sack which the dead man had evidently carried inside his shirt. The leather was dry and stiff, and it ripped when he tried to open it. Within were several fragments of the same ore the Kid had himself found!

Tucking the samples and the remnants of the sack under a rocky ledge, the Kid stuck the rusty six-shooter in his belt and climbed back to the ledge where a cautious look showed that the ladino was gone.

The roan pricked up its ears and whinnied, not at all astonished that this peculiar master of his should come crawling out of the ground. The Kid had lost his rope, which was probably still trailing from the steer's horns, but he was not thinking of that. He was thinking of the murdered man.

When he awakened the next morning he rolled over on his side and stared around the bunkhouse. Everyone was still asleep, and then he realized that it was Sunday.

Wald was nowhere around when the Kid headed for the cook shack. Smoke was rising slowly, for Cholly Cooper, the best cook on that range, was conscientious. When you wanted breakfast you got it, early or late. The Sandy Kid was glad that Wald was not around, for he had no love for his morose, quick-to-anger boss.

It was not a pleasant outfit to ride for, Cooper being the only friendly one in the bunch. Jasper Wald never spoke, except to give an order or to criticize in a dry, sarcastic voice. He was about forty, tough, and hardbitten. Rumor had it that he had killed more than one man. His two permanent hands were Jack Swarr, a burly Kansas man, always unshaven, and "Dutch" Schweitzer, a lean German who drank heavily.

"Hi, Sandy." Cholly waved a fork at him: "Set yourself down and I'll get some coffee. Up early, ain't you?"

"Uh huh." The Kid pulled the thick cup toward him. "Sort of reckoned I'd ride up to the Forks. Few things I need. Shirts and stuff."

Cholly dished out a couple of thick slabs of beef and four eggs. "Better eat," he said. "I wouldn't want yuh pourin' them shirts into an empty stomach."

While Cholly refilled the Kid's cup, he said in a low voice, "What did you all do to the boss? He was shore riled up when he came in and saw yuh hadn't showed up with the rest of the hands."

"Reckon he was just sore. I tied in with an old mossyhorn up in the breaks and lost my rope. Durned steer had one horn, looked long enough for two steers, and a stub on the other end."

Cooper chuckled. "You ain't the first who lost a rope on Ol' Stob! You were lucky not to get killed."

"Rough country, over thataway," the Sandy Kid suggested. "Ever been over there?"

"No further'n the creek, and I don't aim to. Only one man ever knowed that country, unless it was the Apaches, and that was Jim Kurland. He always claimed there was gold over there, but most folks just laughed at him."

"Rancher?"

"No, sort of a prospector. He mined some, I guess, afore he came here. Dead now, I reckon. He headed off into that country about a year ago and nobody ever saw hide nor hair of him again. His wife, she died about three, four months ago, and his daughter works down to Wright's Store. She handles the post office in there, mostly."

Jim Kurland. It was a name to remember. The Sandy Kid knew he was walking on dangerous ground. The killer of Kurland, if it was his skeleton the Kid had found, was probably still around, and any mention of Kurland's name might lead to trouble. It would be wise to proceed with caution.

The Sandy Kid was no hero. He had never toted a badge, and like most cowhands of his day, he looked upon the law as a nuisance originated mainly to keep riders from having a good time. He went his own way, and if someone made trouble for him, he figured to handle it himself. He would be ashamed to ask for help, and figured any sheriff was the same.

He was interested in gold. If there was a mine as rich as that ore seemed to indicate, he wanted it. Why, with a little gold a man could buy a spread of his own and stock it with those new white face cattle that carried so much more beef than a longhorn. A man could do right well with a little money to go on. . . .

When he rode into the Forks he headed right for the store. He was not planning on doing any drinking this day. It was Sunday, but Sim Wright kept his store open seven days a week the year 'round. The Sandy Kid, who was a lean six feet and with a shock of sandy hair and mild gray eyes, swung down from the roan and crossed the boardwalk to the store.

At first he thought it was empty. Then he saw the girl who stood behind the counter, her eyes on him.

He jerked his hat from his head and went toward her. "Ma'am," he said, "I better get me a couple of shirts. Yuh got anything with checks in it?"

"Big checks?" She smiled at him.

"Uh huh, that's right."

She showed him the shirts, one of them with black and white checks as big as those on a checkerboard.

He fingered them thoughtfully. Then he said, "Ma'am, is yore name Kurland?"

"That's my last name. My first name is Betty."

"Mine's Sandy," he told her. "They call me The Sandy Kid."

He hesitated, then slid a hand into his pocket and took out the pocket knife and laid it on the shirts.

Her face went white as she caught it up. She looked at The Kid. "Where did you get this?"

Slowly, carefully, he told her. As he talked, she stared at him with wide eyes. "You think," she asked when he had finished, "that he was murdered? But why?"

"He had gold samples, ma'am. Folks will do a powerful lot for gold. I would myself. I sort of figured I'd keep quiet about this, and sort of hunt that claim myself, and when I found it, I'd stake her out. Then I heard about you, an' I figgered yuh'd like to know about yore Pappy and have him buried proper."

"Who killed him?"

"That I don't know. I reckon if a body was to try, he could find out, but you'd have to keep still about findin' him for a while."

"If I keep still, will you find the murderer? If you do, I'll give you that claim."

"No, ma'am, I couldn't take yore claim. Menfolks in my family wasn't raised no such way. But I don't have a particle of use for a coyote that would murder a man like that, so if yuh want, I'll have a look around in my spare time."

Her eyes were large and dark. It was nice looking into them. The Sandy Kid reckoned he had never looked into eyes that were like hers. And her lips—she had right nice lips. Not too full, and not thin, either. He liked that. Her neck was sure white— She was smiling at him, amused.

He flushed a deep red. "Reckon yuh must think I never saw a girl before," he said. "Well, I reckon mebbe I never did really look at one. Somehow, they never sort of called themselves to mind."

"Thank you, Sandy."

All the way back to the ranch he was thinking how nice that name sounded from her lips.

The Bar W lay like an ugly sore in the bottom of the flat. Three adjoining pole corrals, an unpainted frame bunkhouse, and a ranchhouse of adobe. The cook shack was also adobe, and there was smoke coming from the chimney when he rode in with his shirts.

It was still quite early, for the ranch was only a short piece from town. He unsaddled the roan and walked back toward the cookshack for coffee. They were all there. Nobody said anything when he came in, but Cholly threw him a warning glance. The Kid got a cup and filled it with coffee, then sat down.

"What happened to yuh last night?" Wald demanded, glaring at him across the table.

"Me? I had me a run in with that Old Stob horned ladino. Lost my rope."

"You still got that rock?"

"That?" The Sandy Kid shrugged carelessly. "No, I throwed it away. Reckon it was just iron pyrites or somethin'."

Nothing more was said, but he felt uncomfortable. He had found Jasper Wald an unpleasant man to work for, and the sooner he got himself another job the better off he would be. There was something in Wald's baleful glance that disturbed him.

"In the mornin'," Wald said after a few minutes, "you work that Thumb Butte country."

The Kid nodded, but made no comment. The Thumb Butte area was six miles across the valley from the badlands where he'd had the run in with Old Stob, that red-eyed mossyhorn. Was it chance, accident, or design that had caused Wald to send him to the other side of the ranch?

Yet, the next day, he realized that his new working ground had advantages of its own. He worked hard all morning and rounded up and turned into a mountain corral, forty head of cattle that he combed out of the piñons.

Switching his saddle to a bay pony, he took off into the draws that led south and west, away from the ranch. An hour's riding brought him to the Argo trail, and he cantered along to the little town at Argo Springs. Here was the only land office, within two hundred miles or more, where a mining claim could be registered.

A quick check of the books, offered him by an obliging justice of the peace who also served in five or six other capacities, showed him that no mining claim had been located in the vicinity of the badlands. Hence, if the killer of Jim Kurland had found the claim, he was working it on the sly. He did some further checking, but the discovery he made was by accident. It came out of a blue sky when Pete Mallinger, at the Wells Fargo office, noticed his brand.

"Bar W, eh? You bring one of them boxes over here? The ones Wald's been shippin' to El Paso?"

"Me? No, I just rode over to get myself some smokin'." He grinned confidentially. "The boss doesn't even know I'm gone."

"I wouldn't let him ketch yuh. He's a tough one, that Jasper Wald is. Throw a gun on a man soon's look at him. Got money, too, he has. He's buyin' up most of that Agua Dulce canyon country."

The Sandy Kid rolled a smoke and listened, his eyes sweeping the narrow street with its hitching rails and clapboarded buildings. Jasper Wald was not making enough on the Bar W to buy any land, not even with all his free and easy branding operations. Nothing you could really complain about, but nevertheless the Bar W brand was showing up on almost everything on the range that came within sight of a Bar W hand.

Before he left, the Kid managed to get his hands on the address in El Paso. The boxes were being shipped to Henry Wald, a brother of Jasper, and they were notably heavy.

The Sandy Kid strolled thoughtfully away from the door of the Wells Fargo office, and crossed the dusty street to the saloon. He might as well have a drink while he was here. He pushed through the swinging doors into the bare, untidy bar room. Dutch Schweitzer was leaning an elbow on the bar, staring at him.

"Howdy." The Sandy Kid strolled up to the bar and ordered a drink. "Looks like we've both strayed on the same mornin'."

Dutch looked at him with sullen eyes, "No, I'm on the job. The boss sent me over here. He didn't send you."

"Shore, he didn't. I rounded up enough stock for a full day in that country where I'm workin'. It's dry work, so I ambled over for a drink."

"At the Wells Fargo office?"

The Kid shrugged. He picked up his glass and tossed off his drink. "I'm on my way back," he said, and turned to go. Schweitzer's voice halted him.

"Wait."

The Sandy Kid turned. Suddenly, he felt cold. He had never met a man in a gun battle, but there was cold deadliness in the big German's eyes. The Kid stood with his feet apart a little, and his mouth felt dry. He felt sure Dutch meant to kill him.

Schweitzer had been drinking but was not drunk. The man had an enormous capacity for liquor, yet he rarely drank to the point where he was unsteady or loose talking. Only when he drank he grew mean and cruel.

"You're a smart kid. Too blamed smart," he said menacingly.

Two men in the back of the room got up and eased out through the rear door. The Sandy Kid could see that the bartender was obviously frightened.

Curiously, The Kid was not. He watched Dutch carefully, aware that the man was spoiling for trouble, that he had a fierce, driving urge for brutality. Some inner canker gnawed at him, some bitter hatred that he seemed to nurse for everything and everybody. The Sandy Kid knew it was not personal animosity. It was simply that in these moods Dutch Schweitzer was a killer, and only the tiniest spark was needed to touch him off.

In that mental clarity that comes in moments of great stress, The Kid found himself aware of many things—a wet ring on the bar where his glass had stood, the half-empty bottle near Schweitzer, the two empty tables in the back of the room. He saw the sickly pallor on the bartender's flabby face and the yellow hairs on the backs of Schweitzer's hands.

"You stick your nose into trouble." Schweitzer lifted the bottle with his left hand to pour a drink. Then his face suddenly twisted with blind, bitter fury, and he jerked the bottle up to throw it at The Kid.

Afterward, The Kid could never remember any impulse or feeling. He simply drew and fired without any thought or plan, and he fired at the bottle.

It exploded in a shower of glass and drenched Schweitzer with whisky. He sprang back, amazed, and when he looked up at The Kid he was cold sober.

Slowly, his eyes wide and his face pale, Schweitzer lifted his hands in a gesture of surrender. "I ain't drawin'," he said, astonishment making his voice thick. "I ain't makin' a move."

"See that yuh don't!" The Sandy Kid said flatly. He glared at the bartender, then backed through the swinging doors, and holstered his gun. With a wary eye on the saloon, he crossed to his horse, mounted, and rode out of town.

He moved in a sort of daze. He was no gun fighter and had never fancied himself as such. He was only a drifting cowhand who dreamed of some day owning his own spread. He had never found any occasion for split-second drawing, although he had practised, of course.

He had been wearing a six-gun for years, and he practised throwing it hour after hour, but more to ease the monotony of long nights on night guard than from any desire for skill. It had been something to do, like riffling cards, playing solitaire, or juggling stones.

Like all Texas men of his time he had done his share of fighting and he had done a lot of shooting. He knew he was a good shot and that he nearly always got what he went after, but shooting as quickly and accurately as he had done in the saloon had never been considered.

Out of town, he did not ride away. When Dutch Schweitzer returned he would tell Jasper Wald what had happened. There would be trouble then, The Kid knew, and the least he could expect would be to be fired. Yet there was something he would do before he left town. Riding around the town in the juniper clad hills, he dismounted and seated himself for a long wait.

He saw Dutch ride out a short time later. He saw the streets become less peopled, and he saw the sun go down. When it was dark, he moved down to the Wells Fargo office. When Dutch left he had been driving a buckboard, and that meant something to The Kid.

Using his knife, he cut away the putty around a pane of glass, then reached through and unfastened the window. Raising it, he crawled in.

For an instant he stood still, listening. There was no sound, so he struck a match, and shielding it in his hands, looked around for the box. He identified it quickly enough by the address. It was not large but was strongly built. With a hammer he found lying on a shelf, he pried up one of the top boards. He struck another match and peered into the box. Inside, wrapped in sacking, was a lot of the same ore he had found near the skeleton of Jim Kurland!

He blew out the match, then pushed the board back in place, hitting it a couple of light taps with the hammer. Then he went out, closed the window, and replaced the pane of glass, using some slivers of wood to hold the pane in place.

Jasper Wald then, had killed Jim Kurland and found the claim. Or perhaps he had found the claim first. The ore was extremely rich, and he was shipping it, a very little at a time, to El Paso where his brother was probably having it milled.

A slow process, certainly, but it was high-grade ore, and no doubt Wald had made plans to file on the claim when there would be no danger of Kurland's disappearance being linked with the proceedings. Everyone from the Forks to the Stone Tree Desert and Agua Dulce Canyon knew Kurland was the only mining man around, and also that he regularly penetrated the badlands of the Stone Tree.

The Sandy Kid took to the trail and put the roan to a fast trot. He was foolish, he told himself, to be mixing into something that was no concern of his. It would have been wiser to forget what he had seen after he came out of that crack in the mountain. Even now, he reflected, it was not too late to travel to some far off place like the Blue Mountains or maybe the Grand Canyon country of Arizona, which he had never seen but had heard cowhands lying about.

Little as he knew about gold, he could tell that the ore he had seen was fabulously rich, for the rock had been lined and threaded with it, and being so heavy, it had to be rich ore. Such a boxful as he had seen in the express office might be worth two or three thousand dollars.

Now that he thought about it, he had an idea where that claim was located. Not more than a half mile from where he had jumped into the crack to escape the steer, the plateau broke sharply off in a sheer cliff, some fifty or sixty feet high, that overhung the waterless, treeless waste of Stone Tree Desert and could even open upon the desert itself. That rupture, obviously the result of volcanic disturbance, could have exposed the vein from which the ore had come.

Pure speculation, of course, but The Sandy Kid had an idea he was nosing along the right trail. Also, he was aware that his interest did not arise from chivalry. He was not going into this to help a lady in distress. Trouble with Jasper Wald and his two hard-bitten henchmen was not lightly to be invited, and if he did go into it knowing what he was facing, it was only partly because of the way Betty Kurland had looked at him that he was following through.

It was a fool thing, he told himself. He had no particular urge to get money. Much as he'd like a ranch, he didn't want to have his head shot off getting it. He admitted to himself that if it had not been for Betty, he would never have gone all the way into this fight.

"The devil with it!" he said viciously. "I'll go back to the Bar W an' roll my soogan an' hit the trail!"

But when he came to the last forks, he kept on toward the mountains. He circled when he hit the willows and let the pony take its own gait. He was just edging out toward the cliff edge where he could see over into the Stone Tree when a rifle bullet hit the fork of his saddle with a wicked thwack, and then the bullet whined off ahead of them. It was a wonder it hadn't glanced back into his stomach or hit the pony's head.

The echo of the report drifted over him as he hit the ground running, and he grabbed the bridle and swung the bay pony back into the brush. Then he slid his Winchester .44 out of the saddle scabbard and Injun-crawled toward the cliff edge.

That shot meant that somebody wasn't fooling, so The Kid wasn't planning on fun himself. He was some shakes with a Winchester, and when he got to cover where he could see out, he looked around, trying to locate the spot the varmint had shot from. There was nobody in sight.

The Sandy Kid was not a trusting soul. His past dealings with Comanches had not been calculated to inspire any confidence in the serene and untrammeled appearance of woods or mountains. So, after a long look, he left the bay pony tethered to a bush and crawled to the very lip of the cliff. When he glanced over, he could see something that looked like a pile of waste and rock taken from a mine tunnel, but he wasn't looking for that. All in good time he could have an interest in the gold.

Then, in the rocks further along the rim of the cliff, he detected a slight movement. He looked again, widening and then squinting his eyes. It looked like a boot heel. Not much of a mark at that distance, and not much damage could be done if he hit it.

"We'll scare the daylights out of yuh, anyway!" he said, and lifting the Winchester, he nestled his cheek affectionately against the stock and squeezed off a shot.

Dust obscured the spot for a moment, but no dust could blot out the startled yell he heard. Somebody lunged into view then, and the Sandy Kid's jaw dropped. It was Betty Kurland! She was wearing a man's trousers and a man's shirt, and limping with one boot heel gone, but that hair could belong to nobody else!

He got up, waving his arms, and ran out to meet her. She turned on him, and her own rifle was coming hip high when she got a better look and recognized him. She came on a couple of steps, then stopped, her eyes flashing with indignation.

"I thought you were my friend!" she flared at him. "Then you shoot at me!"

"You shot at me!" he declared. "How was I to know?"

"That's different!"

Such feminine logic was so amazing that he gulped and swallowed. "Yuh shouldn't have come out here," he protested. "It isn't safe!"

"I wanted to find my father," she said. "Where is he?"

He led her to the lip of the cliff, and they found a way down. The Kid wanted a look at that desert, first. They came around in full sight of the mine tunnel and were just in time to see a man climbing out of a hole.

"I'll go get what's left of Kurland," they heard the man say. "They'll never find him here!"

The Sandy Kid was cursing softly, for he had been so preoccupied with the girl that he had walked around, unthinking, and now found himself looking into a gun held by Jasper Wald. The rancher had seen him, even if Jack Swarr, climbing from the freshly dug grave had not.

"Well, now!" Wald said. "If this ain't nice! You and that girl walkin' right up on us!"

"Don't you try nothin'," The Kid said. "This girl is known to be here. If she doesn't show up you'll have the law around."

Wald chuckled. "No, we won't. Not for long, anyway. I'll just tell them this Kurland girl showed up to meet you, and you two took off to get married, over to Lordsburg, or somewheres. They'll figger yuh eloped, and never even think of lookin' for yuh!"

Swarr grinned. "Hey, that's a good idea, boss! An' we can pile 'em in the same hole with her pa!"

"If I were you," The Sandy Kid said, "I'd guess again. I just come from Argo Springs. I know all about that gold ore you've been shippin' to El Paso, and I ain't the only one."

Jasper Wald hesitated. His idea for getting rid of the two had been a sudden inspiration, and a good one, but the thought that The Kid might have mentioned the gold to someone in Argo Springs disturbed him. It would mean he would have to move slowly, or worse, that he was already suspected.

Suddenly there was a clatter of stones, and they looked up. Only Wald, who held the gun on the Kid did not shift his eyes. The newcomer was Dutch Schweitzer.

"Watch that hombre, boss!" the German said hoarsely. "He's gun slick!"

"Him?" Swarr was incredulous. "That kid?"

"How old was Bill Bonney?" Dutch asked sarcastically. "He flashed a gun on me today so fast I never even saw his hand move!"

Angered and worried, Jasper Wald stared at the Kid. Quickly, Swarr explained.

"Aw, boss," Dutch said, "he's lyin'. I nosed around town after he left. After he left me, I mean. He never talked to nobody."

"How did I find out about the gold in that box yuh brought in? Addressed to Henry Wald, in El Paso?" The Kid asked him.

"He must have seen the box," Dutch protested.

The Sandy Kid's mind was running desperately ahead, trying to find a way out. "Also," he added, "I checked on this claim. You never filed on it, so I did."

"What?" Wald's shout was a bellow of fury. His face went dark with blood. "You filed on this claim? Why, you—" Rage drove all caution from his mind. "I'll shoot yuh, blast yuh, and let yuh die right out in the sun! You—"

"Boss!" Swarr shouted. "Hold it! Mebbe he's lyin'! Mebbe he didn't file! Anyway," he added craftily, "why kill him until he signs the claim over to us?"

Wald's rage died. He glanced at Swarr. "You're right," he said. "We can get possession that way."

The Sandy Kid chuckled. "You'll have no cinch gettin' me to sign anything."

"It'll be easy," Wald said sharply, "we'll just start by tyin' up that girl and takin' her boots off. By the time she gets a little fire on her feet, yuh'll sign!"

Dutch Schweitzer glanced at his chief, then he helped Jack Swarr tie the girl. Swarr knelt and pulled off her boots. He drew deeply on his cigarette, and thrust it toward her foot.

Dutch stared at them, his eyes suddenly hardening. "None of that!" he said. "I thought yuh were bluffin'! Cut it out!"

"Bluffin'?" Swarr looked up. "I'll show yuh if I'm bluffin'!" He jammed the cigarette forward, and Betty screamed.

Dutch Schweitzer's face went pale, and with an oath, he grabbed for a gun. At the same time Jasper Wald swung his gun toward the German. That was all the break the Sandy Kid needed. His right hand streaked for his gun-butt, and he was shooting with the first roar from Wald's gun.

The Kid's first shot took Jack Swarr in the stomach as the big man lunged upward, clawing for his pistol. Dutch had a gun out and was firing. The Kid saw his body jerk with the impact of Wald's bullet, and he swung his own gun. Wald faced him at the same instant.

For one unbelieving instant, The Sandy Kid looked over the stabbing flame of his own Colt into the flaring muzzle of Wald's six-shooter. He triggered his gun fast at almost point blank range.

He swayed on his feet, his legs spread wide, and saw Jasper Wald's cruel face turn white before his eyes. The rancher's knees sagged, and he went to the ground, glaring bitterly at The Sandy Kid. He tried then, to lift his gun, but the Kid sprang foward and knocked it from his grasp. Wald slumped over on the sand, his face contorted.

Swarr, The Kid saw at a glance, was dead. Yet it had not been only his bullet, for the German must have got in at least one shot. Swarr's face and head were bloody.

Schweitzer lay on his back, his face upturned to the sun. The Sandy Kid knelt beside him, but a glance told him there was nothing he or anyone could do.

Dutch stared at him. "Never was no hand to abuse women," he said, "never—no hand."

The Sandy Kid turned to Betty Kurland who stood, staring down at Dutch. "He was a strange man," she said.

"Let's get out of here," The Kid said. Taking her by the hand, he led her toward the path down which Schweitzer had come.

On the cliff top, they stood for a moment together. Betty's face was white now, and her eyes seemed unusually large and dark. He noticed then that she hadn't limped.

"Was yore foot burned badly?" he asked. "I didn't think to help yuh."

"It wasn't burned at all!" she told him. "I jerked my foot back as he thrust the cigarette at it."

"But you screamed?" he protested.

"Yes, I know," she said, looking at him. "You had to have your chance to draw, and they hadn't taken away your guns. And I knew about Dutch Schweitzer."

"Knew about him? What?"

"The Apaches killed his wife. They burned her. I thought, maybe . . . that was why he drank so much, I guess."

When they were on the trail toward the Forks, he looked at her, then glanced quickly away. "Well, yuh've got yore claim," he said. "All yuh've got to do is stake it out and file on it. I never did. Yuh found yore pa, too. Looks like yuh're all set. I reckon I'll hug the rawhide and head out of the country. A loose horse is always huntin' new pastures!"

"I'll need a good man to ramrod that mine for me!" she protested. "Wouldn't you do that? I promised you half, too!"

"Ma'am"—The Sandy Kid was growing red around the gills and desperate, for she was sure enough a pretty girl—"I reckon I never was made to stay no place. I'm packin' my duffle and takin' the trail out of here. If anybody comes around askin' for the Sandy Kid, you tell 'em he lit a schuck and went to Texas!"

He turned his horse at the forks of the road and headed for the Bar W. His own horse was there, and since Wald wouldn't be needing this bay pony, he might need him out West there, Arizona way. He sure did aim to see that Grand Canyon down which flowed the Colorado. A mile deep, they said. Of course, that was a durned lie, but she might be pretty deep, at that.

Once, he glanced back over his shoulder. The girl was only a dim figure on the skyline.

"First thing we know," he said to the bay pony, "she'd have me a settin' in church a wearin' a fried shirt. I'd shore be halter broke."

The bay pony switched his tail and picked up its feet in an Injun trot, and the Sandy Kid broke into a song, a gritty baritone that made the bay lay back its ears.

Oh, there was a young cowhand who used to go riding,
There was a young cowhand named Johnny Go-day!
He rode a black pony an' never was lonely,
For a girl never said to him, "Johnny, go 'way!"